Love and a Little White Lie

STATE OF GRACE

Love and a Little White Lie

TAMMY L. GRAY

a division of Baker Publishing Group
Minneapolis, Minnesota

Published by Bethany House Publishers
11400 Hampshire Avenue South
Bloomington, Minnesota 55438
www.bethanyhouse.com

Bethany House Publishers is a division of
Baker Publishing Group, Grand Rapids, Michigan

Printed in the United States of America

ISBN 978-0-7642-3589-4 (trade paper)
ISBN 978-0-7642-3638-9 (cloth)

Cover design by Susan Zucker

Author is represented by Jessica Kirkland, Kirkland Media Management.

20 21 22 23 24 25 26 7 6 5 4 3 2 1

This one belongs to the Lord.

I was discouraged, creatively spent,
and certain my time as an author
had come to an end.
Instead of letting me quit,
He answered my prayer with a story.

Romans 8:28

ONE

I've face-planted myself into rock bottom.

Well, maybe a hammock above rock bottom—one my aunt Doreen graciously set out for me when I found myself abandoned and broke.

She's the provider of the cabin I'm temporarily living in, the four hundred dollars in my otherwise empty bank account, and this current job interview at Grace Community Church, which is highly improbable since I don't believe in God.

Though I have to admit, Pastor Thomas is not what I expected. For one, he's only ten years older than I, and two, he's wearing jeans, a pair of polished work boots, and a tight polo shirt with a stitched church logo over his heart. I say *tight* because the seams along his biceps look like they're crying for mercy. The guy has muscles. And not the I-carry-a-few-boxes-now-and-then kind of muscles. No, these are the I-pump-iron-in-the-gym kind of muscles. Luckily, they're really the only intimidating thing about him.

"So, January . . . that's a unique name. Is there a story behind it?"

I stop from rolling my eyes. No, there is no story. No

rhyme or reason of any kind. My birthday is not in January, it's in August. In fact, there is absolutely no significant event in the month at all. But lucky me, my mom was all about unique, cool baby names. I don't think she ever considered what it would be like to wear the moniker. Then again, my mom often doesn't consider much more than herself. Yet another reason why I'm not returning home. I don't have the money for an apartment deposit, and living with my mom and her newest husband is out of the question.

"No story, I'm afraid. Just my mom keeping me humble. Everyone usually calls me Jan." I offer a self-deprecating chuckle and forget for a second that I'm interviewing with a pastor. "I guess it could be worse: I could be a boy named Sue."

To my utter shock, he laughs. Like full belly laugh, and I realize he actually gets the joke. Almost as if he's listened to Johnny Cash himself. *Wait a second, are pastors allowed to listen to jailhouse country?*

I roll my shoulders, hoping my face doesn't show everything I'm thinking, which unfortunately it has a habit of doing.

"Your aunt was right about you. Quick wit." He points a finger. "That's the sign of a very smart person."

Sure . . . I'll take that. Truth be told, most of my wit comes from clamping down on what I really want to say. Although, with him, I'm finding my usual sarcasm is waning. I like Pastor Thomas. Not in a weird I'm-attracted-to-a-man-of-the-cloth kind of way. Beefy guys have never been my preference and definitely not ones wearing a wedding ring. But he's genuine and kind, and not at all like the two guys who stood on the corner of my apartment complex in college telling me I was going to hell.

"Your aunt says you're originally from Georgia?"

"Yes, sir, I moved to Texas this past August."

"Any particular reason why?"

Now all my wit is gone, and I find myself wanting to stretch out on his leather couch and download all my problems to him. *See, it all began this past May when I met my soulmate while he was stationed at Robins Air Force Base. We fell in love, then he got orders to move to San Antonio, Texas. I gave up my apartment, quit my job, and emptied my savings account to go with him because I thought he was "the one." A month after we moved, he deployed to Afghanistan. Whether from separation or stress or just bad timing, he realized I wasn't, in fact, his soulmate. Julia, a fellow Air Force sergeant, now fits that description. His request for me to move out of his apartment before he returned to the States was polite. At least more so than the engagement pictures he recently posted on Instagram.*

But I don't curl into the fetal position and tearfully share my latest nightmare. Instead, I fight for a smile and pray lightning doesn't make it past the ceiling when I utter the untruth: "I just needed a change of scenery, and Midlothian seemed a good place to start. Plus, I've always loved spending time with Aunt Doreen."

The last part is true. She's eccentric and bold, and despite her annoying habit of slipping Bible verses into everyday conversation, I adore her. She has the biggest heart of any woman I know, and there was no one better suited to be my safety net after the biggest heartbreak in my twenty-nine years of life.

"I'm pretty sure this entire church shares your feelings about her." He leans back and casually stretches his arm over the back of the couch, his triceps bulging. "Did you know she was on the committee that hired me six years ago?"

"Yes, sir, I did. And from what I understand, she's also on the beautification team, first-impressions team, serves as a Bible study teacher, and volunteers as a money counter." Hence the reason I'm sitting in this chair. My aunt has connections.

When I asked her about the pesky little detail regarding my faith, or lack thereof, she waved a hand and said, *"Who knows what the Lord will do in a few months? If they hire you, then it's God's plan, and I'm not about to stand in His way."*

She talks about God's plan a lot. My mom thinks she's an ignorant fool to waste so much time and money on a social club with rules, or so she calls the church. But even I have to admit, God's plan has worked out pretty well for her. Doreen's been married thirty-five years, adopted two boys after dealing with infertility, and is now welcoming her second grandbaby.

"Did she also talk to you about the temporary nature of the job?" His brow creases like it would really bother him if I were to feel misled.

His concern brings an unwelcome measure of guilt and makes the long hair I pulled into a tight bun suddenly feel stiff and itchy. While I promised my aunt I wouldn't lie if directly asked about my beliefs, I have no intention of offering up something that would unquestionably disqualify me for the position.

"Yes, Doreen explained that you're looking for someone part-time for a few months to provide administrative support to one of your staff members who's been 'drowning,' as she called it."

"That's actually a very good assessment of the situation. Which is why I see no reason to delay." He scoots forward and puts out his hand. "Welcome to the team."

"That's it?" The words slip out before I can stop them. "You don't have any questions about my qualifications? My schooling?"

I realize I left him hanging when he pulls back his unreturned handshake and picks up my résumé from the coffee table. "Your background is perfect—multiple jobs and skill sets. I spoke with your old boss yesterday, and he said you broke an old man's heart and that he'd take you back in a millisecond if you wanted. And . . ." He shrugs. "You come with the highest of recommendations from a woman I absolutely respect. That's good enough for me."

My mouth opens, then closes again.

I can't believe it. Me, January Sanders, only daughter of Cassidy Burch, who is a self-professed atheist and currently on husband number four, is now a part of organized religion. I'm pretty sure it's snowing in hell right now. If those two guys preaching on my corner were right, I'll be down there one day soon to check it out.

Pastor Thomas tries again with the handshake, and this time I take his hand and hope he doesn't crush me with his grip.

"Thank you," I say and find I genuinely mean the sentiment. Not just for the job, which I need, but more that I suddenly feel surrounded by warm, fuzzy cotton balls. And since my usual armor is dented, tattered, and virtually nonexistent right now, I don't think I'll survive anything less.

"I do have one other question," he says, and my heart immediately plummets because I know it has to be about my views on religion. Soft, fluffy cotton disappears, the hammock is ripping, rock bottom is getting closer and closer . . . "Your previous boss and your aunt mentioned a unique talent of yours. Something about a photographic memory?"

The adrenaline drop nearly makes me slither from the chair and sink into the carpet. He's asking about my brain, not my faith. That one I can answer without any hesitation. "It's not a photographic memory. In fact, I'm not sure I'd even call it a talent—more like an annoying vice."

He wrinkles his forehead, and I know I'm going to have to explain.

"Okay, I'll just take your office for an example. When I came in, I noticed three things. One, you have a black Sharpie streak on your otherwise pristine walls. It looks smeared, so I assume it's from one of the two boys in your family picture on the desk, and that your wife scrubbed at the mark unsuccessfully. Two, your office chair is slightly tilted, which makes me think you favor one side, probably due to back trouble that I'm guessing is from lifting heavy weights. And three, that yellow sticky note showing halfway out from under your keyboard has the capital letters *TH*, lowercase *inm*, the dollar symbol, and the number 23. Your password, I assume. And you should probably change it because I will remember that sequence until I'm seventy-five and senile."

His mouth is literally hanging open. I get that a lot. What they don't see is the downside.

"Unfortunately, there's an equal and opposite defect," I continue. "I miss all the obvious things a normal person would register. I'll see a small scratch or blemish on the leg of a piece of furniture but miss the fact that the same piece is painted baby blue. My brain trades off what others see for what they don't notice. A gift and a curse. Especially in situations of excessive noise or visual chaos. But don't worry," I quickly add. "I've learned to compensate, so I'll still be able to get the job done no problem."

He slaps his palms on his thighs and stands. "Well, January . . . I mean, Jan, I have a feeling this is going to be a very interesting next couple of months."

I stand, too, only now noticing that he's short. Maybe two inches taller than me, and I'm just five-foot-five and change. "Yes, sir, I'm looking forward to it."

"Oh, and you can stop with the *sir*. People call me Thomas or PT—you know, short for Pastor Thomas." He glances up at the ceiling, a half eye roll, but there's affection in his voice when he says, "The kids from youth group came up with the nickname and it seemed to stick."

I lift my purse on my shoulder as he guides me through the door he left open during our interview. His assistant smiles from behind her desk, as if she, too, is sincerely thrilled to have me as part of the team. Her lipstick is pink, two shades darker than Pepto, and I'm certain it's Clinique's sheer lip color and primer in Bubble Gum. I shouldn't know this, but I do. I think about it so much that I miss her handing me employment paperwork to fill out.

"Sorry." I take the stack, along with a blue pen from a plastic holder.

"No problem." She winks as if Doreen has already shared my secret about both my backward mind and nonexistent faith. "I'll be here if you need anything at all."

I wonder what she notices when she looks at me. Probably not my lip color, which is likely gone since I bit my lip at least sixteen times on the way over here. No, she likely sees what the rest of the world sees: defeated blue eyes, dark brown hair I only bothered to wash because it had been three days and Doreen said my time for wallowing had passed, and a heart that feels too empty to ever imagine it being full again.

I sit in an open chair and look down at the blank sheet that finalizes my employment. It's an uncomfortable feeling when nothing matches the stereotype expected, and so far the people in this building haven't fit with any of the churchy clichés I was certain to find.

A premonition sinks in my chest that Pastor Thomas is exactly right in his assessment: the next several months are going to be interesting indeed.

TWO

The paperwork didn't take much time to complete, which leaves Pastor Thomas's assistant, Margie, with the grand task of showing me around the church, a job she does at breakneck speed.

I nod at each of her explanations, even though I don't understand half of what she's talking about. I recognize some terms and phrases from conversations with Doreen but quickly deduce that working inside the church organization is going to take a lot of bluffing. Christians don't speak in normal terms, choosing instead to say odd things like *The Holy Spirit led us* to do this or that, or referencing children's events with acronyms I'm just supposed to understand. *VBC, or was it VSB? Oh well, I'll figure it out later*.

"Will I be involved in these programs?" I ask.

"Oh no. Ralph doesn't work with kids. You'll be assisting him with Bible study, small groups, outreach events, discipleship, volunteer-led ministries, and pretty much anything that doesn't have a home."

"Ralph? I thought I was working for Eric."

"Sorry. I forget you don't go to our church. Eric Phillips

is the executive pastor. He supervises all the staff, including Ralph and now you. I'm going to take you to his office next."

Which means we're skipping the worship building tour. A relief. One can only feign so much knowledge, and apart from the small chapel where we said goodbye to my pawpaw, I've never been inside a real church.

Margie sweeps through the children's building exit, and I follow, wishing I'd grabbed my jacket from the lobby chair prior to starting the tour. Another reason why I hate my namesake. Apart from day one and MLK's birthday, there is nothing else about the month of January that's enjoyable. The weather is yucky, Christmas is the furthest it will ever be, and worse, summer is still half a year away.

I heave a sigh of relief as soon as we're back in the administrative building, attempting to tuck away the strands of hair that pulled free from my bun. Who knew a church needed a full-sized basketball court to function?

"Okay, here we are." Margie extends her hand to a small hallway across from Pastor Thomas's suite. "On the right is Eric's office, then Teresa, our financial secretary. Straight ahead is Jonathan, our media pastor, and the two offices on the left are for our worship pastor, Brent. Everyone else is upstairs."

"Why two offices for Brent?"

"The second office is for our praise band. They write songs in there and use it for vocal practice. They have a CD out if you're interested."

"Oh sure. Yeah, I'll check that out."

Margie knocks on Eric's door while she opens it. A courtesy more than permission, I guess. "Wait here a second," she says and disappears inside his office.

I hear his "Hello" and then they begin a back-and-forth

exchange on yet another topic that flies over my head. I pick at my nail, reposition my weight from my right to my left foot, and wait for them to remember me.

Just when I'm about to take my chances and step inside, a bellow of laughter steals every bit of my nervous attention. I close my eyes and listen as it comes closer. It's masculine yet light and wonderfully authentic.

Here's the thing about being depressed: you lose all the little joys that make life worth the effort. Laughter becomes a memory and, in some ways, a painful reminder of all you've lost.

Maybe that's why I can't move. Why I'm stuck in the doorway of my new boss's office, determined to wait and see where the beautiful sound is coming from.

My suspense is short-lived. Two young men turn the corner, still talking. They don't notice me staring until they're nearly across the hallway, both obviously heading for the office Margie said was set apart for the praise band.

The taller of the two holds an air of seniority. It shows in his easy stride and the way his gaze transfixes on mine, as if this place belongs to him and he's fully aware of every stranger who walks through the door.

"Hey?" He says it like a question. Probably because I'm psycho-staring.

"Um . . . hi. Sorry, I didn't mean to stare. I just started working here." I clear my throat. "Are you Brent?"

"Nope. Brent's with the sound guy for probably another hour." He grins, and a wide row of white teeth appear. He has a dimple on his left cheek, a small scar on his bottom lip that makes an indention in the tender skin, and a smattering of freckles on his nose that I count. There's fourteen of them. "I'm Cameron." He steps forward and offers me a hand just like Pastor Thomas had earlier. I wonder if that's part of staff training, a firm handshake followed by a wink and a smile.

Makes sense. Church is like any other good organization. You need a sales team.

"Jan." I don't bother with giving him my real name; one explanation on that catastrophe is enough for today.

The handshake is quick, yet I don't miss the roughness of his skin. Different from Pastor Thomas's, whose hand was hardened from lifting. This hand is a musician's, the calluses deep and worn at the fingertips.

"You play the guitar?" I ask, even though I know the answer.

The other guy unlocks their office door and turns to join the conversation. "And the violin and the cello, and pretty much any instrument he picks up. This guy's a virtual Mozart."

Cameron actually looks a little embarrassed by the praise. It's endearing and unexpected. My ex, whose name shall no longer pass through my brain, loved accolades. There wasn't a compliment he didn't enjoy.

"I'm Nate." He, too, shakes my hand. "I'm the one behind the glass wall banging on the drums." Nate's younger than I think Cameron is, not that I'm an expert at judging or anything. If I had to guess, I'd say Cameron's in his twenties, and Nate maybe nineteen. He still has that skinny just-out-of-high-school look, complete with acne on his cheeks.

"Jan," I say again.

"Where will you be working?" Cameron slides his hands in his front pockets and rocks back on his heels a little. He must do this often. The jean material is faded there, and the pocket seams are slightly frayed.

"I think for Ralph? I don't really have a whole lot of details yet. I just know I'm here to help support the staff."

"Ah, well, maybe we'll get lucky and they'll send you our way."

"Not sure if that would make you lucky. Unless you count my third-grade recorder skills a worthy accompaniment to your famed brilliance."

He laughs again, and I find myself leaning closer as if his joyous demeanor might bounce from him to me and make all my troubles disappear.

"I'm an excellent teacher . . . in case you ever want to expand your skills." He reaches two long fingers into his chest pocket and pulls out a small navy guitar pick. "Consider this a coupon for three private lessons."

"Only three, huh?"

"That's usually all it takes for me to see if there's potential."

I take the pick slowly, feeling pretty certain we are no longer talking about lessons. It's then I realize that not only has Nate disappeared into the band room but also that Cameron and I are no longer on opposite sides of the hallway.

Oh good grief! I'm flirting outside of a pastor's office, and so blatantly that a teenage boy felt the need to excuse himself. This is a new measure of low, even for me.

"Does Tuesday evening work for you?"

I'm too horrified to follow Cameron's train of thought. "What?"

"Your first lesson. I'm free tomorrow night."

There's a glimmer in his eyes that I don't miss this time. Probably because I know it's very likely plastered all over my face, too. The attraction is mutual but needs to stay stuffed down and buried under the huge oak tree in my aunt's backyard.

Getting involved with anyone while in my current state of vulnerability is a bad idea. Getting involved with a guy who spends his time singing about a God who I doubt exists, well, that's just reckless. And my days of leaping into the unknown are over. At least until all the broken bones heal.

"No. I'm sorry, Tuesday's bad for me." I take two deliberate steps back, and his smile fades ever so slightly.

"Well, maybe another night?"

"I don't know, but thank you for the offer." I grip the guitar pick in my fist, irritated by how it already feels like a treasure. "Nice to meet you." My goodbye is more curt than I intend, but I don't want there to be any confusion—for either of us.

Margie and Eric are still engaged in deep conversation when I finally enter his office, but they both stop talking as soon as they see me. I've obviously interrupted something important. "I'm sorry. I thought maybe you'd forgotten me. I can go back out into the hallway until you're ready."

"No need. Margie and I are finished." Eric again shatters any cliché I had about church staff. No suit and tie, no wire-rimmed glasses or Bible in hand. Instead, he has a full gray beard that comes to a point, a plaid shirt that could be a twin to the one Nate is wearing, and black skinny jeans. Since when did senior adults get so trendy?

"You must be January. I can't tell you how thrilled we are that you're here," he continues with yet another Grace Community Church handshake. "Have a seat."

Margie excuses herself with a tap on my shoulder. "Come see me before you leave, okay?"

"Sure." I take the cushioned chair across from Eric's desk, hoping the sting in my cheeks is from the blistering wind and not from how his enthusiasm makes me feel like a fraud.

Eric moves fifteen of the papers spread out over his desk

into a nice neat pile; he clasps his fingers together and gives me his wholly undivided attention. The intensity makes me feel like I'm about to be inducted into a very private club. "So, here's the deal. We are majorly understaffed, and until we find the right permanent hire, we desperately need your help to get us through this transition. Ralph especially has taken the brunt of our busyness. And now on top of his daily tasks, we just started a new prayer initiative that he's spear-heading."

"Okay." A framed picture of a lion sits on his desk. No kid in it, just a lion's head staring at me as if I'm some kind of threat to this place. I quickly redirect my focus to my new boss and push the unease aside. So what if I'm missing a fun-damental part of working here? I can still help. Can still give whatever task they assign one-hundred-percent effort. "I'll be happy to help any way I can."

"If you're anything like Doreen, I have no doubt you will." His cell phone rings, and he presses a button before looking up. "So, when are you starting?"

No one has said. "I guess tomorrow?"

"Good. Good. I'll talk to Ralph this afternoon."

I stand because Eric's phone rings a second time. "You can get that. I'll go check in with Margie before I leave and see you in the morning at . . ."

"Eight-thirty is good. That's when everyone gets going." He answers his phone but tells them to hold a second. Setting the device back on his cluttered desk, he once again zeroes in on me. There's a tiny mole just a centimeter below his lash that he should probably get looked at. It's angular and dark.

"January," he says, and I quickly stop obsessing over his skin. "I really do appreciate your being here. You have no idea what an answer to prayer you are."

That itchy feeling returns, and I blame Doreen for buying me generic fabric softener. "Thank you. I'll do the best I can."

And really, what else can I offer?

I'm not who they think I am, nor whom they need, but in this case I intend to pull a page from Doreen's handbook. If this is their God's plan, then I'm going to ride it as long as I can.

THREE

Because this season of my life seems to be steeped in irony, it should come as no surprise that I'm currently living in a bridal cabin on thirty acres of land that's filled with romantic walkways and structures.

Not that I'm complaining, because I'm not. This land has been in our family for four generations, and the beauty, along with the serenity, is probably the only reason I'm not still curled beneath my covers refusing to get out of bed. My daily walks have kept me sane, and today's walk is no exception. I only wish it wouldn't remind me of how estranged my family has been for years.

I blow on my frozen fingers when I reach the top of the hill and sit on a bench that overlooks the entire property.

When my pawpaw died a decade ago, he willed his sixty acres to both my mom and aunt to be divided up evenly. Doreen turned her portion into an amazing wedding venue—the Boots and Lace Ranch. A name that so perfectly describes my aunt and uncle that it makes me smile every time I say it out loud.

B&L has four cabins that collectively sleep thirty people,

two reception barns, and three different ceremony locations, though the third is currently under construction. My cabin is off from the others with a single bedroom, full kitchen, and a quaint but elegant bathroom. Doreen had it built for the bride and groom in case they wanted to stay on-site, but more often than not the parents of the bride rent it out, since the newlyweds are often eager to go and begin their honeymoon.

I offered to vacate the cabin when the venue was in use, but I believe my aunt's exact words were, *"Pishposh. The day the mighty dollar takes precedence over my niece is the day the good Lord needs to take me up to heaven."*

A smile forms and then immediately fades when my gaze drifts to my mother's side of the property line.

Unlike my aunt, who has carefully cultivated every blade of grass, Mom returned to Georgia the minute the ink dried on the title and left her inheritance to rot. Not that any of us were surprised. Mom fled to Georgia at seventeen with fifty bucks in her pocket and only returned for short visits after I was born. I once asked her why she hated Texas so much. Her face paled and she said that some stories were meant to stay in the past.

I didn't understand that theory until recently, but now I get it. Pain is easier to deal with when it's left untouched. The land has been no exception.

Doreen offered to buy her out, but she refused, sparking another fight that has yet to be resolved. For ten years now, Mom's thirty acres have sat neglected, becoming more and more overgrown with brush and wildlife.

It's odd. Every time I look past the small fence that distinguishes one sister's inheritance from the other, I think of how the contrast is a direct reflection of their personalities and lifestyles. Even more disturbing is that I feel like the fence in the middle, my life a mix of neglected chaos and carefully tilled love.

Sighing, I stand, even though I just got here. It's out of the ordinary for me. On the bad days, I've been known to park myself here for hours. This bench is my favorite spot on Doreen's land because it's located right next to a hundred-year-old live oak whose branches make an eighty-foot diameter canopy. The trunk is close to six feet wide and sturdy. It's the most popular of the ceremony locations, and it's easy to see the appeal. There's something safe about a piece of earth that's withstood Mother Nature's wrath for so many years. Even alone, I feel empowered. I can't imagine what it would feel like as a couple, promising to love each other for a lifetime. At the rate I'm going, I'll probably never know.

The trek back to my cabin is the same one I've taken every day since moving in. It's been showered by a monsoon of tears, though each day seems to bring less of an ache with it, as if every step is a stitch in my heart. I hope so, at least.

There's two hundred feet of flagstone between the oak tree and Doreen's new gazebo area. I step on each stone, avoiding the cracks and the grass poking from beneath them. As soon as I clear the hill, I see the same two commercial trucks that have been there nearly every day since I moved in: Kyle's Construction and Landscaping.

At least now the heavy equipment is gone. It's been nonstop noise since the New Year. They poured concrete last week. Had about twenty guys out here scraping, coloring, and stamping. The effect is beautiful. Three circular slabs, stacked to create rounded steps that lead to the crowning feature . . . a gazebo that hasn't been built yet. I've seen the drawings, though, and it's a masterpiece.

I wave at the father-son duo, who are currently walking the

area, inspecting each section. As is our routine now, Mr. Kyle Senior waves back, while the younger, broodier Kyle ignores me completely. It's harder for him to do so today since he's just walking the site, and I think I get a barely perceivable nod, though I can't be sure. All the same, I take it as an invitation and do something I've never done before—I walk in their direction.

Maybe it's from the high of my interview this morning or just the small measure of friendliness I received, but I'm fueled in a way I haven't been since the breakup.

"Hey, guys," I say when I get close enough for them to hear me. "This looks fantastic." They colored the three slabs differing shades of barn door red, each getting lighter as they approach the center, then stamped the surface so it looks like stones pressed together. "It's artwork on the ground."

Mr. Kyle grins at his son. "Yeah, Dillon certainly has an eye for design. I take back all the arguments I made about staining the concrete." He pushes his son's shoulder affectionately as pride fills his weathered face. It's a good face, too—solid bone structure, a thick, wide jaw, and distinctive cheekbones that are rarely seen on a guy. And he smiles a lot. In fact, I don't think I've ever seen him not smiling in some capacity.

Dillon has the same handsome face, but somehow it's more striking on him. Maybe because Dillon does not smile. Ever. Or at least not in my vicinity.

"How long till you start building the gazebo?" I ask, mostly because Dillon's continued silence is making this chitchat uncomfortable.

"A lot sooner if Doreen would quit tweaking the drawings." Mr. Kyle winks at me, his affection for my aunt seeping through his teasing. "In the meantime, we have an endless list of smaller projects we can knock out instead."

Dillon pitches his eyebrow at his father, and the old man retreats. "Sorry . . . *Dillon* has a list of projects to knock out. One of the perks of being the owner and the boss." He laughs at his comment as if it were a punch line, and maybe it is, but I don't get the joke. Apparently neither does Dillon, because the only movement he's made is to go from looking at his dad to looking directly at me. And not in a casual way. No, his perusal is intense and invasive, like he can see right into my empty chest and peg me for the lovestruck fool I was.

I tug my jacket tighter until I feel less exposed. "Well, I don't want to keep you. Just thought I'd come take a look."

"Glad you did. You're welcome anytime."

"Thanks." I back up and focus on Mr. Kyle's worn boots. They're crusty brown and ugly, but it's better than acknowledging Dillon's laser gaze, which hasn't found a new target.

I spin around and step quickly onto the path, chastising myself for taking the detour in the first place. I'm almost through my second internal tongue-lashing when the pounding of footsteps halts me mid-step.

"Hey . . . January." The voice is not Mr. Kyle's. It's smooth and deep with a slight rasp. Life is so unfair. A man that moody should not be so darn attractive.

I turn and swallow, irritated that Dillon's voice could have such a profound effect on my whirling stomach.

"You dropped this." He stops a foot away, his hand outstretched with one of the three business cards I picked up from the church. It must have fallen out of my coat pocket.

"Thank you." I take the card, careful not to touch any portion of his skin, and tuck it back in my pocket.

"You look . . . better today," he says and then immediately focuses on his boots, which are systematically scraping a smear of mud from the stone. "Less . . ." He shakes his head. "Never mind."

My cheeks blaze because I know exactly what he's witnessed. That I've been a walking zombie for weeks. That the stains on my cheeks haven't been from the wind but from my stupid broken heart. But I also know you don't say that to someone, especially when it's the first ten words you've ever bothered to utter.

He turns to leave, and though I know I'll regret it, I can't seem to stop the words that go flying toward his back: "It's nice to meet you. This weather sucks, doesn't it? What's the business card for? Are you settling in okay?" I'm breathing so hard, my chest literally hurts when he turns back around and looks at me like I've lost my mind.

"What?"

I cross my arms as if trying to ward off the cold, even though I feel nothing but furious heat. "Those are all phrases that would have been appropriate to say to me for our first conversation. Not point out how pathetic I am." I know I'm overreacting, but I can't seem to stop the flow of anger that's had no landing point until now.

His surprise turns to indignation. "I never said you were pathetic. Just that you look better. And you do. Your hair looks shiny and clean, and your makeup isn't streaked down to your chin."

"Is that supposed to be a compliment?"

"No. It's a statement of fact."

"Well, next time keep your facts to yourself. Or here's a thought—say something nice instead."

"Aren't pretty words exactly what got you in this mess?" He steps closer, and it's incredibly difficult not to punch him in the face. "I don't do flowery nonsense. I say what I mean, and from what I've heard about your supposed Prince Charming, you could use a little honesty in your life."

My mouth drops open, and I'm not sure if I'm more shocked from his statement or from the fact that my aunt Doreen apparently can't keep a secret. Treacherous tears fill my eyes, and I hate Dillon Kyle right now more than any other person on earth. "You don't know anything about me."

"Sure I do" is all he says before returning to his trek back to the gazebo.

"Hey!" I yell when he's far enough that I trust myself not to attack. "I look less what?" He stops but doesn't turn or answer my question, which only makes me more determined to know. "Come on, Dillon, you said you don't sugarcoat. What were you going to say?"

He glances over his shoulder, just enough that I see his profile and maybe even the slightest hint of contrition. "Broken. You look less broken."

FOUR

I'm shaking by the time I slam Aunt Doreen's front door. "Did you tell Mr. Kyle about what happened in San Antonio?"

"Well hello to you, too." She appears as if out of a TV sitcom from the fifties, with a towel in her hand, an apron wrapped around her waist, and an expression that's one part scolding and the other part concerned. "Any particular reason you're shouting at me from the doorway?"

I close my eyes and quietly take two deep breaths. Sometimes I forget how different Doreen's house is from the one I grew up in. Yelling was natural there. Here it's an anomaly. When my heart rate calms, I try again. "I talked with Dillon today, and he seemed awfully informed on my colossal lack in judgment. He wasn't all that sympathetic about it, either." I know my voice is accusing, but if she's planning on spilling my secrets to the world, she should at least give me a heads-up.

"Dillon Kyle is an angry young man for reasons that have absolutely nothing to do with you." She wraps an arm around my shoulder and squeezes me to her chest. I can't help but acquiesce. She smells like cinnamon and a perfume I would hate in the store but love on her because it makes me feel safe. "But, yes, we did tell his father what happened, because Robert is a very dear friend of ours and I wanted someone I trust watching out for you." She walks me toward the kitchen. "Plus, your uncle can't keep a secret to save his life, and they're fishing buddies."

"Great," I moan. "The whole world is going to know I'm a fool."

"Falling in love does not make you a fool."

"No, but moving halfway across the country on a whim sure does."

Doreen kisses the top of my head. She's two inches taller than I and four inches taller than my mother. It seems fitting since she's always been the older, wiser one. "Well, look at it this way: if you had gotten married, it would have been one heck of a romantic story."

I snort but find the tears receding and my temper completely gone. "Dinner smells good."

She unlatches her arms and returns to the stove. Only then do I notice what she's wearing beneath her lime green apron: black slacks, a blinged-out hot pink sweater, and stiletto boots.

Yes, my sixty-year-old aunt has more style and grace than I'll ever possess, especially when my daily choice of attire lately is sweat pants, fuzzy boots, and my ratty old junior college sweatshirt.

"Well, are you going to leave me in suspense or tell me how the interview went today?"

I pick up a carrot and sneak it into my mouth before she turns. "It went well, I guess. They hired me."

She spins around so fast that bits of sautéed onion fly from the spoon. "They did?"

I get her surprise. I'm still questioning if I imagined the whole thing. "Yeah. Not one inquiry about my job performance or my personal beliefs. I guess they assumed since you're so holy and dedicated, I must be, too." I slip that last part in as a warning. My aunt put her name and reputation on the line for me, and I'm not exactly the most trustworthy of choices. I dropped out of college after only two semesters, quit my first three "real" jobs, and until he-who-will-not-be-named came along, I went through boyfriends nearly as quickly as my mom did.

Unfortunately, there's a lot more of her in me than I like to admit.

Doreen nods as if she gets an answer from some unseen being. "Well, it is what it is. I hope you see this as an opportunity and take full advantage of the kindness you've been shown."

"I do, and I will." Not just for me, but also for her. Then I think of all the people I met today and realize I want to do it for them, as well. There's something special in that office, a feeling I can't quite define but know I need more of.

She stretches her arm out and pulls the cutting board away before I can eat any more of her chopped goodies. "Can you grab me the chicken stock?"

"Yep." I rummage through her walk-in pantry and take out two large cartons. I can tell by the ingredients that we're having her homemade chicken soup tonight, and my stomach delights as the smell of seared vegetables fills the kitchen.

Yet another difference between my mom and aunt. Mom's idea of cooking is opening a box of Hamburger Helper.

As I set the cartons on the counter, my eyes flicker to the invoice on the fridge. The letterhead matches the side of the trucks perfectly, *Kyle's Construction and Landscaping*, and the amount due is enough to make my insides turn.

I've always known my aunt and uncle are wealthy, but I'm quickly learning that my idea of wealth and their reality are not even in the same stratosphere. Probably an added bonus as to why my mom resents her older sister so much.

"Why are you suddenly so quiet?" Doreen asks, and I realize I've been staring at the invoice for longer than is natural.

"Sorry. I was just thinking about—" I nearly speak the truth when that familiar twist stops me; mentioning the fallout with my mother always makes Doreen's mood plummet, and I don't want to do that tonight—"what you said regarding Dillon and his being angry. What happened?"

Doreen sets the spoon against the pot and affectionately tucks a piece of hair back from my face. "That's not my story to tell."

"Well, his dad doesn't seem to share your same integrity." I stubbornly fold my arms. "Dillon knows my sordid past. I think it's more than fair that I know his."

"Maybe so, but I'm still not going to be the one to tell you." I pout and she gives me her signature scolding eyebrow. The one I've seen both my cousins imitate. "Let me put it this way. I would think that you, after all the hurt you've experienced over the past few months, would offer a little grace back to someone who is hurting, too."

"You are far too noble." Dillon Kyle looked nothing like a man in pain, but then again, Doreen's love for the weak and wounded is why I'm here in her kitchen.

She grabs a towel, and I know I need to move or she's going to snap it right at my bottom.

I scurry away. "I'll set the table."

"Add a couple more place settings."

"What? For who?"

Doreen's grin is downright smug. "I invited the Kyles over after they finish for the day."

My mouth slacks, and she nearly squawks with laughter.

"Just kidding. See, an old woman can have a sense of humor, too." Her wink warms my insides as the last bit of tension from the day rolls completely off my shoulders.

Okay fine, maybe Dillon wasn't too far off base in his assessment.

I do feel a little less broken.

FIVE

I show up at Grace Community at exactly 8:25 a.m. dressed in my best church-appropriate clothes and ready to kill it on my first day. The sun's shining and is supposed to stay that way until this evening when a dreaded cold front is forecast to blow in. Until then, though, I'm going to soak up every ounce of this sixty-five-degree day and count it as confirmation that I'm exactly where I belong . . . well, minus the whole believing in a higher power thing.

Head high, lungs full of excited breath, I knock carefully on Eric's open office door and get a cheery "Come in!"

He looks just like he did yesterday, except his jeans are lighter and his shirt is blue. He's also moving before I make it past the threshold.

"Perfect timing. I have a meeting in ten minutes, and I want to get you settled first."

We walk—well, he walks while I speed-step to keep up. I'm starting to understand why everyone in the office wears casual shoes. They all seem to move like racquetballs in a men's over-forty tournament.

Ralph O'Neal, the discipleship and education pastor, is

located on the second floor of the admin building, along with several of the other ministers. Or at least that's what my cheat sheet says. I had Doreen give me a rundown of the staff members and all the special committees in the church. Not only is the page full, front and back, but she said tomorrow she'd get me a list of all the Bible study and life group leaders. It's the first time since high school that I truly value my ability to quickly memorize names and facts. I never realized the enormous amount of people it took to keep a church running.

We take the stairs because Eric says the elevator is slow. Personally, I think they must have a Fitbit contest going on. A sheen of sweat is already forming across my forehead and I still have five steps until I reach the top.

"I met with the personnel team last night," Eric says when I finally catch up with him. "Their goal is to start advertising this week for a permanent hire, so we're thinking four months for sure, maybe five, if that works for you."

I quickly do the math. That would be nine months from when I made the fateful decision to leave my hometown and follow a guy to San Antonio. And a year from when we began our tumultuous romance.

"I think your plan sounds perfect." And it does. When I return to Georgia in May, I'll be a different person. Not just less broken but healed. "Plus, it's a great opportunity to widen my résumé."

Eric stills for a brief moment, and I'm learning that when he has something important to say, he always stops moving and looks directly at me. While it's unnerving, I also kind of respect the gesture.

"Your flexibility and positive attitude are such a gulp of fresh air right now. Our church is exploding, and yet I feel as if Satan is attacking our staff on every side. He wants to take us down because of the work we're doing for the Lord, and it's not going to happen. Not on my watch."

I'm grateful when he returns to his remote-control-car speed and quits with the demon talk. I've never been one for horror flicks and certainly not in the building where I plan to spend every weekday. Yet Eric talks about the devil as if he's real and not just some made-up character to scare children into listening to their parents.

Mom believes in fate and karma. I don't believe in anything except my own abilities. Good things happen when you work hard, and bad things happen when you're stupid. San Antonio, stupid. Grace Community, hard work. Well, at least I think this job will be a good thing. I swivel my head to check the edges of the hallway, half expecting a masked man in a red suit and horns to come popping out, and rush to catch up with Eric.

He stops a few strides later at a closed door. "This is it."

It's the only office door I've seen closed in the building, and I have a sinking suspicion that Ralph is not going to be one of the overtly friendly ones I've met so far.

Eric knocks and a gruff "Yeah?" echoes under the door, confirming my apprehension. Oh well, it's just for a few months. I can endure anything for that length of time.

As we walk into Ralph's office, my brain nearly explodes. The problem with categorizing useless details to an obsessive level is that stimulation overload is a real thing. Not only is the office twice the size of all the others I've seen, but it's also a complete disaster. Like a serious you-may-need-to-be-on-*Hoarders* kind of mess.

My glance darts across the room. The corners are filled with cardboard boxes, not labeled but overflowing with small magazines named *Quarterly*. Paper and trash fill the floor around Ralph's desk even though he has two good-sized trash cans, both of them overflowing like the boxes. There are four bookshelves in the room, which are packed tight. Books are stacked in front of the vertical rows to the point I can't even read the spines.

A small table—maybe an intended workspace—is shoved against the back wall and completely covered with craft supplies and what looks to be old media equipment. The serial number on the TV is KR786W79V. I focus on that number, and slowly the ache in my head starts to subside.

"Now you know why we make him keep his office door shut," Eric whispers to me, and I think he means it to be funny, but I'm still way too close to panicking to find any humor in the situation.

"Where am I going to sit?" It's a selfish thing to ask, I know, especially since it's fairly obvious that this poor guy is completely swamped, but there is no way I can be of any help in a space this full of stimulation.

Eric frowns like he can't believe he didn't think of that little detail. "Hmm. Well, the band room is unused most of the time. I'll get you a key, and you can work there for now."

I think of Cameron, and my chest flutters. His guitar pick hasn't left my person since he gave it to me. It's tucked in the hidden pocket on the inside of my skirt, pressed against my hip bone. The comfort a tiny piece of plastic gives makes no logical sense. But even now, my palm is pressed against the spot and I feel some of the tension fade. "Thank you."

Ralph stands as we shove aside stray boxes and progress to the center of the room. My eyes lift toward the ceiling. The man's a giant, the kind who has to duck so that the light fixture doesn't brush the top of his head. I stand there seriously wondering if I need to buy some magic beans and call myself Jack.

"Ralph, this is January Sanders. She'll be assisting you for the next few months while the prayer initiative gets squared away." He looks around the room. "And she can help you with any other projects you have."

Ralph doesn't look pleased, nor does he offer his hand like everyone else I've met here has. "Does that mean we're not getting a permanent minister? Because you promised me when you tacked on these new initiatives that we'd hire someone for pastoral care."

"And we will, just as soon as we find the right person." His voice turns authoritative. "In the meantime, January here is very proficient at organizing."

Not sure where Eric got that tidbit from, but okay, I'll do what I seem to do best here: smile and keep my mouth shut.

Ralph presses his lips into a line and looks down at me. "Sorry about the mess. This is what happens when you have one person doing a ten-person job." It's not just bitterness in his tone, it's utter defeat, and suddenly Ralph doesn't seem so intimidating. In fact, my heart fills with an odd feeling. I don't even know what to call it, only that I really want to help this man.

"Well, now you have two people, or maybe two and a half, if you count it in feet."

My joke seems to make his face relax slightly, the redness easing a little from his cheeks. Now they're more reddish-orange, matching his hair and the curly strands on his forearms. Ralph reminds me of an old Scottish highlander, lacking only the beard and the accent, though imagining the lilt when he talks might keep things light between us. And maybe I'll throw in a kilt, since his clothes look like they were pulled from his bedroom floor this morning. His short-sleeve, button-up shirt has so many wrinkles, I lose count after I get past the first arm hem.

A ding sounds from Eric's pocket, and he pulls out his phone. "I have to run." He glances between me and Ralph like he feels bad for leaving but has no choice. "You two get acquainted and I'll check in later." He slides his phone back and turns to escape, stopping only to tell me he'll leave the band room key with Margie.

The air turns awkward almost immediately after. "Well, any idea what you need me to do first?"

Ralph walks to the back wall, picks up an overflowing box of thin one-sided cards, and stops in front of me. "Sort these."

I realize he's waiting for me to react. "Oh, sorry." I adjust my purse on my shoulder and take the box from him. It seems bigger and heavier in my arms, but then again, he's likely more than a foot taller than me and easily a hundred pounds heavier.

"For now, just separate them by medical, family, job, and any other grouping that stands out." He tugs open a drawer in his desk, fiddles around, then pulls out a bag of rubber bands. "Once we get a good idea of what we've got, we'll start distributing them among the staff." He sets the bag on top of my teetering pile of papers, and I know at any minute a cascade of white is going to spill over.

I carefully adjust and dare to ask a really stupid question. "What are these?"

"Prayer requests from the congregation. We get about a hundred every Sunday and even more through our website." There's far more than a hundred pieces of paper in this box. Ralph must sense my confusion and adds, "We're a little behind, as you can see. These go back to October, so you may find that some of them have already been answered. You can make a stack for those, as well."

"You're telling me you guys read all of these every week?"

"Not just read them, but pray for them all week, and ideally we'd like to follow up with the members." A sigh of resignation fills the room. "Unfortunately, right now we're lucky if they make it out of the box."

It's weird; I've always heard people promise to pray or say they will, but I never really paid much attention. I thought the words were throwaway phrases, like *Let's get together* or *I'll call you*, to end the conversation and get on with the day. But Ralph seems genuinely concerned over the untouched pile of papers staring back at us. Of course, considering the state of his clothes and his office, his frustration might have nothing to do with the prayer cards at all.

"Well, don't worry. Every one of these cards will see the light of day." I internally cringe as I realize I'm the one who will now be reading each request. Worse, I know every word will stick in my brain until the unforeseeable future. I back up to the doorway before he can read the apprehension on my face. "I'm going to set up in the band room, unless you had somewhere else you wanted me to sit?"

Ralph snorts and spreads his octopus arms. "And get an OSHA violation for dreadful working conditions? No, I wouldn't do that to you. At least not until you get as jaded as the rest of us."

Again that pressure hits my chest, like I should say or do something. But I'm helpless. I'm a temporary Texan in a temporary job with a temporary faith. If this building of believers can't find the right words to take away his unhappiness, then I certainly can't. "I'll be back when I'm finished."

"Sounds good."

I hear his door shut again when I'm ten steps away and within arm's reach of the elevator. Juggling the box to one side, I reach out to press the down button when a hand beats me to it. Next thing I know, the box is taken away.

"I've got it."

"Thanks." I turn toward my knight and swear the guitar pick heats up in my pocket, as if some life force is surging from its owner. "You again?"

Cameron's smile is as warm as it was yesterday. "I do work here from time to time." He peeks into the box of prayer cards. "I guess you have your first assignment."

"Yep. Sorter extraordinaire." The elevator opens, and it dawns on me that he might be using the band room. "I was going to set up in your practice space, but I don't have to."

"No, please do. I'd love the company."

"What about the rest of the band? Won't they mind?"

"Brent and I are the only ones on staff. Nate takes classes at UNT, and Brian and Darrel have succumbed to full-time respectable jobs." He smiles at me over the box, and I watch the elevator doors trap me inside. "Looks like it's just you and me."

Suddenly, I feel the need to grab an empty prayer card myself. I'm starting to believe it's going to take divine intervention to keep me away from a guy like Cameron.

SIX

We've recycled every bit of small talk I can think of by the time we reach the band room. I've learned that Cameron's last name is Lee, that he's kid number three of four, turning twenty-nine at the end of February—almost exactly six months younger than me—and lives in a small three-bedroom apartment with two other bandmates, eight minutes' drive from the church.

He sets the box down and stretches his hand to the top of the doorframe. "Don't tell anyone about my hiding spot." He swivels his head like James Bond in a takedown. "Margie threatened my life if I kept forgetting my key, so desperate measures had to be taken." He slides the key into the lock while I watch him with a goofy smile on my face. The same goofy smile that got my heart pummeled only months ago. My grin immediately fades.

Cameron turns the key and opens the door. "You can have the desk. I'm going to be working on a song and tend to pace when I get stuck."

"You write music, too?" Is there anything this guy *doesn't* do? He's cute, kind, acts like a gentleman, is a musician for crying out loud, and he has a great sense of humor. I'm so busy getting annoyed at his perfection that I nearly miss the tension that comes with that question.

"I *did* write music." Cameron is no longer smiling. He shoves the key back to its hiding place as if it wronged him in some way. "Now I stare at a blank sheet for two hours."

I want to ask why, but everything in his body language keeps my mouth tightly closed. We all deal with sore subjects. This is his, and I'm not about to stand here and press on the bruise.

Instead, I peruse the space in a way I couldn't the last time the door was open. A wave of relief slams into me. The room is not only clean and free of clutter, but whoever decorated the area must be part engineer. Every piece feels as if it's been measured to be the perfect distance from the adjacent wall.

Cameron walks to the side of the room designated as a seating area with a full couch, two big club chairs, and a love seat. Framed pictures of the band and their album cover the wall, each impeccably spaced at what looks to be three inches. Turns out Cameron is as photogenic as he is talented.

"That one was taken in Arlington." He points to an eleven-by-fourteen frame of him hunched over his guitar, his sweat-soaked hair draped over his forehead and fingers contorted in a way that doesn't seem real. In this picture, Cameron looks like a full-on rock star. "There were twelve bands at a free concert, and we got to be on the same stage as For King & Country and Mercy Me. It's still the pinnacle of my music career."

"How long ago was that?" My shoulder brushes his, and tingles tiptoe down my arm and into my fingertips. I should move away, but I don't. It feels good to feel this way again, even if it's equivalent to lining up in front of a firing squad.

"September." His voice is laden with disappointment. "I

was sure that concert would be the launch we needed, but apart from a two-month spike in iTunes downloads, nothing's come from the exposure."

"Music is a hard business to break into." I flinch when I realize my insensitivity. "Sorry. You don't need me to tell you as much."

His smile returns, and it's so welcome I nearly sigh in relief. It feels wrong to see Cameron sad. He's too . . . I don't know, just too delightful to be anything but happy.

"It's all about God's timing. I know this, but it's hard to be patient."

And there it is. The reminder I need to get refocused and forget whatever crazy thought I had about me and Cameron sitting in a tree. "Speaking of timing, I should probably do some real work. Or at least look like I am."

"Right, I can see how they may expect as much on your first day." He winks and returns to the hallway to retrieve my box of prayer cards.

I slide four music binders into a stack on top of the desk and set them carefully on the floor. All that's left on the surface is a laptop, a set of keys, and a baseball cap.

"I'll take those." Cameron puts the box on the corner and fills his arms with the rest of the items.

"You're a Rangers fan?"

"Since I was old enough to throw a ball. Mom and Dad took us to every opening game. They still do." He plops the hat upside down on the coffee table and tosses his keys inside. He's gentler with his laptop. "You ever been?"

"To a Rangers game? No. But I went to a Braves game once." I was ten and Stepdad #2 was trying to bond. It's the only good memory I have of him. "It was fun. Especially since I got to eat all the cotton candy I wanted."

He grabs a guitar from among the three on the far side of the room. "A girl who eats sugar. I didn't know those existed anymore."

"I am rare."

Cameron pauses and stares with a look I feel all the way down to my toes. "That you are."

I want to ask him how he could possibly know that when we've had only two small interactions, but at the same time I somehow feel a similar assuredness. That beyond the music, there's something inside that makes him unique. Special.

My cheeks heat and I focus on the box. The room suddenly feels stuffy, and I struggle out of the cardigan that covers my thin blouse. One thing I learned quickly in Texas is to always dress in layers.

The plucking of guitar strings fills the space and relaxes me. Cameron's back is to me, and he's hunched over like he was in the picture, only this time he stops every few chords and writes in the notebook in front of him. The starting and stopping doesn't bother me, but he seems to get more agitated with each strum.

I turn away because it's none of my business and I'm already more invested than I should be. I'm here to help Ralph, not Cameron, and to do that I need to sort a thousand prayer requests.

My fingers lift the first one from the stack, and I stare at the elegant handwriting:

> I'm a terrible daughter. Four months ago I put my mother in a nursing home because she no longer had the capacity to care for herself and needed full-time nursing assistance. Forcing her to leave her home of fifty-five years was the hardest decision of my life and has damaged our relation-

ship immeasurably. She's called me a traitor, a liar, a thief, and many other words I won't repeat. Now, to my dismay, the doctors have told me she's going blind. Her eyesight has been deteriorating for a while, but as of this month she cannot even read the largest font on her Kindle. For her, this is a tragedy nearly as great as moving. Reading is her favorite pastime and now even that pleasure is gone. I know I need to visit more, to be her eyes for her, but I can't seem to get my feet to move. I feel lost and completely depleted and truthfully very angry at God and at her.

Please pray for the Lord to give me perseverance and forgiveness. And to bring someone into her life who can fill the gap until I find the strength to take my rightful place by her side once again.

Every part of me that might have approached this task flippantly withers and dies. I turn the card over. The woman didn't leave her name, but she did write her mother's down. Sandra Cox. Serenity Hills Nursing Facility, Midlothian, Texas.

With shaky fingers, I set the card down. It's the first time in my life I want to believe there's a God somewhere who might hear this poor woman's prayer.

~

Two hours pass before Ralph ducks through the doorway, and I'm pretty proud of the progress I've made. Cameron gave up on the song writing about forty minutes after he started and said something about adding lyrics into the computer for Sunday. He still hasn't returned.

"How's it going?" Ralph looks even more foreboding from my seated position, so I stand to get a little leverage.

"Good. I've gone through about a hundred and fifty and sorted them in the piles you mentioned. The medical one was way too big, so I've done subcategories with ones that have follow-up information and ones that are anonymous." I point to my two highest stacks. "I can call and get updates on those if you'd like, before we pass them along."

It sounds crazy, but I think I actually see the stress roll away from his eyes. "This is excellent, January. And while it's a great idea to get updates, let's wait until we're all caught up. The last thing we need is someone complaining that their best friend's cousin got a call and they didn't."

I think he's joking until I realize he's not. "People would actually complain about that?"

He snorts, and I'm learning that he makes that sound every time he finds something to be ridiculous. "People would complain about the color of my shoes if we let them." He puts out his hands, palms up. "Go ahead and give me what you have so far."

I hand over the four stacks but find myself hesitating as I let the follow-up medical one go. Sandra's card is at the bottom, and every loop and period in her daughter's handwriting is etched inside my head.

"What if I wanted to, um, do one of them myself? Is that allowed?" The words come out before I realize the impact of what I'm asking. Not only am I stepping way over the line, but I'm also taking away someone else's prayer for that woman.

"Sure. Of course you can." Ralph's voice hitches in surprise, yet I don't think it's because he knows I'm a fraud. I think it's more because he long ago stopped looking at this stack of cards as anything more than another task on his to-do list. "Which one?"

The sudden searing guilt makes no sense. I don't believe in God, so these prayers are empty anyway, right? Still, I make no move to take Sandra's card from the pile.

"I have it already. You can take all those." It's not totally a lie. I have it in my head as clear as if I'd taken a photocopy. There's no reason to keep the card for myself. Sandra's daughter asked for prayer, and I have no doubt she didn't want it to come from someone like me.

SEVEN

As far as first days go, today could definitely be counted as a success. I finished half of my sorting task, and since Ralph had left the office for a hospital visit, Cameron insisted on showing me around the sanctuary before I left for the day. Surprisingly, I feel none of the apprehension I did yesterday about stepping into the worship building. I don't even check the sky for lightning.

Probably because Cameron is a much more pleasant tour guide than Margie.

"So, how did the song writing go?" I ask because he only came back to the office once, and that was just to ask me if I wanted something for lunch. I declined, having brought a thermos of Ramen noodles. *Yeah, I know, it's one hundred percent salt. Don't judge.*

"Terrible. I've rewritten the same verse at least fifteen times." He shakes his head and swipes his keycard over the sensor. "I've been mentally blocked since the concert."

"I'm sorry."

"Thanks." His tone indicates he doesn't want to talk about it, so I refrain from asking any more questions.

We turn a corner where Cameron flips up four different

light switches. The auditorium comes to life, and I'm stunned by what I see. Three huge projector screens, a state-of-the-art sound system, and laser lights. I always pictured sanctuaries to be filled with long pews and solemn music, but this building resembles a rock venue much more than it does a church.

"Over here," he says, pausing on a set of stairs at the far end of the stage.

I follow him up and through a wide black doorway. It leads to a bright hallway that I assume is where all the backstage magic happens.

We pass a control room, and then he points to an open space that looks a lot like a teachers' lounge. "This is where we hang out before and during the service when we're not onstage. And to the right is Pastor Thomas's quiet room."

"He needs a quiet room?" For some reason I picture Pastor Thomas humming *ohhhmmm* with his massive legs crossed, his meaty fingers making a circle. "What does he do in there?"

Cameron pauses like he's never bothered to ask that question. "Well, I assume he probably prays or talks through his sermon. More than anything, it's a peaceful area where he gets settled before going out to preach in front of thousands of people."

I halt. "Wait, thousands? How many people go to this church?"

"We run two services . . . so, not counting kids, we probably have close to twenty-five hundred attending each weekend."

"Two thousand five hundred?" That many people really give up hours of their weekend to sing dull songs and listen to some guy talk for thirty minutes? "Wow. I had no idea."

"You don't go to church here?" Cameron tilts his head and studies me. "Where do you go?"

I give myself a mental head slap and toss out the best excuse I can come up with on the fly. "Well, I just moved to town a month ago, so I'm still trying out different ones."

"Try here, then." He says this as if it's the easiest decision in the world. And truthfully it's tempting, because I would love to see him onstage.

I shrug. "Maybe I will."

"Good. Because now I'm gonna show you the best part." He grabs my hand to pull me along, and as much as I try to ignore the pulse of excited tingles his touch brings, the effort is futile. If today has shown me anything, it's that I'm hopelessly attracted to this guy. Which is why I should be anywhere but stepping onto a church stage with him.

Cameron, on the other hand, inhales as if the wood platform is his lifeblood. He lets go of my hand and walks to the center. Spreading his arms, he says in an exhale, "This is my favorite place in the world."

I walk forward slowly until I'm standing at his side, sharing the same view of fifteen hundred empty stadium seats. I don't feel elated like he does, more like terrified and overwhelmed, but I still smile and say, "Yeah, it's incredible."

"I was five the first time I performed in front of an audience, and I knew, even back then, that music was my future. It's like the world stops for those brief moments and all I can feel is the pulse of the crowd and the beat in my chest."

I'm drawn to his passion, mostly because I've never had any of my own. I've walked through life bumping along, figuring out what's easiest and moving on when it gets difficult. "It's good that you know exactly what you want."

"Is it? I'll be twenty-nine soon, working two part-time jobs to keep my dream alive, and sometimes I think it's never going to happen." He looks at me and there's apology in his eyes, like he knows this conversation is much too deep for two people who have only just met. "Sorry. I think the abysmal writing this morning got to me a little more than I realized."

I pat his arm and try to lighten the mood. "You're too young to give up on your dream. Wait until you're thirty at least."

That has been my go-to answer for years.

Not married? Well, I'm not even thirty yet.

No solid career? I'm still in my twenties. This is the time to explore my options.

Will you move to San Antonio with me?

I shake off that last question before it ruins my mood. In hindsight, I can now see that my yes was not just rooted in love but also in fear. I was turning twenty-nine at the end of the summer and felt as if the banker was about to call in all of my it-will-happen-when-I'm-thirty debts.

Cameron's eyes spark back up, and I guess I'm not the only one who finds solace in pushing off decisions until we cross into the next decade of our lives. It feels good that the two of us have that in common at least.

He glances toward the electric piano at the back of the stage. "Wanna break some rules?"

"On my first day?"

"Eh. It's a tiny rule, and I break it all the time." He walks to the keyboard and sits. "I'm new at the piano, so be kind." Seconds later, a beautiful noise escapes from his fingertips. I guess Nate was right when he said Cameron could play any instrument. He sounds nothing like a novice.

I smile when I recognize the song. It's the same one Doreen played at Pawpaw's funeral.

Cameron watches me more than his fingers, which is an art in and of itself. "Even with all the new music out there, 'Amazing Grace' is still my favorite."

"Mine too." Not that I know any others. "It reminds me of my grandfather." I move closer, and he begins to sing. Everything inside of me melts. His voice is, I don't know, shockingly unique. Raspy and coarse when in the lower register, yet smooth when he reaches the higher notes. I'm no musician, but I'm fairly certain Cameron has the most perfect tone of anyone I've ever listened to.

He finishes the second verse, and just when I think he's about to go into the third, he switches up the melody, sends his fingers across the piano faster, and belts out something about chains being gone and being ransomed and amazing love.

It's a version of the song I've never heard before, and it sparks something uncomfortable in my chest. There's too much emotion when Cameron sings, as if he's not just singing the music but living and breathing it in. They're more than words to him. He's pouring out his heart in such an authentic and beautiful way that I almost understand giving up a Sunday morning to come watch it.

The piano slows again until the sound fades out in one long, elegant note. And when the stage around us goes quiet, I can't move or speak. I feel as though I've been taken on a journey through a deeper part of his heart and maybe mine, as well.

No wonder women worship rock stars. I think a part of me just fell in love with Cameron Lee.

EIGHT

I'm still sporting a cheesy grin and humming the words to "Amazing Grace" when I park my car in front of my cabin. The cold front has held off, and for the first time in over a month, my upcoming walk feels more like a victory lap than a mourner's march.

In fact, I'm in such a good mood, I don't even flinch when I notice the Kyles' white truck parked two spots down from mine. Grabbing my purse and keys, I slide from my little Prius and slam the door.

"It's about time."

I wish I could say I didn't know that voice, but I do. It's the same deep, aggravating tone that got under my skin last night.

Dillon emerges from around a pillar and takes two steps down. He's in his typical jeans, work boots, and T-shirt ensemble. How he doesn't freeze is beyond me, but then again, every inch of him is covered in lean muscle. "Doreen said you got off at four."

"I do, but I stayed late."

"Already? Not really a good precedent to set, especially at a place that works their staff so hard."

"How would you know?"

"Who doesn't know?"

Whatever. I am not going to let Dillon get to me today. I think back to Cameron's voice and the way his head tilted toward the ceiling in absolute surrender. A floaty smile emerges, and I know that Dillon notices because his eyebrow lifts. I choose to take the high road and ignore it. "What's so urgent, anyway?"

"Rain is coming, and while I'm pretty sure I fixed the roof leak over your bathroom, I want to draw a circle around the water stain so I can see if it grows any tonight." He picks up his toolbox when I get to the top of the steps and stands there, waiting for me to open the door.

"You could have just asked Doreen for an extra set of keys."

"And invade a woman's bathroom without her knowledge or permission? No thanks. I like my head attached to my body."

A smile slips through, even though I had determined never to speak to the man again. "I take it you have sisters?"

"Nope. Just a wife." His curt tone is as jarring as his words.

"You're married?" I glance down at his left hand. It's as bare as it was the other day. Not even a white line where a wedding band should be.

"Divorced." He impatiently sets down the toolbox, and I realize I haven't moved since he said the word *wife*. "Do you need me to do that?"

"No. Sorry." I twist the key and push open the door. A burst of honeysuckle fills my nose, thanks to the candle warmer I have plugged in. The scent is my favorite because it reminds me of the plants that hang along Doreen's wooden fence surrounding the pool. Mom always let Doreen have me one month out of the summer, and my cousins and I would splash and play until our fingers wrinkled. I quit going when I turned fourteen, too interested in boys and friends to be bothered with family.

"It's clean, so go ahead and do whatever you need to," I mutter, wishing I could go back and knock some sense into my younger self. Apart from coming to my pawpaw's funeral, for fifteen years I let my only contact with Doreen be quick phone calls and an occasional Christmas present. Yet, despite my neglect, she took me in and lifted me onto my feet without a second thought.

I set my purse on the kitchen counter and watch as Dillon hauls in a six-foot ladder. He's careful not to bump or scrape the floors or walls, which makes me understand a little why Doreen gives his family all her business. Well, that and his dad being Uncle Jim's fishing buddy.

The reminder nips at my conscience as Doreen's admonishment comes back to me: *"I would think that you, after all the hurt you've experienced over the past few months, would offer a little grace back to someone who is hurting, too."*

Yeah, yeah, okay. Dillon is divorced, and having watched my mom go through three nasty ones, I know it's a vicious way to end a relationship.

I grab a cold bottle of water from the fridge and go to offer him one when I hear a rattle and a curse coming from the bathroom. "Need some help?" I call, determined to be the bigger person.

Another rattle and then a grumbly, "Yes. Can you hold this ladder still?"

"Sure thing." I make my way to the bathroom and have to hold in my amusement. Dillon is standing on the second-to-top rung, bracing himself against the wall while the ladder is teetering to the left. I quickly hold it secure. "You should really be more careful, you know."

He glances down at me. "And here I got the impression that you wouldn't mind seeing me fall a few notches."

"Whyever would you think that?" I ask innocently even though the image is rather appealing.

He stretches out and makes his first mark with a pencil. "Our last encounter didn't exactly lend to your being the newest member of my fan club."

"True, but I've chosen not to hold your bad behavior against you."

"See, that's where we differ." He finishes half of the circle and has to readjust to get to the other side. "You think telling someone the truth is bad behavior, whereas I think skirting your real thoughts and feelings is the most hateful thing you can do to another person."

I shouldn't take his words as a snub, but I do. "Sometimes the truth does more damage than a lie." Or in my case, a small little white lie that isn't hurting anyone. In fact, it's helping a whole group of people.

"So says every liar I know."

"Hey! Do you want me to hold this ladder or not?"

He actually chuckles, and it surprises me with how nice the sound is. "Tell you what, you give me one example of how a lie made a situation better and I'll stand corrected." He finishes his pencil loop and straightens his body so that I can let go of the ladder without him falling.

I'm still trying to come up with an answer that won't incriminate me when his work boot hits the tile floor. Sandwiched in the tiny bathroom, he's closer than I expect, our hips only a foot away. I try to back up, but my backside hits the sink.

"Can't think of anything, can you?" His voice is smug, as if he doesn't notice our awkward proximity.

Unfortunately, I do notice, a little too much. I slide to the left, eager to put even an inch more of distance between us, when a flash of color makes me freeze. "They're brown," I say with a catch to my voice.

"What?"

"Your eyes." I study them, fascinated, and lean in close enough that I feel his breath come faster. "With gold flecks that look like little floating stars."

"Little floating stars?" His surprise is mixed with jest, and I'm immediately horrified.

"I didn't mean that the way it sounded."

"Good, because it sounded like you were about to write a sonnet about my eye color." He's still grinning, which only causes my face to flush.

"Don't flatter yourself." It's then that I realize our chests are practically touching and I stumble back. "My awe has nothing to do with you and everything to do with the weird way my mind works."

"Sure it does." He draws out his words, and even though I can tell by the glimmer of amusement in his gaze that he's messing with me, I still succumb to his goading.

"Seriously. I never notice eye color. Ever. I'll notice a tiny scar someone got when they were three or a stray hair they missed when they shaved. But never the color of their eyes."

Dillon rests his elbow on the ladder rung, and I swear his eyes get warmer, like a thick cup of hot chocolate I want to swim in. "So you're telling me that in twenty-nine years you've never once noticed the color of someone's eyes?"

"Not unless I make a mental note to do so, and even then, it's a quick check mark. Blue, green, hazel. Usually a very dull detail." I search my memory bank for Cameron's and come up empty. It bothers me, almost as much as the fact that Dillon pegged my age to the year. Add in his wealth of knowledge regarding my new employment and suddenly his earlier comments about lying feel very personal. "How is it you know so much about me?"

"I ask."

"Well, stop." Stupid Uncle Jim. He raised two boys and obviously requires a lesson in a woman's need for a little anonymity. "Unless you want me poking into your personal life, too."

"Go ahead. I have no secrets." He says it as if he wants me to ask, and it bothers me that I want to know.

Bothers me so much that I slide to the corner, as far as I can away from him, and say, "Well, some of us like our privacy. Please try and respect that."

"Whatever you want." His face morphs back into the same irritation he's worn since I moved out here. He lifts the ladder, turns it sideways, and hauls it through the bathroom door. "Watch the stain tonight and let me know if it grows any."

I follow him into the living room and out the front door, rubbing my arms to ward off the chill I suddenly feel. "Okay." I can't quite place the sick feeling in my stomach. Guilt? Shame? A little of both? Is it really so heartless to ask the guy not to pry into my life? We are strangers after all.

Dillon tosses the ladder into the back of his truck without another word and gives a two-finger salute before he disappears behind the driver's door.

The first drops of rain come shortly after.

Figures.

That man is a walking storm cloud, and once again he's rained all over my happy mood.

I shut the door harder than necessary and plop down on the small leather sofa. His comment about the cruelty of withholding truths is still a bur under my skin. My huff echoes through the empty cabin. Working at Grace Community isn't hurting anyone.

In fact, tomorrow during lunch I will prove exactly how wrong Dillon Kyle's theory is.

Sandra's daughter asked for someone to stand in the gap for her, and she will get just that. I may not pray to some imaginary being, but I can certainly read to a blind old woman.

NINE

I'm ashamed to say I fell into the worst kind of female stereotype. Not only did I get up an hour earlier than necessary to carefully blow-dry and curl my hair, but I also wore completely impractical shoes and a silky jumpsuit that is far too dressy for the casual atmosphere at Grace Community.

So you can imagine how silly I felt when I found out that Cameron doesn't come into the office on Wednesdays. At least not until six, when they have praise team practice.

Now my feet and my pride hurt. Worse, I can't get it out of my head that I don't know Cameron's eye color and yet practically melted into Dillon's. I examine every picture on the wall in the band room, but none of them gives me any clue. They're either in black-and-white or Cameron has his eyes closed, lost in whatever private place he goes to when singing.

I run my finger along the glass, tracing the line of his cheek, until I realize that someone could easily walk in and catch me obsessing. I've done it once again—leapt from one crush right into another one. And worse, this one is wrong on so many levels that I can't even list them all.

Frustrated, I grab my keys and lock the office door behind me. It's close enough to lunch that I can leave without apology and hobble to my car, because two blisters have already formed on my big toes.

I looked up Serenity Hills Nursing Facility last night and discovered it's only ten minutes from the church. Kicking off my shoes, I start the car, determined to do something positive with my day.

The words from the prayer request cascade through my mind as I drive, the details flashing as if on a TV screen. Sandra Cox, pulled from her home of fifty-five years, loves to read, thinks her daughter is a traitor.

At least I can relate to that last one. My own mother hasn't spoken to me since I told her I was staying in Midlothian with Doreen. She thinks I'm picking sides when really I'm just trying to survive. And since neither of them will tell me exactly what the fight is about, it's a little unfair to expect me to shut out the only stable person in my life right now. But Mom doesn't listen and she doesn't forgive . . . not even her only daughter.

I take my final turn into the parking lot and find an open space. The Serenity Hills Nursing Facility is actually pretty lovely, though smaller than I expected. The building is red brick trimmed with white wood, and despite it being the middle of winter, fresh mulch and bright green shrubbery line the entry. This place obviously keeps a paid landscaper.

The thought immediately jolts me, and I lean closer to the windshield, checking each side of the parking lot for the distinctive white Kyle truck and logo. My relief is almost enough to make me not cringe when I put my shoes back on. Almost.

I manage to make it down the sidewalk and into the building without painful tears but have every intention of begging for a couple of bandages. It is a medical facility, after all.

Or at least that's what it looks like. A large nurses' station is the first thing I see, beside two office doors marked *Admissions*. I force my feet to move until I can lean on the counter. A nurse looks up and smiles. Her canine teeth are crooked while all the others are straight and white. And while the wide smile might seem warm, the lack of makeup and glimmer of moisture in her eyes makes me wonder if she's having the same kind of month I am.

"Hi, I'm here to see Sandra Cox. But first, would you happen to have some Band-Aids?"

Her brows move, and I can tell I've surprised her with the question.

"New shoes," I say, and since she's a woman, it's all I need to say.

She stands and pulls a first-aid kit from the cabinet behind her. "Is there a special occasion?"

"Nope. Just trying to impress a guy." I have no idea why I'm being so open and honest, but something about this woman reminds me of Doreen, though she's probably only in her fifties.

"Were you successful?" She hands me three bandages, and I immediately go to work on my feet.

"Not at all," I sigh. Destiny has given me a cold slap in the face. Whatever stupid romantic notions I dreamed up yesterday need to be crushed.

The nurse is back in her seat when I straighten, the pain substantially lessened now. "Thank you so much."

"You're welcome. Sandra's in room 205. It's down the green hallway."

"Green hallway?"

She points to her right, and I realize that once again I failed to notice the most obvious thing about the interior. The nurses' station is a hexagon with four hallways, the entrance, and a large dining room feeding into it. Each hall is a different color: blue, green, yellow, and an orangey-red. It's on the walls, the carpet, and even the room signs that jut out from the doorways.

"It helps the residents find their rooms easier," she explains.

"Makes sense." I point to Sandra's hall and wish I could just once be a little normal. "Green, got it."

I follow the carpet until Sandra's room number appears and carefully knock on the door.

"Come in." The voice is shaky and deep, but definitely feminine.

I step inside, only now considering that this woman doesn't know me and I don't know her, and explaining myself is going to be very interesting.

The room is single occupancy, with a small hospital bed on one side and a sitting room on the other. Sandra's in a pink recliner with a blanket draped over her legs and a Velcro strap around her waist that appears to be hooked to some kind of machine. An alarm, I decide.

"Hi, Mrs. Cox, my name is Jan." I consider mentioning the church, then decide not to. There's probably some kind of protocol when visiting, and knowing my luck, I'm doing it all wrong. "I'm here to read to you for a little while."

Sandra turns my direction, and while I can tell she has some vision, there's a vacancy in her eyes that highlights her blindness. "Oh, how sweet. Please . . . please . . ." She reaches out her hand, wrinkled and trembling.

I see she wants me to take it, so I do. The skin is remarkably thin and soft, yet her grip is firm. She pulls me to the chair next to her.

"I've been ever so lonely," she says, her hand still a vise on mine. "But I won't be here too much longer. My daughter is coming to take me home any day now."

I feel the same pressure in my chest that I did when I first read the prayer. I know Sandra isn't going home but have no intention of saying so. "Do you have a favorite book?" I ask instead.

"Yes. My Bible. It's in the nightstand by my bed." Her voice turns more eager while dread layers mine.

"Your Bible? Isn't there something else you'd rather read?"

"Oh no, dear. My Bible is first, then the other stuff."

I stand and walk across the room, completely flabbergasted as to why this lady would continue to read her Bible when the God she prays to has allowed this to happen to her.

Still, I cater to her wishes and head for the large-print, leather-bound Bible she requested. It's massive, a good four inches thick, the binding frayed from overuse. A few stray pages slip out as I carefully pick up the fragile copy. Returning to my seat, I cradle the book. I may be agnostic, but even I have some reverence for the Bible. Any book that can withstand so much scrutiny over thousands of years deserves a little respect.

"Okay, where do we start?" I ask.

"Luke. It's my favorite."

"Really? Why's that?" I flip past a few silky pages and find the table of contents. It takes me toward the back.

"Because it's all about forgiveness, and my heart doesn't feel a whole lot of that right now."

The comment is so similar to her daughter's that I nearly reveal the reason I came. But for some reason, I feel this pressing on my throat to keep silent, so I do and instead turn to the first verse. "'Many have undertaken to draw up an account of the things that have been fulfilled among us . . .'"

~

I'm actually a little disappointed when my phone dings that our time is up. We switched from the Bible to a fictional story about a young Egyptian girl who's sold into slavery, and I'm right at the part where she meets her new master.

I set her e-book reader on the chair as I stand. "I'm afraid I have to get back to work, Mrs. Cox."

"Will you come back soon?" She reaches out for my hand again, and I feel a surge of affection this time when I take it.

"Yes, ma'am. Tomorrow at the same time."

She exhales and smiles. "You, my sweet Jan, are an answer to prayer."

The words bring a scowl to my face. She's the second person who's said that to me this week and I don't like it. "Oh, I wouldn't go that far. I'm just trying to do a little good in a very rough world." And heck, if Mom is right about karma, it's time to turn some of it into the positive.

"We don't always know when God is using us, my child, but I guarantee He is."

I pull my hand away. This is one side effect I hadn't anticipated when taking the job. All these people ever talk about is God doing this and God doing that. Well, so far my life hasn't exactly been roses and cupcakes, so even if I were to believe in their lunacy, I'd certainly have a few choice words to say to the man, none of which would include a *thank you*.

"You have a nice day, Mrs. Cox. I'll see you tomorrow."

She's still talking when I escape from the room. The air

feels hot now and weighted, and all I want to do is get back in my car and drive and drive until the feeling goes away.

I make it down the hall and nearly to the exit when I see a flash of curly orange hair that's too familiar to ignore. I press my back against the wall and slide out of sight. Ralph is here, and while my need to hide makes no sense, I want to shrink into the walls. Sandra Cox's words burrowed under my skin, and now I feel as though my deception is plastered all over my face.

"You can't just show up here, Ralph." It's from the nurse who gave me the bandages. The one who looked as distraught as I feel.

"What do you expect when you don't answer my calls or my texts?"

"What's the point? Nothing has changed. And I refuse to be second in your life. Not anymore."

His sigh holds that same frustration I heard when he asked Eric for more help. "You know I can't do what you're asking. There's expectations. My reputation to consider."

"Is your reputation more important than me?" Her voice is so broken I know tears are coming, and I feel sick eavesdropping on their conversation. Sicker still that their back-and-forth sounds clandestine, especially since I know that Ralph is married.

I glance around for any sort of escape and realize the entrance to the women's restroom is only inches away from me. I push through the door and immediately go for the sink, my stomach turning so hard I think I might start retching.

Ralph is a cheater. Just like my ex. And my three stepfathers.

Heck, just like every other man in this stupid, twisted world.

I turn on the faucet and am splashing cool water on my face when the bathroom door swings open. It's the nurse, and there are tears streaked down her cheeks and red rims around her eyes. But none of the friendliness I felt toward her earlier is there. I want to yell at her, remind her that families are devastated when a partner strays. I know this truth far too intimately.

But I don't say any of those things, just watch as she goes to the sink next to me and grips it like she might throw up.

"I saw you duck in here," she says quietly, though her throat sounds constricted. "Thank you." She looks at herself in the mirror. "Twenty-six years. You'd think I'd know by now that he will never change."

Twenty-six years? My brain throbs as if it knows it's missing something critically important. That's when I catch her reflection and see the bright red nametag she's been wearing all day. *Victoria O'Neal*. Ralph's last name. Ralph's wife.

He's not cheating after all.

The responding relief makes no sense, but I want to crumple to the floor and burst into tears myself. I know I shouldn't hold him to a higher standard for working at a church, but I do. Just like Cameron and Eric and even ultra-perceptive Margie. I want them to be better than the rest of the world. Need them to be.

Victoria is still looking at herself in the mirror when she says, "I left him a week ago. Packed a bag and went to stay with my sister. I thought it would wake him up."

My head spins, yet so much of what I saw in Ralph now makes sense. The rumpled clothes, the frustrated, bottle-tight responses, the plea for Eric to give him some relief. That poor man is losing his wife. No wonder he seems ready to break down.

"Well, he did come here." It's the best I can offer without telling her I'm his temporary assistant. That would probably not go over too well at this point. "And from what I saw, he looked pretty upset."

"Not enough to go to counseling. Or enough to work less, or even enough to do something as simple as bring me flowers." She shakes her head again and looks back at the sink. I see another tear fall. "It's just time to accept that we don't know each other anymore. Not since our kids left."

I don't answer because I really have nothing more to offer. Longevity in relationships has never been something my mom or I have been able to achieve, whereas Victoria has over two decades of experience. But it does seem especially tragic that a marriage can sustain that much time and still fall apart.

"My mom's been married four times. None of them to good guys." I don't know why I'm telling her this. I never talk about my mom, or my childhood for that matter. "If you've made it twenty-six years . . . I don't know, but if it were me, I'd fight like hell to make it last." I realize as soon as I speak that the *h-e-l-l* word isn't really accepted in Christian circles. Or at least Doreen used to fuss at me when I'd use the term as a kid. Always cracked me up, because if she'd walked down the halls of my school and heard the language there, she'd probably go into cardiac arrest.

Victoria doesn't seem to care about my terminology. She just keeps sniffling and looking down at the sink.

I don't know what else to say, so I simply pass behind her and offer to give her some privacy. Doreen would have prayed for her. Would have held her hand and spoken some great wisdom or truth. I don't have any of that to give; if I did, I wouldn't be staying in a wedding cabin, licking wounds from one relationship while wearing completely ridiculous shoes for another one.

Suddenly everything about Cameron feels stupid and silly. We have nothing in common. And like Dillon so ineloquently pointed out, anything that does start will be based on a lie. Been there, done that, and it never ends well.

When I get to my car, I'm feeling more defeated than I have in days. If people like Ralph and Sandra, who have devoted their entire lives in service to their God, are struggling this much, how is there any hope for me?

TEN

The day finishes as lousy as it started. Ralph is distant, moody, and curt, and I can't really blame him because now I know his secret and it makes me look at him differently. I'm fully aware of my hypocrisy even if it is justified. It's human nature to judge people by their weaknesses. And everyone in this church would do the same if they knew mine.

I leave as soon as the clock strikes four, since I'm on a part-time schedule—Monday through Thursday, eight to four. They don't have me come in on Fridays, as almost the entire staff works Sunday through Thursday. It's a weird system but seems to be the accepted schedule in this church culture. I'm grateful for it today, though, because my capacity to smile and act like all is well is sorely limited.

Unfortunately, coming home doesn't ease my mood any, especially when I see that Dillon has been in my bathroom. The ceiling is fixed and primed. He left a paint can in the corner, which will likely be gone tomorrow.

Knowing he was here without me, even though I pretty much gave him permission last time, leaves an acidic taste in my mouth. His words have continued to seep into my bones, and with each pang it brings a familiar burn of anger to the surface. No one invited him to give commentary on my life, though he seems determined to do just that since our first conversation.

I slam the bathroom door and tear into my bedroom, tossing aside my jumpsuit for a much more suitable pair of jeans, long-sleeve T-shirt, and walking shoes. I nearly moan when I put them on.

My walk will make me feel better. It always does. I'll walk out this feeling of unrest, of disappointment and self-reflection. I'll remind myself that my time in Texas is temporary and best served if I stay away from forming a relationship that will undoubtedly lead to more pain.

I shut my door to the cabin at the same time my phone buzzes in my pocket. For a second, I think it might be my mom, and for that brief period of time I feel a surge of hope that maybe she's come around.

It's not my mom, though. It's Doreen, asking if I'll be coming to dinner.

I text back a yes because I don't think I have the capacity to be alone tonight. I feel this tug inside of me, this wrenching and twisting that is as unwelcome as it is uncomfortable.

I was so stupid taking that prayer card, thinking I could help someone else when my entire existence is one big do-over right now.

"I'm sorry, Mrs. Cox," I say out loud as I take that first step. I won't be going back to that nursing home. If her God wants to use someone, well, it's not going to be me.

"You're awful quiet tonight." Doreen's watching me with the keen eye of a parent as I push around the contents of my plate with a fork. "Something wrong?"

"No. Just tired." I glance up and smile at her to make my case, but I can already tell by the gleam in her eyes that I'm not going to be let off the fishing hook anytime soon.

"Tell you what—since you seem to be finished, why don't we go out on the patio and let Jim clean up tonight?"

I can tell my uncle wants to protest as much as I do, but Doreen's tone isn't up for negotiation. To further her stance, she stands and slides her plate on top of her husband's. "I'm going to go light the fire pit. Jan, get a jacket on; it's cold outside."

"Sorry," I mumble to my uncle as I walk past him with my barely eaten dinner in hand. "She's mother-henning tonight."

"No worries, Teapot. Doing the dishes every once in a while keeps me out of the doghouse."

I don't know why Uncle Jim calls me Teapot, but he has for as long as I can remember. It warms me now, that consistency he's always shown. Unlike Doreen, Uncle Jim doesn't like crowds or gatherings or big displays. He's all quiet strength. Introverted and amiable, but when needed, he stands up as the clear leader of his family. He's the most steadfast male figure I've had in my life, and I don't know why, but I set down my plate and hug the back of his shoulders.

It's awkward because neither of us is prone to affection, yet I can't seem to help myself. Everything in my psyche is off today, which makes my impending discussion with Doreen even more terrifying. She reads me way too well.

I set my dishes in the sink, grab my coat, and take the dreaded steps out the back door and onto the patio. She has the fire pit going, a blanket wrapped around her legs, and a determined set to her chin.

"Sit," she says, patting the cushion next to her. I do as she asks, because that's just how it is between us. "Now, tell me what's going on with you."

I want to talk about my horrible day. About the disappointment of Cameron being absent, the thrill of helping Sandra only to have it crash down around me by seeing the degradation of Ralph and his wife. But instead I find myself asking a question I never have before.

"Why didn't you ever take me to church?" The words make her sigh and lean back on the love seat we're sharing. Still, I press. "I came every summer for a month, and yet I have no memory of going to any sort of church function."

"It was a stipulation your mom gave me. You could come and stay with me, but if you returned home quoting Bible stories or singing hymns, she'd stop the visits altogether." Doreen looks at the arbor overhead. "It was a struggle every year, knowing what you were being cheated out of but fearfully unwilling to step over Cassie's clearly drawn line."

It jars me for a second, hearing my mom's childhood nickname come out. Her given name is Cassidy Elizabeth Sanders. Same last name as mine because my father split a month before I was born. She's changed hers four times now, Burch being the latest one and maybe the best of the four. I don't know, I've only spoken with him a handful of times, the second being their wedding day.

Even when I lived in Georgia, I stopped going to my mom's house. Too many memories there that would nip at my serenity. Instead, we'd meet for lunch or she'd come to my small one-bedroom apartment. Our relationship is not like Doreen's and mine. My mom isn't a nurturer or even a mother really.

She's always been the needy one and I'm her strength, even when I have none left. Our twisted relationship is why I knew I couldn't go back to my hometown, back to her complaints and needs and endless frustrated commentary about her newest deadbeat husband. Yet, at the same time, I find myself missing her more and more each day. Because even though she'll never win Mother of the Year, my mom has been the most consistent source of love in my life. Without her, I really am alone.

"Do you remember our weekly 'girl day'?" Doreen's question pulls me from the recesses of my mind.

I'm grateful. Days of reflection annoy me. They don't come often, and when they do, I feel no capacity to handle the self-examination.

"Of course I remember. They were my favorite." We'd leave the boys behind, go have breakfast, then do some shopping in Arlington.

"They were every Sunday morning for a reason." She sits straight again and runs a loving hand down my cheek. "I guess I always hoped our closeness would one day open the door that your mom seems so determined to seal shut."

That uncomfortable feeling slams into me again and I stand, needing to move as much as I have all day.

Doreen must see my discomfort because she doesn't tell me to sit back down. Instead, she curls the blanket in her fists and says, "It's okay to ask questions, Jan. And even more okay to seek answers. You're not betraying your mom by doing so."

Tears prick my eyes. It's a backward mentality, I realize that. To hate how my mom leans on me to the point of breaking, and yet I feel completely empty because of the distance. I wonder if they have chapters on this in psychology class. If our messed-up relationship can be defined by some four-syllable word in a textbook somewhere. I wish someone would highlight the chapter and give me a solution, because right now it feels hopeless.

"I'm already betraying her," I say, which is exactly how I feel. Being with Doreen, working at a church, it's everything my mom loathes. "Her ultimatum at Christmas made it clear that she believes I am."

I spent the holiday in Texas with Doreen, Uncle Jim, and my two cousins and their families. Doreen is twelve years older than my mom, so even though Doreen was in her late twenties when she adopted her two sons, and Mom had me at only nineteen, both my cousins are married—one with a kid, the other with a bun in the oven. Meanwhile, I can't even seem to make a relationship last more than seven lousy months.

"Cassie is . . ." She pauses like she's really trying to find the right words. "Well, she's complicated. Mom died when she was so young, and your pawpaw, though he tried, was too overcome with grief to be the kind of father she needed."

"You turned out okay."

"I had my mom for seventeen years. Cassie had her for only five. We didn't have the same childhood." The sadness in her voice is palpable, and I sit back down because I've done it again. Brought up the one subject that seems to deflate that powerhouse spirit in my aunt.

Something horrible happened between my mom and aunt the week before Pawpaw's funeral. Something bigger than normal sibling arguments, and afterward nothing was the same. They fought over the will, the funeral service, even down to what clothes he'd be buried in. My cousins and I quietly stayed out of it and slowly watched the demise of a sisterhood.

"I'm sorry. I shouldn't have dumped this on you." I wrap an arm around her shoulders and rub her upper arm. "Mom will come around. For both of us, I'm sure."

"That's what I pray for every day." Doreen lays her hand on my cheek again and smiles. "You know, it's been an awful long time since we had a girl day. I think maybe we're overdue."

Her offer surprises me and brings a new wave of emotion. "I'd love that."

"It's a date. I'll pick you up Sunday morning at nine."

I know she's giving me an out. Time to process these new thoughts and feelings I'm having without the pressure of stepping into Grace Community on a Sunday morning. It's a sacrifice for her that I don't miss or take lightly.

And never in my life have I loved my aunt more than I do right now.

ELEVEN

I'm feeling so much better when I wake up on Thursday morning that I nearly cheer when I see the sun through my windows. The bad thing about my mind is that once a thought takes hold, it snakes and burrows until I grab the unwelcome intrusion and rip it away. The good thing about my mind is that once I do, I'm free. No more self-reflection and no more burden of conscience.

To prove I'm a changed woman, I make a point to dress down, even though I now know Cameron's schedule down to the hour. He works a half day Monday, long enough to go over any issues from the weekend, Tuesday and Thursday all day, and of course Sundays.

I don leggings, a long, comfy sweater dress, and pull my hair into a loose braid. It's getting way too long, practically past my shoulder blades, and I put finding a new hair stylist on my growing list of to-do's.

The drive to Grace Community is a 9.6-mile stretch of back roads and periodic stoplights. It takes me sixteen minutes to get there, even with the church located on the south side of Midlothian. Aunt Doreen's wedding venue isn't technically in the same zip code. My mail says Maypearl, but that tiny downtown is seven minutes away. Basically, I'm living in the middle of nowhere. And oddly, I like it.

"It's a new day," I practically sing to myself as I park my car. I'm even early by ten whole minutes. Yay me.

I use my security badge to access the building and take the flight of stairs to Ralph's office, hoping I can get all three Bible study resource boxes downstairs before he walks in. Another sorting task, only this one involves data entry and Excel tracking, which I'm good at but seriously hate. Too many numbers exhaust me and slow down my productivity. Like a computer on ultra-download because my mind won't forget one lousy decimal place.

My hope of a stealth entry is quickly dashed when I see the light peeking from under Ralph's door. I knock quietly, dreading our interaction and wishing I'd never seen him pleading with his wife to come home. It's an image that won't leave me anytime soon, and one that plays all-too-familiar havoc with my heart.

The door swings open like a ghost is in the room since Ralph remains seated at his desk. The benefit of long arms.

"Good morning," I say in my brightest, cheeriest, you're-not-going-to-spoil-my-mood-today voice. "I'm going to grab these boxes and head downstairs and out of your way."

He grunts. That's it. A grunt. My giant metaphor is taking all kinds of warped shapes as I look at the man's back. Wasn't there some kind of golden harp in "Jack and the Beanstalk" that sang and gave the giant peace? Maybe I should send Cameron up later and have him sing "Amazing Grace" to Ralph like he did for me.

Somehow I know it won't have the same effect. An over-email breakup after a shaky seven-month relationship is nothing compared to the demise of a twenty-six-year marriage.

I pull the first box away from the wall and pause when I find a photo frame trapped behind it. It's the desktop kind, five-by-seven, and looks as if a child made it. The frame lies on its side, forgotten, but I can see the young family through the glass. Ralph and Victoria, two small boys, a baby, and a golden retriever.

I don't know why, but I pick up the frame carefully, as if it were made of gold and not plaster, and bring it over to my grumpy co-worker. "You have a really beautiful family."

Ralph looks up from his head-cradled position, his eyes turning their attention from the pages on his desk to my proximity next to him. He sees the picture immediately, and I swear his entire body deflates.

With a gentleness unfitting to his stature, the man takes the frame from my hand and stares at the glass.

"How long ago was this taken?" I ask because I fear if I don't remind him I'm still here, he might start weeping.

"Almost nineteen years ago, at Easter. My oldest was only six."

That means he and Victoria raised three small boys, who couldn't be more than a couple of years apart. No wonder they've forgotten how to just be a man and woman now that the nest is empty.

"And the youngest? Where is he now?"

"Texas A&M. He's studying to be a veterinarian." The sadness in his voice sounds the same as it did in Victoria's. Loss. Not like with a death, but more the end of an era.

I wonder if that's what Mom's feeling with my being gone, as if a part of her has been stripped away.

"Your wife must be an amazing woman. Three kids. I can't imagine."

If it's possible, his face turns more somber. "She is."

I go back to the box and heave it into my arms. "My mom always liked flowers. Roses, red ones."

He twists in his chair, and I ignore the small narrowing of his eyes and keep with my nonchalant demeanor. "Did you know that January is the most neglected month for flowers?" I have no idea if this is true, but that's not really the point. "No one ever thinks to send them. Which is a shame because it's a pretty dreary month, and sometimes flowers just make everything better." I make my final trek to the door, feeling rather smug at my crafty suggestion. Now, hopefully, Ralph is smarter than Jack's giant and gets his wife a bouquet big enough to bring her home. "I'll be back for the other two boxes once these are organized." My smile is bright and innocent. "Need anything else?"

He shakes his head like I bashed him with a bat. Not really my intent, but if the man doesn't stop moping and fight for his marriage, I may need to consider it.

My earlier decision to forgo the nursing home at lunch is tossed out the minute the elevator doors close. Not only will I read to Mrs. Cox today, but maybe I'll also poke Victoria's memory a little. I'm not going to let them throw away twenty-six years and a Partridge family like the one I saw in that picture.

Not when I know exactly what it feels like to have none of the above.

Cameron strolls in around nine-thirty, and I nearly jump from the desk chair and hug him. Not just because he's become a beacon of light somehow, but also because this current task of tracking which classes want which Bible study material—small print, big print, Old Testament, New Testament, young adult, senior adult—is literally the most detestable job I've ever had. I mean, seriously, how many different ways can a person study the same book?

Doreen's been a Christian for over forty years now. My guess is she can smack her hands together and say, "Yep. Done with this now." Instead, she teaches, which . . . okay, yeah, is pretty admirable.

Cameron must notice my especially grateful expression because his brow shoots up. "You look ready to bolt. Like a trapped koala whose keeper just left her cage open."

That makes me smile even bigger. "Why a koala?"

"I don't know." His neck turns a little pink, and my heart goes pitter-patter. "Your sweater's fuzzy and it's the first animal that came to mind." I love that he blushes. It's sweet and innocent and such a refreshing change from the men I'm usually exposed to.

"Well, you're actually not too far off base." I close the laptop and stretch. "I'm tracking all the Bible study guides the classes are using, and I think I may go permanently cross-eyed. Supposedly, it's been a free-for-all the last two years, and now Pastor Thomas wants some accountability."

He grimaces. "Yikes."

"I know. Feel like distracting me for a while?"

"I'd love to, but unfortunately I have my own horrid task."

"Do you? Maybe we can trade." I slide up onto the top of the desk and cross my legs. Everything about the way I'm leaning toward him undermines my I'm-not-pursuing-anything mantra that's been going through my head the last two days, but I can't seem to help it. I'm inexplicably drawn to Cameron; it's as instinctual as a moth to a buzzing electronic shocker and likely just as suicidal.

Yet here I sit, smiling, leaning forward, hoping the joyous high-on-life feeling I get around him never goes away.

"Not sure you'd enjoy this job any more than your current one." He tosses his keys on the coffee table and slides his hands back into his pockets. "Every week we live-stream our services and then post it into our sermon history. This Sunday's copy got corrupted somehow, so I have to go back in and recompress it."

"A musician and a computer genius. Impressive."

"Genius is taking it a little far, but I have learned some digital tricks, mostly for recording."

That reminds me of what Margie said the first day. "You have an album out, don't you? What's the name? I'd like to download it."

"No need. I still have about a hundred copies to off-load." Cameron takes two steps to a filing cabinet and opens the top drawer to expose a pile of CDs. He grabs one and stares at it a little too long. Almost as if it hurts him to see a reminder of his dream.

"You okay?" I slip off the desk in an unsuccessful attempt at gracefulness and end up having to catch my dress before it sneaks up past my hips. Cameron doesn't even notice, which confirms my concern.

Finally, he closes the drawer, plastic case in hand, and turns. His smile is there, but it's lackluster, as if someone has sprayed film over a window and acts like the view is no different.

"Expectations can be very defeating," he says as he hands me the CD. "We released this six months ago. All seven songs on here are original, and two of them even got some play time on our local radio station. My songs are tracks two, five, and six."

"Are you singing them?"

"Only track five. The rest are Brent's vocals."

The plastic is cool against my fingertips, and I feel the significance of what he's passing to me. His dream. His victory. And possibly his failure. A treasure even greater than the guitar pick tucked away in my leggings, though this one will not be so easy to hide. I press the CD to my chest. "I can't wait to listen."

We stand there, me staring up at him in absolute admiration. Him staring down in sad acceptance. Maybe we're not such a bad match after all. He needs to be uplifted right now, and I need something to believe in.

"Are you still interested in giving me lessons?" The words flow before I can change my mind. Not that I want to.

"Very much." He takes a step closer, if that's possible. "Why don't we start a warm-up session this Saturday?"

"Yeah?" I'm practically giddy, which is silly and exhilarating at the same time.

"Yeah." He seems to like the idea more now than when he suggested it. "A friend of mine's band is playing at College Street Pub. He wanted me to come by and see if maybe, I don't know . . ." His voice fades as if he's about to expose a secret he shouldn't. "We can get some dinner and listen if you're up for it?"

Dinner and live music. That's a date in my world. I'm going to assume it's one in his world, as well. "Sounds perfect."

I back up a step, because now I have something to look forward to and I don't want to spoil the moment. I jumped in fast and furious with my ex and lost my head before I ever hit the ground. This time I'm going to be wiser and maybe even play a little hard to get.

I keep the CD pressed close when I sit back down. There's a happy swirl of anticipation and attraction in the room, and I think both of us are still blushing when he clears his throat.

"I better, uh, get to work." He cocks his head toward the door, since all the video equipment is in the worship building and that's where he's supposed to be right now—not in the band room, flirting with me and making plans for the weekend.

I set the CD next to my laptop, having every intention to play it the minute he walks from the room, and scoot into the office chair. "Yeah, me too."

"Okay then. See you later?" he asks with an adorable awkwardness. It's so incredibly refreshing that I want to start giggling.

"Definitely."

He leaves, and I watch the doorway for a good two minutes after it's empty. Anywhere else, a man like Cameron would be haughty and arrogant. Would have women lining up in front of him just to kiss one of his dimples. But not here. In this bubble of a building, in this world that makes me feel encapsulated in a warm blanket, Cameron looks at me as if I'm just as worthy as he is.

I remove the CD from its case, slide it into my laptop, and hit track five. Beautiful acoustic strings begin a ballad, and the rasp of Cameron's voice makes me close my eyes.

Hard to get? What a joke. He had me the moment I heard him sing that first note.

There are two dozen red roses sitting on the nurses' station desk when I enter Serenity Hills on Friday. The rose heads are big and full, and I'm especially proud of Ralph for not going with the cheap grocery store ones like Stepdad #2 always did after he and Mom had a fight.

I lean my forearms on the counter and look for Victoria.

She's not behind the desk. No one is, in fact. Carefully, I move toward the bouquet and smell the rich scent, the soft petals tickling my nose as I lean forward.

No one has ever given me flowers, and for a moment I wonder if Cameron will on our date. I can already picture the buds popping from the vase, announcing to the world that January Sanders snagged the cutest, sweetest guy in the world.

A rustling of papers has me straightening as I watch Victoria return to her desk.

"Maybe he heard you after all," I say, then realize a *Hello, remember me from the bathroom?* may have been a better opener.

"Maybe. It's certainly in miracle territory." Her lips move slightly into a smile she looks like she's fighting. "What about you? No Band-Aids today?"

"Nope. Just comfortable flats and a date for Saturday." That makes us both laugh, because it's amazing what can change in just forty-eight hours. It's also amazing how incredibly likable Victoria is compared to her broody husband. Maybe opposites really do attract and that's why they've worked for so long.

"So does this mean you're going home?" I ask, ready to make another check mark on my list of good deeds. *Watch out, karma, I am on a roll.* "You two can have a candlelight dinner and reconnect."

She picks up a file and hugs the contents to her torso. "Oh, if only life were that simple."

My chest caves as if she pounded it with a hammer. She didn't see the way Ralph looked at that photograph. Didn't see the heartbreak when he agreed his wife was incredible. These weren't just flowers on her desk; they were an outstretched hand, a plea for his partner to come home.

"But the flowers?"

Her gaze softens. "They are beautiful."

"Yes, they are. But more than that, it's a gesture that he's listening. Isn't that what you said you wanted?"

She shrugs as if she knows I'm right to point it out but still wants to remain stubborn. "It is."

"Okay then." I hit my palm on the counter like a gavel. "Call your man. If for nothing else than to thank him."

Her gaze narrows, yet there's affection in her expression. "You're not the type to refrain from speaking your mind, are you?"

Her question sends a jolt through me. "Actually, I usually don't say a word." The realization percolates. "I guess I can't accept your letting twenty-six years go."

Victoria walks to her flowers and removes the card from its plastic holder. She hands it to me, and my heart pulses faster.

Ralph's messy handwriting is quick and to the point, like him. *I miss you,* the card says.

I feel an inexplicable desire to cry. The kind of runny-snot cry that comes after watching *The Notebook.*

I clear my throat and hand the card back to her. "I think it is that simple."

TWELVE

By the time Saturday rolls around, I'm convinced that Father Time has a master's degree in torture. Fifty-five hours have never gone by so slowly, and yes, that's exactly how long it's been since Cameron asked me out on this date. Fifty-five hours, twenty-two minutes, and . . . I stop there, because knowing the seconds is a little too pathetic, even for me.

He just texted he was on his way over, and now I'm pacing my living room, stopping every third lap to check the mirror for obvious flaws.

None so far.

My dark hair is shiny and curled, a process that took well over an hour and gave me two finger burns. Worth it.

My makeup has recovered from the fiasco that was me trying to do eyelash extensions tonight. I can even see out of my right eye again, which is a bonus.

My outfit is from one of those send-a-box services that comes complete with high heels, jewelry, and a handbag. It's trendy and cute, and even though I have to suck in my gut because these jeans hug every curve, I do feel a little like

America's Next Top Model. Now if only I could stop falling off my shoes.

I check my watch, take a deep breath, and shake out my hands as I begin my laps again.

The sound of gravel crunching makes my heart plummet and soar at the same time. I itch to swing open the front door and fall into his arms like we're cast in some cheesy musical, but I wait until I hear the car door slam and his footsteps on the front porch.

Mom always said to make the guys knock at least three times. If I get to one, I'll pat my own back for monumental self-control.

The knock finally comes, and I swing the door open immediately after.

"Hey." I know my voice is breathy and schoolgirl, but I haven't seen him since the day he asked me out, and all my expectation is rewarded by his knockout smile.

"Hey yourself." His gaze sweeps over me, and it's like tiny feathers touching my skin. "You look beautiful."

"Thank you."

He looks pretty amazing, too. Dark jeans replace his normal faded ones. There aren't even frays on the pockets, which means he either just bought them or doesn't wear them often.

I grin at the effort, hoping it means he's anticipated this night as much as I have.

Cameron moves so I can lock the door, though the act does feel unnecessary since there is no wedding scheduled this weekend.

"This place is amazing." He grips the porch rail and stares at the expanse of trees toward the setting sun. It casts an orange filter on his cheek that makes me want to pull out my camera and capture the image forever. He turns, and I jerk my head back to my task before he catches me staring. "We have time if you want to show me around?"

I think of my shoes, which are totally impractical for a walk, but I don't seem to have the ability to say no. Luckily, there's enough flagstone to keep a relatively flat surface. "Sure."

I set my new handbag in one of the rocking chairs and walk toward the steps. Cameron waits like the perfect gentleman, allowing me to go first before following. "You're lucky it's quiet," I say. "Doreen has a four-hundred-person wedding booked next weekend, so the area is going to be a madhouse."

He quickens his steps until we're walking side by side. "You're not bothered by all those strangers milling around your cabin?"

Hmm. Good question. "I guess I haven't thought about it. It's the first wedding she's had since I moved in. January is her slowest month."

Cameron slips his hand in mine like it's the most natural thing in the world to do. "Well, be sure to lock your door and maybe have a friend come over or something."

My heart is going to be a melted puddle by the time this date is over. "I'll be sure to do that." I glance up with a flirty smile and hope he knows exactly which "friend" I want to come over. Small hint, it starts with a *Cam* and ends with *eron*.

I laugh at my own silliness, and it makes his eyebrows crinkle adorably. "What's so funny?"

"Nothing." I take a deep breath and wonder how everything could be going so right in such a short period of time. "I'm just really glad you're here."

He squeezes my hand tighter. "Me too."

We clear the first hill, and I soon realize that taking Cameron around the venue is like bringing a teenage girl to the mall. He stops at every curve, touches every tree, and has pulled out his phone at least ten times to snap a picture. Some are selfies, others scenery shots with a combination of guitar picks he carries. None of me, but that's okay. Expecting as much would be a little neurotic.

"Sorry," he says after the latest photo by my favorite oak tree. "Our band has a pretty significant social media following, so I'm always looking for content."

I put out my hand for his phone and slide through the multiple shots. His creative genius expands well past music. Each picture is artwork. The frame, the angle, the lighting. I'm quickly learning that being with a guy as talented as Cameron is going to take an extra measure of self-esteem. "You're really good at this."

He shrugs like he did when Nate touted his music skills. "It's fun most of the time." As if he can sense he's been distracted, Cameron slides his phone back in his pocket and takes my hand again.

His skin is warm and comforting, and I find myself snuggling closer as we turn back for my cabin.

"How do you get large catering trucks down that entry road?" he asks. "I kept praying no one was coming the other direction."

"Yeah, it's a tight fit. I guess Doreen just warns them." The wedding venue has only one entry road, a narrow caliche drive that dips and curves before widening. Flood markers follow the ditches along the side, but Doreen says they haven't had an issue in years. "There's a better easement through the adjacent property, but the owner won't let anyone use it." I leave out that the owner is my mom and Doreen's only sister. I want nothing but happiness in tonight's date with Cameron.

"Has your aunt looked at expanding the road?"

"I don't know." I shrug. "We don't talk business. Just shoes."

"Shoes?"

"Yes. My aunt Doreen has the largest shoe collection of any person I know. Easily two hundred pairs."

"I really didn't need to know that."

I spin, halting our forward progress, and stand in front of him. "Ah, don't judge. Everyone has something they collect. Like you with your guitar picks." My right hand is still tucked into his left one, and neither of us lets go. He looks down, his grin matching mine, and I realize that in my heels I'm much closer to his mouth than usual. Close enough that if I just lean slightly forward . . .

"Is that Dillon Kyle?" Cameron's words are equivalent to a fire hose exploding against my stomach.

I check behind me, and sure enough, fate and karma have conspired to slap me in the face. Dillon is pushing a wheelbarrow of mulch right toward us. "You two know each other?"

"Yeah, forever." He sounds happier to see Dillon than he is to see me, and I try not to let my irritation show as he disentangles his hand and moves around me to speak to his friend. "What's up, man?"

Dillon looks up at the same time Cameron approaches with arms spread, and who would have guessed, he looks just as thrilled to see Cameron. They give each other a quick hug, and I hear the standard "Hello, how are you? Whatcha been up to?" from each of them. It's annoying, especially since I'm just standing here, arms folded across my chest.

I drop them to my side when Dillon acknowledges my

presence with a chin lift and a raised brow. He doesn't say a word, but I can feel his judgment gnawing at my neck. *Liar, liar, pants on fire*.

"Do you usually work out here on the weekends?" Cameron asks.

"When I'm in the mood." Dillon tugs off his stained leather gloves and tosses them on top of his mulch pile. I hate the amusement in his eyes, the same expression he wore the last time he had me cornered. "What are you guys up to?"

"Bryson's playing at College Street," Cameron says. "You should come. The whole crew will be there."

I fight to keep my face placid. The whole crew? Like in a group date?

Dillon takes his eyes off me for only a second. "Thanks, but I still have a lot to do. Just tell everyone I said hi."

"I will, but it'd be nicer if we actually saw you once in a while."

Dillon shifts, and it's the first time I've seen him act even a little uncomfortable. "I'm getting there. It's just going to take time."

They exchange a look of understanding that makes me feel like I'm missing the entire middle part of a story. And while my mind tells me I should care, all I can feel is an immediate need to get to the car, grab a Sharpie, and black out the last five minutes. Nowhere in any of my Cameron-slash-first-date fantasies did Dillon Kyle make an appearance.

I hug my arms as if a huge gust of wind just blew through. "Wow, it's getting chilly. Are you ready?"

As I'd hoped, the gentleman breeding in my date takes over and he backs away from Dillon and his intrusive wheelbarrow. "Yeah, we should probably get going."

Cameron moves down the path, leaving me a sliver of

space along the flagstone to pass by Dillon without my heels sinking into the grass. Head down, I focus on my shoes, concentrating on a small defect in the stitching. My intent is not to be rude, but I don't want to see him or talk to him. It took me an entire day to recover from our last encounter.

To my relief, Dillon doesn't make any attempt to speak to me, either. I catch up with Cameron two strides later and wrap my arm around his elbow for the warmth and support I suddenly need.

I hear the click of the wheelbarrow behind me, and swirls of mocha-colored eyes with small gold flecks fill my mind. "Wait," I say, clamping his arm like I might trip.

Cameron leans down because my tug doesn't really give him any alternative. "You okay?" The angle is exactly what I need to finally see his eyes.

Blue. A surprisingly simple blue.

"Yep." I smile when Cameron's eyes crinkle adorably. "Now I'm perfect."

THIRTEEN

The twenty-minute ride to the restaurant confirms my nightmare. Tonight's date is a group one. And not just any group. Four of Cameron's closest friends, two of which are his roommates. Talk about throwing me into the fire without so much as an air tank. Or maybe this is a normal thing among singles in the church. I have no idea. But between Dillon and now the addition of four strangers, my hope for an intimate, romantic evening is gone.

I look out the window and try to get all my pouting out before Cameron finishes messing with the playlist on his phone. If I wasn't so disappointed, I might find his excitement over sharing all his favorite songs endearing. Instead, I sort of wish he'd pick a genre and stick with it.

Maybe the blues.

Was supposed to have a date with my dream guy . . . Na Na Na Na Na . . . even curled my hair . . . Na Na Na Na Na . . . Then came my storm cloud . . . Na Na Na Na Na . . . and it turns out they're old pals . . . Na Na Na Na Na . . . and now I'm on a group date . . . Na Na Na Na Na . . . and my pants are so tight I can't breathe . . . and I got the blues . . .

"Jan? Did you hear me?"

I jerk so fast I hit my head on the window. Ouch. "Sorry. Zoned out for a second."

"I was just pointing out the courthouse."

Through the windshield I see the towering building signifying the center of not only downtown but also the county seat, and for a moment I forget that I'm bummed out. The building is spectacular. Nine stories with a clock tower that looks exactly like it belongs in the fifteen hundreds. Nearly every corner is made up of turrets with large red-and-cream stone and arched windows, and the front is adorned with tall granite columns that touch ornate sandstone lattice.

"Wow," I muse as we drive past, turning a corner to see that the design continues around the side and back. "Are those faces carved in the lattice?"

"Yep. They call them unrequited love carvings. Some say that the stonemason who did the detailing fell in love with a girl, and the more she ignored his affections, the more devilish the carving became."

I grimace at the thought of being immortalized in such a twisted way. Poor girl.

Cameron passes through two more stop signs and the courthouse is well behind us now, but my thoughts are still with the stonemason and the girl, my heart torn between which one I relate to more. If I were to carve the face of my ex, would it be a beautiful sculpture representing the man who said "I love you" the first month we dated, or would it be the gut-wrenching version of the man who broke my heart through email? I honestly couldn't say. Bitterness is a vicious thing that can bring out the worst in all of us.

"We're here." Cameron parks the car and says we'll need to walk a little.

I don't mind. The downtown area is beautiful, and the

weather isn't so bad tonight. Maybe some cool wind on my face will cast away the last of my negativity and get me ready to meet this group of his.

"So, go over the names of all your friends for me again," I say as I join him on the sidewalk. Unfortunately, my brain does not remember details I hear, only see, which means unless the person is wearing a nametag or I happen to peruse a guest list, I'm guaranteed to forget it at least once.

Cameron slips his hand in mine, and just like that my apprehension fizzles away. Maybe instead of being so put out, I should see meeting his friends as a sign that he's planning on my being around for a while.

"My apartment mates are Brian and Darrel." He grins. "They're very different and very distinguishable when you see them. Brian wears glasses and has a girlfriend, Kalee, so she'll probably be here, too."

"How long have you guys lived together?"

"Only for the past two years, even though I've known them, I don't know, about seven years now. We met when I joined Grace Community's praise band after college."

I nod, repeating the names in my mind ten times each.

"The other two are Darcy and Alison. Again, very different and very distinguishable. Alison is dating Bryson, who started Black Carousel five years ago with Mason, the lead guitarist. The five of us have known each other since elementary school."

Five guys and three girls. I can't help but wonder if Cameron's invite has more to do with evening the odds than spending time with me. It wouldn't be the first time I've been used to fill a void or make an ex-girlfriend jealous. I grit my teeth and push away the thought. This isn't my life in Georgia. I can only assume that these people are different, as well.

He stops in front of a battered redbrick building with a large flat awning over the door. A few empty wooden tables and chairs flank double glass doors, and a large window has *College Street Pub* spelled out in cursive white etching.

Loud chatter spills out as the doors open, and Cameron steps back, letting me walk through first. This is another aspect of Texas culture that I'm liking a lot. Even young boys will hold the doors for women, as if it's as much a part of their upbringing as using utensils at dinnertime.

The restaurant is small, and Cameron spots his group immediately. They've pushed two tables together near the stage, and large glasses of water and what looks like tea cover the wooden tops.

My mouth goes dry as we approach, and I can't help but notice that Cameron doesn't take my hand again. I'm not sure why it bothers me, but it does.

I do a sweep of his roommates' faces. The three guys couldn't look more different. Cameron's over six feet, has a solid frame, and a clean-cut, wholesome face that could easily grace the cover of a religious magazine. Whereas Darrel, the one without glasses, has a style that will unfortunately forever haunt my generation. Skinny jeans, a man bun, and a beard that reaches his collar.

Brian is soft and pale and should really consider new frames, since the ones he's wearing only magnify his chubby cheeks. He's holding hands with a girl to his left. Kalee, I remind myself. She's cute. Bright red hair with freckles covering every inch of her skin. So much so that her shoulders appear dark brown. She has a birthmark near her elbow that's pink and freckle-free.

"Hey. You must be Jan." Brian's whole face lights up when he grins, and his gentle handshake warms me like an old comfortable coat. "I've heard lots about you. I'm Brian, and this is my girlfriend, Kalee." He glances over his shoulder, and Kalee offers a timid wave. She's obviously the shy one of the two.

"It's nice to meet you," I say, and truly mean it.

Darrel simply lifts his chin at me and goes back to tapping on his phone. *Not so nice to meet you* is what I want to say to him, but just smile instead.

Brian sits back down, and one of the other girls jumps from her chair, giving Cameron a hug so tight I want to pry her hands off, and not just because she's overly affectionate but also because Cameron's body seems to meld into hers.

She lets go of him, and the next thing I know, her long, skinny arms are around me in a hug that no stranger should ever give another stranger.

"I'm so happy to meet you," she says in my ear, and I glance at Cameron with *help-me* eyes. He grins, obviously not so great at reading facial expressions. "I'm Darcy," she says after finally releasing her viselike grip. "And this bozo didn't tell us you were coming until twenty minutes ago. If he had, I would have at least worn a nicer shirt."

It's only then that I notice her outfit. Loose jeans with two holes, brown work boots that rival Mr. Kyle's in both style and ugliness, and a green shirt that says *Made You Look*. Yet somehow with no makeup that I can see, straight brown hair that looks simply brushed and not styled, and an outfit that's more fit for the yard than an evening out, Darcy is flat-out one of the most naturally beautiful women I've ever seen.

I want to hate her, but for some reason I can't seem to. She's too darn sweet. And she's linked her arm through mine like we're lifelong friends.

"You know, you're the first girl Cameron has brought to meet us in years." She narrows her eyes at my date. "Usually he hides them far, far away."

"And you can see why," he says defensively, pointing at how she has me trapped next to her. "Jan's arm is practically turning purple."

"Please, you're just scared I'm going to spill all your sordid secrets." She winks at me. "Not really. Cam has no secrets. No skeletons and no vices. It's pretty pathetic, actually." She tugs me toward the seat she has saved. "As his best friend, I should at least have a little dirt on the guy."

Great. Darcy is not just his incredibly beautiful friend, she's his *best friend*. And I've basically stepped into the first season of *Dawson's Creek*. What do you bet that in the next ten seconds Darcy will hop up onstage, sing some beautiful ballad, and Cameron will discover how blind he's been and give me the *It's not you, it's me* speech.

But that doesn't happen. Instead, we sit, Darcy to my right, Cameron to my left.

The other girl turns and leans around Darcy to introduce herself. "I'm Alison. The normal one in the group."

Her assessment is pretty spot-on. She's exactly that, average. Pretty face but not especially striking. Medium build, nice skin, and brown hair. Her clothes are dressy but not overly so, and she's the only girl wearing jewelry—a small silver cross that falls within the V in her shirt.

"Nice to meet you." Gosh. I need to get some new material. I sound like a wind-up toy. "You're dating Bryson, right?"

"Yep." She smiles, and it's etched with an infatuation too intense not to be a new relationship. "Saying that sounds so weird. We've been 'just friends' forever."

Darcy leans in like she has a secret and whispers, "Don't let her fool you. She's been hung up on Bryson for years now."

"I think it's nice when you start out as friends first." Not that I'd know. All of my relationships, short or long, were based on attraction and intrigue.

Cameron scoots close enough to wrap his arm around the back of my chair and addresses Brian from across the table. "Did you see Brent's notes on the last song of our set? He emailed them an hour ago."

"No shoptalk," Darcy demands before Brian can answer the question. "You always do this, and I'm not going to spend another Saturday night talking about the Sunday morning song set." She rolls her eyes my direction. "Maybe he does have a vice after all."

"I'm just checking," he says, then leans in closer to me. "Sorry. Won't happen again."

Darcy snorts. "Yeah, right."

I can't help but smile at the face she makes. Eyes crossed, tongue out, and completely unattractive. She doesn't seem to care. In fact, I've never met another person so comfortable in her own skin.

Speaking of skin . . . Cameron's fingers are gently rubbing my exposed neck, and I nearly close my eyes and moan. Not really. That would be awkward and not at all appropriate while discussing church music.

I do glance up at him, though, and his neck flushes that adorable pink. To make sure he knows I'm more than okay with the public affection, I place my hand on his knee and lean closer.

"So what do you think of everyone?" he whispers, his breath on my ear shooting very non-platonic tingles down my spine.

I twist to look at him. "They seem really nice." What else can I say? It's hard to make an assessment after only a few verbal exchanges.

"They are, and I can tell they like you."

"Yeah? How?"

"I've known these guys so long I can read their body language like sheet music. Especially Darcy. She's usually the hardest on me."

Total shocker . . . not. I'm more convinced than ever that there's a story between these two.

The band comes out and I turn back around, snuggling into the crook of his right arm. His other hand joins mine on his knee and laces our fingers together. It's enough to push all thoughts of Darcy out of my mind.

Tonight isn't about the past.

It's a fresh new beginning for both of us.

FOURTEEN

I sneak away to the bathroom after we eat dinner and immediately unbutton my jeans with a huge exhale. Fashion or not, I'm throwing these suckers in the not-until-I'm-skinny-again pile as soon as I get home.

The door swings in, and I jump from my position against the sink and try to redress myself before I'm exposed. No such luck.

"Don't do that on my account," Darcy says, amusement lacing every syllable. "I'll honor the sanctity of the ladies' room and not say a word."

I don't trust her one bit, but the screaming red line across my abdomen is hurting enough that I lean back and let the front of my pants stay flapped open. "I tried that outfit-in-a-box thing. Great concept . . . not so much on the execution." Especially when the measurements I uploaded were pre-gallon-ice-cream indulgences and pre-fourteen-hour sleep fests. In other words, my stupid ex not only stole my happiness but also a dress size.

"You'll get no judgment from me. I groom dogs for a living, so being hair-free is about as good as it gets." She slides next to me and mimics my relaxed posture. "I'm actually kind of relieved to see you like this. I was pretty intimidated when you first walked in."

"By me?" The question comes out so fast I see spit fly across the floor. Yeah. Real intimidating. "Why?"

"Besides the fact that Cam's been talking nonstop about you since Monday, you're also very stylish and beautiful. And you have incredibly good posture." She stands a little straighter until her shoulders are back like mine.

"The posture is courtesy of my mom. She used to smack me on the head whenever I slouched." The beautiful thing, well, that's from her, too, although I've never thought much about it. Mom is the one who turns heads when we walk into a room. She's forty-eight but looks twenty-five, has the kind of figure most women—and men—dream about, and spends at least half her paycheck on making sure that never changes. "The rest is very sweet of you to say." I turn my head, feeling the need to reciprocate her honesty. "Truth? You intimidated me, too. You're very comfortable with yourself, and—" I bite my lip, then force myself to continue—"there's the best-friends-with-Cameron thing. Boy-girl friendships always have some kind of buried feelings. Based on how friendly you're being, I'm now guessing it's on his part more so than yours."

She's quiet for a moment as if chewing on all I've just said. "You're very perceptive."

"So I've been told."

Darcy again pauses, and the more she hesitates, the more nervous I get. Finally, she sighs. "Cam's feelings wore off a long time ago."

Though deep down I knew there had to be history, hearing it still feels like being punched in the stomach. "So you two dated?"

"No, nothing like that. He just hinted at possibly evolving our relationship when we were seniors in high school, and I turned him down as gently as I could."

"How come?"

"Well, for one, we have the whole I've-known-him-my-entire-life thing to overcome. There are some images a girl can't get out of her head, and believe it or not, Cam has not always been the handsome, suave man he is now. He used to be a band nerd with braces." She scrunches her nose. "Plus, our dreams are completely incompatible. I want to be an international missionary, and he wants a career in music."

I work to keep the shock out of my expression. I imagine missionary work is common in Christian circles, but to me it's an insane concept.

"So, even if I was willing to settle for friendship and forgo passion, which I'm not, we'd fail before we ever started." She turns and leans her hip against the counter. "But that's all ages ago. And right now you're the first thing that's made that man smile in months. Which makes you top shelf in my opinion."

I shouldn't care this much about her admission, but I want to do a happy dance in the middle of the bathroom. "Same here. He's the only bright spot in my life right now."

She pushes away from the counter. "In that case, suck in the gut, baby, and get back out there. As for me, I really did come in here to pee."

I laugh because I can't help it when in the presence of someone who seems to say out loud every thought in her mind.

Darcy pokes her head out from the stall before completely closing the door. "Oh, and when he grills you on what we talked about in here, just tell him *chicken coop*. He'll be too embarrassed to say another thing about it." The door shuts a beat later, and while I'm dying to know the story, I'm totally not comfortable talking to her while she does her business.

I suck in a breath, pull the clasp of my jeans until it connects, and drape my shirt to hide the muffin top. No more Ramen noodles. Just salad and celery and . . . never mind. The minute I think about dieting, I immediately crave a cheeseburger. I'll just up my daily walks and add some sit-ups at night.

Armed with a plan, I exit the bathroom and rejoin the group.

Cameron twists in his chair like he's been watching for me, and that wonderful warm splash of happiness returns. I'm not even bothered by the knowledge that he pursued Darcy years ago. I've liked plenty of guys in the past, and none of them have ever looked at me the way Cameron does—like I'm special and worthy of respect.

"I was beginning to worry," he says when I sit back down. "You two were in there a long time."

I don't want to embarrass him with whatever inside joke is behind the chicken coop, so I simply lace my fingers in his. "She was just telling me how great you are. I happen to agree."

He rewards my comment with a heart-stopping grin that produces not one but two dimples. "You do, huh?"

"Very much."

He motions toward the guys plugging in their guitars onstage. "And the band? Did you like them?" The timid way he asks makes me wonder if there's a deeper purpose behind the question. I hope not, because I don't have a whole lot of positive things to say about them.

"Yeah, they were good."

"You don't say that with any kind of excitement."

That's because Bryson's band reminds me of every other cover band I've heard. They'll probably do this kind of thing for a few years, maybe develop a small following, and then eventually fade into oblivion. But I'm not about to tell Cameron that. "Sorry. I'm not really a music critic, so I probably don't know what to look for."

"Okay." He slides me back to our position where his arm is around my shoulder and I'm leaning against his torso.

Unfortunately, even my toned-down answer must bother him, because Cameron's oddly silent through the whole second set, and even after, when Bryson comes and sits with us.

Not that the guy does anything to improve the evening. I'm not sure if it's the lackluster performance or the obvious irritation between him and the rest of the band, but Bryson's presence is equivalent to a boiling pot of water.

Plus, his eyes keep flashing to mine like I'm the one causing the tension at the table. At least I'm attempting to make small talk and not ignoring everyone, including his supposed girlfriend.

I lean close to Cameron, my ability to hide my sheer dislike for his friend nearly depleted. "I'm kind of tired. You about ready to leave?"

He squeezes my hand twice and then lets go. "We're going to take off," he announces to the group and begins to stand.

I'm out of my chair just as quickly.

"I thought we were going to talk," Bryson says, his voice low and accusatory. He eyes me again, and it hits me why he bothers me so much. He doesn't seem to belong in this group and certainly doesn't fit the image I have of Cameron's world. In fact, Bryson's the first person I've met from Grace Community who reminds me of my old life.

"Tomorrow." Cameron pushes in his chair and then mine. "I have to be up at the church by seven. Brent's not happy with our new song."

"Another reason right there, Cam." Bryson's tone gets even more serious and I can see Cameron tensing under his stare. "You can't do this forever."

I glance at Darcy right as she smacks Bryson in the arm. Good. I want to peg him one myself. A big fat knuckle sandwich to his face.

"What?" he says, rubbing the spot. "I'm just stating a fact."

When Darcy doesn't argue, Cameron shoves his hands into his pockets. "We'll talk about it later. I'm going to get Jan home."

Cue fake smile. "Good night, everyone. It was so nice to meet all of you."

A cascade of verbal goodbyes come, but I'm so over being there that I don't bother to wait for them before turning for the door. Cameron's behind me but still manages to reach out and push the door open before I get to it.

"Thanks," I say, then wrap my coat tighter because the temperature outside is easily twenty degrees colder.

"Did you have fun?"

"Yeah. I like your friends. Especially Darcy and Brian." Mostly only Darcy and Brian, but Kalee was nice, too. Just really, really quiet.

"Yeah. They're great."

I hate how every word feels stilted now and how his expression matches the same one he had when he stood on the stage and talked about how frustrated he was with his career. I feel certain he's wrestling with something but have no idea how to even approach the subject with him.

So instead I ask about one of the songs he played on the

way up and we do the music thing all the way back to my cabin. It cheers him up a little, but he still seems like he's walking wounded.

"Well, thank you again for dinner," I say as he parks the car.

"I'll walk you up."

"Okay." My arms and legs tingle as I step from the car, slipping a mint in my mouth just in case he ends the night with a kiss.

I come around the car, and we walk up my three front steps together. He pauses at the door but makes no move to touch me. I'm not really sure what to do at this point. Do I go inside? Step closer? Say good-night?

"Can I ask you a question?" His voice sounds so sad I immediately forget about the will-he-kiss-me-or-not scenario and rest my hand on his arm.

"Of course. Anything."

He motions to the rocking chairs on my front porch and we sit, even though my hands are turning to ice. I know forty degrees is not very cold for some people, but this Southern girl likes the sun.

"Part of why I wanted to take you tonight is because you're the only one I know who might be able to give me an unbiased opinion."

I'm not sure how to take that comment, so I just stay quiet.

"Bryson wants to fire Mason, and he's asked me to take his place as lead guitarist. In addition to getting full creative freedom, he's promised to give me one song a night as lead vocals. But he wants my decision by next week."

"What's that mean for the church band?"

Cameron rubs his hands together and then leans down and sets his elbows on his knees. "I'd have to quit. Bryson says there's way too much travel to commit to Sunday morning worship."

"But Bryson's band isn't Christian. I mean, some of those songs they played were pretty dark and angry." Two things Cameron is not.

"I know. That's why I'm torn." He cradles his head in his hands. "I want to play inspirational music, but the market is so small and every great church has someone just like me."

"No, they don't." Okay, so maybe I'm guessing on that one, but I know talent, and Cameron is well above average. "I may be overstepping here, but what you sang for me the other day, it meant something. It inspired me. You inspire me. And tonight, well, it was just another average band."

"A band with gigs lined up for the next four months. Some decent places, too. And Bryson says they're this close"—he sits up and gestures with his thumb and pointer finger until they're an inch apart—"to getting a spot at the Mohawk in Austin. That will catapult them, and if I add some strings to a few of their originals, it'll take the sound to a whole new level."

I want to say *If Bryson lets you*, but I don't. I know they've been friends most of their life and I don't want to insult him. All the same, though, the idea of Cameron playing backup in a substandard band feels completely wrong. "Just be careful. You're special, Cameron, and not everyone can handle that. I would hate to see you reduce yourself just to make him look better." Because the truth is that Cameron is far superior to Bryson in every way. And the minute Bryson realizes it, he'll not only take the one song away that he promised, but I have no doubt he'll also make Cameron's life miserable until he quits.

"Bry would never do that. I know he's a lot to take in at first, but deep down he's a good guy."

I silently agree to disagree with that one.

Cameron slaps his thighs and stands. "Well, thank you. It was nice to hear a different perspective."

"You're welcome," I say, though I seriously doubt I was any help at all. I walk to my door, knowing a kiss is out of the question. The mood is too heavy, and neither of our minds is in the right place for it now. I slip my key into the dead bolt when I feel his hand encircle my arm.

"Come here," he says, gently tugging me.

I acquiesce immediately and find myself enfolded in his arms.

The hug is so unexpected and odd that it takes me a second to lift my arms and wrap them around his torso. When I do, his hug gets tighter and he drops his head to the crook of my neck, inhaling as if he needs help breathing.

My eyes close and I let myself be still, to feel the warmth of his body next to mine, the security of his arms, and the vulnerability of holding someone so openly.

Never in my wildest dreams would I have envisioned a hug being more intimate than a kiss, but this one strips me bare, my eyes filling with tears as I allow the pain of the last couple of months to pass between us.

I press my forehead into his shirt and catch the mildest scent of Irish Spring soap. I want to bottle it, spray it on my pillow, and feel this way forever.

"Thank you," he says, pulling away.

I swallow back my tears and look up at him. This perfect, beautiful man who has no idea how incredibly unique he is. "Whatever you decide, just don't change, okay?"

His smile is real for the first time in hours. "I promise." He steps away, and I know he's waiting for me to go inside. I finish my task of unlocking the door and wave before closing it behind me. The air is thick with promise and I touch my mouth, feeling my lips as they stretch with pure happiness.

The euphoria lasts only a few minutes before I tear off my shoes and jeans, my smile growing even more now that I can move without pain. I walk to the kitchen in my underwear, grateful there isn't a soul for miles, and strongly consider mimicking the scene from *Risky Business*.

Instead, I think through the evening and let the floaty cloud feeling come again. I rehash my night filled with careful touches, hidden smiles, and the friendly admission that Cameron has been thinking about me as much as I have been thinking about him.

My inner Tom Cruise wins and I do a slide to the fridge, my bare feet moving a mere six inches before they catch against the tile floor. Slide, stumble, whatever. I still want to giggle.

I grab a cold bottle of water from the fridge and am halfway through twisting off the cap when I see a mason jar stuffed full of golden Copper Canyon daisies sitting on my kitchen table. I recognize them from Doreen's greenhouse.

Only two other people have access to both Doreen's place and mine—the Kyles. And since Mr. Kyle has never stepped foot into my cabin, I can only assume the gesture had to come from Dillon. But why in the world would he leave me flowers?

Stepping closer, I peek out the kitchen window. Unable to see anything in the dark night, I opt to close the blinds. Me in my underwear is not really a sight I want exposed at this time, especially to a guy who prides himself on telling me the truth. Yeah, definitely switching to salads.

Confirmation comes as soon as I pick up the card balancing against the glass. The distinctive Kyle logo is etched in black against a white background, just like their trucks. I flip the business card over and see the words *For your next sonnet.*

I reread the line several times, hoping it will suddenly make sense. And then it does. The daisies . . . they look just like little golden stars. Despite my better judgment, I gingerly touch Dillon's attempt at a peace offering. Maybe I was being too harsh when I ignored him earlier.

Leaning over, I sniff the blooms, catching a hint of citrus, and set the card back where it was originally.

I shake my head and walk toward my bedroom. What a strange night this turned out to be.

FIFTEEN

As far as girl dates go, this one is pretty phenomenal. Doreen and I have already hit five of my favorite stores, and despite my protests, she bought me three really cute outfits and two pairs of shoes. I even feel pretty in the new purchases, despite my eight-pound expansion.

Now my feet are warm and bubbly, and the massage chair I'm sitting in is doing its magic on the tension in my lower back. I mean, seriously, who needs church when you can get a pedicure at noon on a Sunday? Heaven on earth. Right here.

"Stop moaning," Doreen says through closed eyes.

I poke her arm. "That was you, not me."

"I can't help it. How have I never done this before?"

Doreen is one of those women who visits the beauty shop every week for a wash and style. She goes to the same lady who's done her hair for the past thirty years and gets her version of a mani-pedi at the same time, which is basically just a recoat of color and a little filing. I say you can't call it a pedicure if there isn't a massage chair, minty exfoliation scrub, and a hot towel.

"Because you live under a rock in a town of a thousand people." Or at least that was what the internet said when I looked up the population of Maypearl.

"Got news, missy. You live under that rock now, too."

That I do, and like her, the small-town mind-set is growing on me. Slow and creepy, like algae in a pond.

"So how was your date last night?" Her eyes are still closed, but a smug little smile is now on her lips.

I twist in my chair. "How did you know about my date?"

"Small-town privilege."

I roll my eyes because she's never going to tell me who spilled the beans, though I have a guess. Margie Singleton may be a rocket moving in a thousand directions, but she knows every little thing that goes on at Grace Community. Especially the social comings and goings of her favorite guitarist.

"Well?"

I roll my eyes. "It went fine. Cameron's a nice guy."

"And you've shared with him your feelings on religion?"

"No." My chair suddenly feels uncomfortable. "But I don't see why that's relevant."

"If you two are dating, it's absolutely relevant."

"We're not dating. We drove in the same car and had dinner with some of his friends. It was no big deal."

She turns her head and raises a perfectly plucked eyebrow. "Did he kiss you?"

"Doreen!"

"What? It's a fair question."

"Yeah, if I was sixteen, not twenty-nine." I mash my lips together and cross my arms. She's ruining my happy hangover and my massage. "But no, he did not kiss me. Satisfied?"

She settles back in her chair and closes her eyes. "Don't let that boy fall for you without him knowing the truth. It may not be a big deal to you, but for a Christian, it's important to be equally yoked."

Equally yoked? "What on earth are you talking about?" I can usually follow Doreen's analogies, but this one is beyond me.

Her eyes pop back open. "A yoke. You know, the thing they put on oxen when they drive a plow?"

"You're comparing us to farm animals now?" I start laughing. I can't help it.

"Ugh. Never mind."

Her exasperation makes me laugh harder until soon she joins me. The two of us make such a spectacle that our pedicurists start talking in another language to each other with their glances flicking in our direction. I imagine what they're saying about us and it makes me double over. Tears sneak from my eyes, and pain shoots through my stomach muscles before I get myself back under control. "Thanks, Doreen, I needed that."

"I wasn't trying to be funny," she grumbles.

"I know." And because I love my aunt Doreen so much, I concede. "And don't worry. If Cameron shows any signs that he's getting attached, I'll tell him."

"Thank you."

We both go quiet, and I watch as the lady scrapes and lotions up my poor feet. The abuse I've put them through this week shows, and I vow to wear comfy shoes until all my blisters heal.

"Hey, Doreen?"

"Yeah, honey?"

"Do you know Sandra Cox?" I don't know why my thoughts

drift to her. Maybe because the blisters make me think of Band-Aids, Victoria, and the nursing home. I know, my brain is weird.

"Of course I know her. She's been a member of Grace Community as long as I've been there."

"Did you know she's in a nursing home now?"

"Yes, I did. We bring an audio recording of the sermons to our shut-in members. She's one of the members on our list."

Why does that not surprise me? Just when I think Aunt Doreen couldn't do more, she adds something else to her expansive repertoire. "But how do *you* know her?"

"I found a prayer card from her daughter." I readjust, careful not to move my feet as the lady is now applying color. "It's probably totally against the rules, but I've been reading to her since . . . you know, she's going blind." Oddly enough, I've come to look forward to the hour visit. Even yesterday, before my date, I went by for a quick pop-in, just because I didn't want her to wonder where I was.

Doreen reaches over and squeezes my hand. "That's incredibly sweet of you, Jan. Her story is a very tragic one."

"There seems to be a lot of those." I pick at my fingers, allowing my mind to drift to the hundreds of prayer cards I've memorized. "I never realized how many people are hurting around us all the time. But every day, Ralph is flooded with emails asking for prayer." I shrug. "I guess it must be therapeutic in some ways to think a higher being exists when life feels out of control."

"Therapeutic?" Doreen shakes her head much like I did when she was talking about the farm animals. "No, Jan. Prayer is not a feeling. It's a power source, and those who tap into it get far more than a warm fuzzy. They get the strength to move mountains."

"Then why can't she see?" My question comes out harsher than I intend, but the thought invades my mind every time she has me read another chapter in Luke. Jesus healed the leper and the paralyzed man, so why not Mrs. Cox?

"That's a good question. One I don't have the answer to. Faith requires trust even when we don't always understand His purpose."

I snort. That word *faith* always seems to be their answer for everything they can't explain. Including the whole earth being millions of years old, which is Mom's favorite go-to whenever people start in on the religious talk.

"I just don't really see the point if it doesn't change your situation."

Doreen pats my hand like she would a small, ignorant child. "Prayer is not about changing your situation, although sometimes God grants those requests. It's about changing your heart. The difference between you and me, dear, is that when the bad times come, and they do for us all, I have comfort and peace. And I'm sure you've already noticed that Sandra does, too."

I don't have a rebuttal for that one because she's right. Sandra has an eerie peace about her. Even when she's complaining or admits her frustration, she always follows it up with some kind of positive statement.

My problems, especially in the last few months, pale in comparison to hers. And yet, after the breakup, it was a week before I could pull myself out of bed long enough to call Doreen and ask for help. Another week before I had the strength to pack up the belongings I'd only just unpacked a few months before. And seven more harrowing days before I finally left my ex's key with the landlord. The only time I felt even a little comfort in that span was when Doreen picked up the phone, and the feeling dissolved the minute I said goodbye to her.

"You've gone awful quiet over there," she says.

"Just thinking."

Doreen reaches over and pats my thigh. "Good. You just keep on doing that. The answers will come."

SIXTEEN

When I walk into Grace Community on Monday morning, my stomach is a cageful of butterfly wings. I know one night does not a relationship make, but I still expected some kind of correspondence from Cameron. Even an *I had a great time* text would have been sufficient. Instead, I spent half the evening watching *Gilmore Girls* on Netflix and checking my phone every two minutes.

Determined to no longer be "that girl," I head straight for Ralph's office, not even allowing myself a peek into the band room. I can do aloof and unaffected.

Maybe. I hope.

At this point, I'd take anything above stalker girl, because that was how I spent the other half of the evening—looking at every picture and comment on his Instagram page. I have Cameron's face memorized—the genuinely happy moments, the picture poses, even the pensive artistic profile shots that highlight the slope of his nose and straight chin.

My fingers tap my thigh as I wait for the elevator. Every inch of me vibrates with the need to walk backward, turn the corner, and demand to know if Saturday was a real date or not.

The elevator pops open and I rush inside, grateful to have the decision taken out of my hands. I press the second-floor button and settle against the metal wall, only to see the object of my affection turn the corner right as the doors begin to close.

The butterflies panic and so do I. I've never done indifferent very well, and since there's only been one other guy I felt this strongly about, I'm pretty certain I'm going to fail miserably at it again.

"Jan! Wait!" Cameron calls and jogs toward me.

I stick my arm out just as the doors are about to shut, and before they're fully open again, he's there, only two feet away and pressing his hand against the seam to keep it open.

"Do you have a second?"

"Um, sure," I say as if it's a decision and not the best question I've heard all morning. I follow him to a more private spot near the restrooms. "Is everything okay?"

"Better than okay." His dimples appear, and the torn-up deflated expression he wore most of the night on Saturday is nowhere to be found. Standing in front of me is the same joyous boy who handed me a guitar pick the day we met. I'm so happy to see this version that I feel the elation all the way to my toes.

"I spent all day yesterday praying about what to do with the band," he continues, "and you were right. It's too early to settle."

Relief stretches through every muscle. "That's great. I really think you're making the right call."

He steps closer and takes my hand. I hope he can't tell that it's trembling. Yes. This is what I've been reduced to in the presence of Cameron Lee—a trembling stalker girl who lives for his smile.

"You're the only one who understood why I hesitated. The only one to remind me what my true dream is, so thank you." He lets out a single laugh. "Everyone else is so ready for me to stop moping they'd probably encourage me to jump off a cliff at this point."

Joining Bryson's band would have been exactly that, but I don't say as much.

"They just want you to be happy. Good friends always do."

"And now I have one more person to add to that friend list."

I smile through my disappointment. I don't want to be just another one of his friends. "Yes, you do."

He gives my hand a squeeze. "Well, I have to run. Brent gets moody if we're late."

"Yeah, me too. I'm sure Ralph is wondering where I am."

"Okay. See you later, then?" He's already jogging back toward the band room before I have a chance to answer, so I don't bother. The question was obviously just a formality.

I trudge to the stairs, forgoing the elevator now that it reminds me of him. This is good. It's better to know up front than to wonder how he feels. It never would have worked between us anyway. He's the type to pray all day before making a life-changing decision. I'm the type to go visit a tarot card reader and believe her when she told me I'd already met my soulmate. That was twenty dollars and seven months I'll never get back.

Ralph's office comes into view quicker than I want it to, and chances are he's likely as grumpy as I am. What a pair we'll make today.

Only I become zero for two in my clairvoyant abilities.

Not only is Ralph not grumpy but he's also whistling while he works, lifting books from his overcrowded shelves, reading the spines, and then dropping them into one of two boxes at his feet.

I clear my throat, because this version of him is super unnerving.

"Jan! Great. I have a big project for us today." He turns and smiles. I think it's the first time I've ever seen his teeth. They're not bad. Straight enough to assume he had braces at some point. "You don't mind a little housekeeping, do you?"

"In this office? No." I cringe every time I come in here, so spending the day making it somewhat livable is welcome. Plus, it keeps me out of the band room and away from Cameron's let's-be-friends mantra.

Setting down my purse, I move to the bookshelf he's finally organizing. "What would you like me to do?"

He points to one of the boxes that's nearly full, then to the empty bookshelf by his desk. "Organize these by type, leaving some spaces so we can add more."

"By type?"

"You know, Bibles, Christian living, apologetics. That kind of thing." He drops another book into the box. "Think of a Christian bookstore."

"Oh yeah. Okay." I push the box because it's too heavy to carry and bite my lip all the way across the room. Not only have I never stepped foot into a Christian bookstore, but I don't even know what the word *apologetics* means. Abandoning the box, I circle back and grab my phone. Thank goodness for the internet. "You seem cheerful this morning," I say as I casually set my phone on an empty shelf.

"I do?" He shrugs like he's not aware he's been stomping around and pouting for a week. "Hmmm."

"Anything new happen?"

"Not really. My wife's been out of town and she got back this weekend, so there's that."

My smile is almost giddy, much like Ralph's. Victoria went home after all. Now I just have to help him keep her there. Flowers. Check. Time together was the next thing she listed.

I set the first book on the top shelf. Lucky for me, it is titled *A Christian Lifestyle*, so that was a no-brainer. "Your wife is a nurse, right?"

"Yep. Out at Serenity Hills."

"Don't they usually work shifts? Like two days on, three off or something?" I set another book on the shelf, trying for nonchalant.

"Three on, two off. Why?"

"Just curious." I go back to my task, set aside the books I need to look up, and focus on filling the Bible shelf. After enough time has passed to avoid suspicion, I say, "I had a friend who was a nurse, and she loved that schedule. She and her husband would go on these romantic getaways, just the two of them reconnecting." I glance at him over my shoulder. "Do you guys do that, too?"

Ralph's bushy eyebrows bunch together. "No, not really. It's hard for me to take time off."

"Well, I'm here now. When's her next two-day break?"

"Thursday and Friday, but we both have a lot of vacation time we haven't used."

"Perfect. You should plan a trip this week. Go look up a place, call her boss, do the packing and everything." I clutch my hands to my chest, let my expression go dreamy-eyed. "It's so romantic."

"It's irresponsible," he says, dousing my mood. "I have to order all the Bible study guides this week. And then there's my weekly hospital visits. I still haven't sorted through Sunday's prayer cards." His voice drops with each sentence as the reminder of his workload comes crashing down on him. "Not to mention, I haven't even told you about the breakfast ministry we do on Tuesday and Thursday mornings, or the thrift store, or any of the special projects they've laid on me recently."

I step forward, determined to get this guy to see that sacrificing his family for any reason, even a noble one like working in the church, is not acceptable. "Ralph. I can order the guides, do the breakfast thing, sort through the prayer cards, and visit anyone you need me to."

He drops two more books into a box and kicks it out of the way. "You don't know the order numbers or what class gets what books. That alone would take me a day just to train you."

"Senior adult four, *Bible Studies for Life*, order number 005075046.2019-SPR, eighteen copies, plus four in case of visitors." Score one for my brain and the stupid spreadsheet he had me fill out all last week. "Young adult, ninth and tenth grades, *Explore the Bible*: *Joshua, Judges, and Ruth*, order number 005792020, thirty-eight copies plus five for guests."

He's looking at me like my head just exploded in front of him.

"I can do this, Ralph," I say again, more deliberately this time. "Go spend some time with your wife—as much as you need. After all, you said she's been out of town, so I imagine you miss her."

He swallows. "You're sure? Because the order has to go in this week or we won't get it in time."

"Absolutely positive. This kind of stuff is easy for me."

He pauses as if he's actually considering my offer. "I guess maybe Eric could cover pastoral care for the week, and then you'd really only have the admin and maybe a few critical tasks that wouldn't take too much knowledge." Ralph stands straighter and abandons his book-dropping project. "And I could take you with me to breakfast tomorrow morning. Nora and her crew do all the hard work. I really just oversee it and make sure they feel supported."

"Sounds like a solid plan."

"We start prepping at six-thirty in the morning."

I put a hand on my hip. "Are you trying to talk me out of helping you?"

He sighs. "It's just a lot. And you've only been here a week."

"That's more one-on-one training than most people get. And like you said, Eric will be doing the ministry stuff, and he or Margie can help me if I get stuck on anything else."

He still looks unconvinced.

"Ralph, let someone else wear a shiny red cape every once in a while. Please, go be with your wife." I'm not sure if it's the reminder of Victoria or the plea in my voice, but I can sense the minute he caves.

"Okay . . . I'm going to do it, then." He walks to the door, and I swear there's an extra skip in his step. "I'll be right back. I just need to let Margie know that I'm taking the rest of the week off."

"Good for you." I sound like a cheerleader at a football game, but who cares. I know for him that this decision is like crossing the goal line for a touchdown with three defenders hanging on him.

I turn back to my task, feeling a strange satisfaction. It's been coming a lot lately. With Mrs. Cox and Victoria. Now with Ralph.

Doreen talks a lot about being "called" to this or that ministry, like it's somehow beyond her control.

I'm starting to wonder if that's another side effect of being at Grace Community, because I feel it, too. This sense of purpose and duty that goes beyond just wanting to get my own life under control.

January's Calling—to help the wounded and brokenhearted.

I scoff at the absurdity and slide another Bible onto the shelf.

SEVENTEEN

I slam my car door and drag my exhausted body to my cabin. I swear I probably burned ten thousand calories running up and down those stairs today, trying to keep up with all the information Ralph was throwing at me. Not that I have a reason to care about losing weight anymore. Apart from a quick "Hi, how are you doing?" in the hall, Cameron has shown no interest whatsoever in setting up another date. Either he's been as busy as I am or I'm completely off his radar now that he has purpose again.

My foot hits the first step when I notice my front door is wide open. Weird.

I search for the Kyles' white truck, which is nowhere to be seen, and my eye catches a long trail of blood droplets. They zag up the stairs, over the threshold, and into my living room, which thankfully has hardwood flooring. I set my purse on the rocking chair and pull out my phone, ready to call for backup.

"Hello?" I call while approaching the doorway. "You should know I've already dialed 911, so if you plan to hurt me, your DNA is all over my front porch." I poke my head inside, and it doesn't take long to spot the culprit or reason for all the blood. Dillon is hunched over my kitchen sink, his body contorted as he tries to get his right elbow under the stream of water.

I rush over and drop my phone on the counter when I see the two-and-a-half-inch gash in his arm. "What did you do?"

"Caught a nail." He pulls several paper towels from the roll and presses one to the wound. "It's not that deep. I just need to get the bleeding to stop enough to close it."

"With what?" I stare at the floor, the contents of the farthest junk drawer scattered everywhere. "Pens and batteries?"

He crouches down and picks up a bottle. "Superglue."

"Superglue! On your arm?" The man must have lost a lot of blood.

"Stings like the devil, but it works." He twists his injured elbow and attempts to reach the cut with his left hand. "I just . . . can't seem . . . to get to it." He gives up when blood gushes again and then presses the towel harder. "A little help might be nice."

"I'll drive you to the hospital, but I'm not supergluing your cut." I make a face when I look closer at the wound. "You probably need stiches."

"I don't." He leans his hip against the counter, his bicep flexing as he readjusts the towel. "Trust me, this isn't my first rodeo with an injury. I nearly lost a finger last year."

I feel an uncomfortable twist in my stomach as my eyes travel from his arms to his chest. He's in a T-shirt today. A thin one that looks a size too small. Annoyed, I drop to the floor and begin picking up the junk drawer remnants. "As encouraging as that little tidbit is, I'm still not shoving superglue into your bleeding flesh."

"Fine. Will you at least find the first-aid kit, then? It's not in the bathroom where it's supposed to be."

"That's because I moved it."

"Why?"

"To make room for my toiletries. That bathroom is small enough without it being a storage room." I stand and cross my arms. "I do live here, not that you seem to recognize that."

"Hey, you're the one who told me to get a set of keys."

"I know I did." I mash my lips together, and just when I come up with a jarring comeback, I spot the wilting daisies on my table and all the frustration dissolves. For some reason, I like seeing traces of Dillon in the cabin. It makes the space feel less lonely. "Come on. I put it in my bedroom."

Dillon seems apprehensive but follows me into the room. It's one of my favorite spaces. Bright white walls, a large king bed with a floral print duvet cover, and an old white antique dresser. I open the closet, push aside a few shoeboxes, and grab the kit.

Dillon is still standing by the doorway as if the floor might swallow him up. I guess I understand. I'd feel weird walking into Dillon's bedroom, too. The thought brings another round of pesky butterflies, and I no longer want to do this in here. "We should probably go back to the kitchen. I don't want your blood to stain my comforter."

He backs up, letting me pass by him. "How very kind of you. I take it nursing isn't on your long list of professions."

"Actually, I did try being a nurse's aide once. I lasted a week." I pull out two dining chairs and have them face each other. "Now sit, before I show you why they frowned at my bedside manner." I pat the wood seat and Dillon chuckles. I like how I always seem to make him laugh, even when I'm not trying to.

As soon as we're positioned, I slowly remove the stained towel from his arm. He's right. The cut is messy and long but not terribly deep. The kit has antibiotic cream, Q-tips, gauze, and what do you know . . . skin adhesive.

He sees it at the same time I do. "I told you. Superglue. Only they charge more for this one."

"Because it's designed for skin, not plastic."

I tug his arm closer and make the first sweep of cream. He doesn't move, not even to flinch, when I know it must hurt. Instead, he watches me, intently, and it makes my hands start to shake. I finish the cream and wipe away the excess with sterile gauze.

"A Band-Aid isn't going to be enough," he says when I hesitate.

"I know. I've just never used Dermabond before."

"Close the wound and apply. It's real simple." His voice is calm enough to make me believe him. I grab the small capsule, crush the ampoule, and carefully brush it over the line I formed by pinching his skin.

"So how did your date go this weekend?"

I freeze for a millisecond, then continue, knowing he purposely waited until I was stuck before asking me. "It wasn't a date. We just hung out with some of his friends."

"Maybe that's what it ended up being, but you certainly dressed up as if you were going on a date."

I glance up and meet his gaze. "Do you want me to do this or not?"

"Do you always shy away from tough conversations, or is it just with me?"

I think of Doreen and scowl. Okay, so maybe I do skirt hard topics, but not everyone likes conflict. Some of us prefer avoidance. Hence the continued silence with my mom, and my fabulous ability to change the subject. "You and Cameron seem pretty tight. How do you two know each other?"

He grins like he's caught on to exactly what I'm doing, but answers anyway. "We grew up together. Went to the same church since kindergarten, same high school, hung in the same circles. I'm a year older, but Grace Community was small back then, so we all ended up being combined."

I want to ask about his ex-wife, if she was also in those circles, but decide against it. "He mentioned they hadn't seen you in a while. How come?"

Dillon's mouth tightens, but unlike me he doesn't redirect the question. "I see no point in living a lie. Church isn't really where I want to be right now, and since we were all raised to hold each other accountable, I know they'd spend the whole night trying to get me to come back before I'm ready."

Silence fills the space, and I gently blow against the adhesive to make sure it's dry. He flinches then, and goose bumps appear across his skin. I look up, confused. "Did I hurt you?"

"No." He clears his throat. "I think the Dermabond is set by now."

I ease my fingers away, half expecting the skin to pop back open. It doesn't, and now the bloody mess is simply a long, thin red line. "All better."

He rises from the chair and gathers the trash. "Thanks. I'll grab a mop."

I watch him work, moving around the cabin as if he'd once lived here. "Is Doreen your company's only client?"

Dillon pauses by the broom closet, and his eyebrows squish together. I'm learning that he does that every time I say something he thinks is crazy.

"I just ask because you're always here," I explain.

"I like it here, and while Doreen is certainly not our only client, she is our favorite one." He pulls a mop and bucket from the recesses of the space. "We actually have offices in Waxahachie, Ennis, Corsicana, and Mansfield."

"Oh. That is big."

He does his chuckle-snort thing. "Yeah. Big enough that both my dad and I have the luxury of choosing our projects. This place is mine." He props the bucket under the faucet. "I've worked at B&L Ranch since the day Doreen decided to make it a wedding venue. I designed this cabin for my senior project and started construction right after graduation."

"So you're the one to blame for my not having a tub."

He cuts off the water and glances behind him. "There's only so much you can do when given a maximum of eight hundred square feet."

"Yeah, yeah. Just admit it. You're a man so it never crossed your mind."

He carefully sets the bucket on the floor and glances up at me through his eyelashes. "I admit it. I saw absolutely no need to put one in here." His grin is daring and alarmingly handsome.

"Knew it," I say, though it's hard to do so. Once again, Dillon Kyle has hit me with an entirely new perspective and left me scrambling for unshakable ground. "Wow. An architect."

"Yep, with a minor in landscaping." He straightens and crosses his arms. "What did you think I did for a living?"

"I don't know. I never thought much about it." I just always took it for granted that he was the one out here watering the plants, trimming trees, fixing . . . whatever.

"That's flattering."

"I didn't mean it like I don't care. I just figured you and

your dad mostly did work for my aunt is all." He raises his eyebrow, and I feel my cheeks flush. "Here, I'll do that. You get the sink and countertops."

He sets the mophead in the water and offers the handle to me. The minute I grab hold, he pulls it back, forcing me to stumble closer.

Our faces are only a foot apart, much like they were in the bathroom when I noticed his eyes. The same eyes that have me captivated even now.

"You can't truly know someone from a distance, January. Every one of us has our own set of secrets and demons and quirks. You just have to decide if it's worth taking the time to learn them. And if you're willing to let someone close enough to learn yours."

His unyielding gaze makes my chest feel like bursting. There's too much context in his statement, like he's asking me for something I'm not ready to give.

When I remain silent, he lets go of the handle and returns to the sink. I study the sudsy water and watch the swirls of soap until my phone buzzes on the counter.

Dillon gets to it before I do and hands it to me. "Looks like it was a date after all."

I glance down, and my heart triples its speed.

Cameron.

I drop the mop and answer before you can say *spit shine*. "Hey. I'm so glad you called."

"Yeah? Is this an okay time?"

"It's perfect."

Dillon waves me away as if I'm an annoyance and picks up the abandoned mop. I go for an evil eye stare, but I'm pretty sure it fails because he just shakes his head and chuckles under his breath. I'm starting to wonder if that particular response of his has a deeper meaning, yet I can't think about that right now.

Cameron clears his throat. "So, the rumor mill has been buzzing today about Ralph. You prepared to fly solo already?"

"It's only sort of solo. Eric's picking up most of the work," I say, excusing myself to the porch and shutting the door behind me. "Ralph's showing me how to run the breakfast in the morning and then taking off."

"I guess that means you won't be working in the band room for a while."

I cover the mouthpiece and blow out a relieved breath. He sounds disappointed. "Probably not. I've been running around like a madwoman just trying to write down a third of what Ralph does, let alone do it for him."

"When does he get back?"

"Not sure. He said it depended on the amount of time off Victoria could swing."

"Well, that stinks. Work is far better when you're around to distract me."

"Yeah?" I sit, grinning and twisting my hair. "In that case, I'm sure I can find a moment or two to come bother you."

"I'd like that, and . . . if you're free next Friday, maybe we can even try hanging out without Margie spying on us."

I silently kick my feet back and forth and thank karma again for this beautiful man. "Won't your roommates do the same thing?"

"Nope. As luck has it, they're both going to a concert that night in Dallas."

"What about the rest of the crew?" My question feels bold, but no way am I doing another group date. Not until I know where we stand.

"Actually, I was thinking just you and me this time." His

voice hitches a little, and it comes off like he's nervous I'll say no. It's so cute I want to stand in my chair and dance.

"Sounds perfect."

I hear a faint exhale and nearly smack myself for second-guessing things. Cameron isn't like other men. I keep forgetting that.

"So it's a date?"

"It's a date."

"Good." He pauses, and I hear voices in the background. "Well, I better . . . uh, get back to the guys. See you tomorrow at work?"

"I'll be there."

"Bye, Jan."

I stand, the ground feeling suspiciously like cloud nine, or ninety-nine, or nine hundred ninety-nine. Whatever combination works. I'm so euphoric when I walk back into my cabin that I slip on the wet floor, my feet going two different directions while my phone crashes and slides under the couch.

"It's wet. Be careful."

I'm halfway into the split position when my foot stops moving. "Thanks. You're extremely helpful." Hopefully, Dillon speaks sarcasm because it's oozing from me. I rock back and forth trying to keep from toppling over. "You know, I didn't just stand there and watch when you were bleeding all over my sink."

He strolls into the living room, clasps his hands around my elbows, and lifts me back on my feet. It's effortless, like I'm nothing more than a speck of dust. "Happy?"

Oh yeah, he knows sarcasm.

"Yes, actually I am." I consider sticking out my tongue but don't. There comes an age when it's no longer cute, and I think I crossed that threshold years ago.

"Everything's blood-free again, so I'm out." He lets go and tugs open the door, not forcefully but definitely with a little attitude. I'm not sure what I did to upset him, but his mood has certainly plummeted. "Don't forget there's a big group here this weekend. You may want to bunk with Doreen a couple of nights."

I tilt my head. "Are you worried about me?"

"A single girl out here alone, yeah. I think you need to take precautions."

"Okay. I will."

His forehead wrinkles like he's surprised I'm not going to argue with him. I guess that's fair. We do spend most of our time arguing. "Alright. Well, I'll see ya around." He steps outside, and for some reason it bothers me that he's once again leaving frustrated. I don't want there to always be contention between us.

"Hey, Dillon?" I call. He stops and turns, his eyes meeting mine. They seem sad. "Thank you for the daisies. They made me happy."

Some of his weariness falls away, and I'm granted a rare authentic smile. One not steeped in additional context. "You're welcome."

EIGHTEEN

The sky is still dark when I step outside Tuesday morning, and for the fifth time I wonder what I was thinking when I encouraged Ralph to go on vacation.

"You were thinking about Victoria," I say out loud, chastising my selfishness. Ralph has been doing this job for years without a break. I can handle a small portion for a few weeks. I hurry down the steps and into my car, my breath a white vapor against the cold morning air. The coffee I drank isn't working, and I yawn hard enough to force an eye shut as I start the engine.

Carefully, I ease my way out of the parking lot and slow to a crawl when I exit the property. I hate driving this road in the dark. Even more frustrating is that I know there's a wide two-lane road that leads from the main highway into my mom's property and continues all the way to Doreen's side, but Mom had it barricaded after the funeral. A decision made solely out of spite.

I sigh and flick on my brights. I nearly broke down and called her last night, but ended up going to bed instead. If she did answer the phone, I'd have to come up with something to tell her about my job. And admitting to my mom that I'm now working at a church would take a measure of courage I haven't quite mustered.

The main highway finally appears, and twenty minutes later I'm pulling up in front of the downtown building where breakfast is served.

It's six-thirty in the morning, so the streets are barren, as is the parking lot minus Ralph's truck and three other vehicles. He steps out of the driver's side after I park and gives me a small wave. He's dressed in jogging pants, a light jacket, and tennis shoes. Not exactly breakfast-serving attire.

"You ready for this?" he asks in a voice that is as much teasing as it is worrisome.

"Sort of. How many people usually come out?"

"Fifty to a hundred. Used to be more, but the economy has improved some."

He unlocks the door while I wait behind him. It's a rusty contraption that takes him several attempts and lots of jiggling to open. "This lock is old, but give it a few tugs and it'll catch." Finally, he pushes the door in and wiggles the key back out. "Here." He offers the key, and I take it, even though I don't want to. If a four-minute jiggle is considered functional, I'm terrified to see what's inside.

"I won't be the first one here, will I?"

"Not usually. But I want you to have it just in case. We have three regular volunteers and they're stellar. Nora and her husband run the kitchen. Although Nora's dad has been in and out of the hospital, so she's been pulled away quite a bit. And Pete serves and entertains."

"Entertains?"

"You'll see." Ralph extends his hand, and I walk into the lobby of the building, eager for some warmth. What I get instead is a face-to-face encounter with a massive yellow reptile behind a thin piece of glass.

"What in the . . ." I jump back, knocking into Ralph with the force of a volcano. "There's a snake on the counter."

He steadies me with two solid hands on my upper arms. "That's just Monty. Pete brings him for the kids."

The lobby area is only about sixty square feet, most of it being the check-in counter and a small lounging area. The two double doors across from the entry are open, exposing a large dining space already bustling with activity.

I ease as far around the snake cage as possible, and I swear the thing lifts its head to get a better feel for how good I'll taste. "He's looking at me," I say, sliding along the chair since I can't go farther back.

"Doubt that." Ralph's mouth twitches upward at my terror, and I think I may like the old brooding version better. "Poor guy was born without any eyes."

I pause to look closer at the snake's head, trying to keep my stomach from revolting. It's hard to tell, but sure enough, the scaled skin continues right from the head to the nose.

Good grief. A blind snake is chilling out in the lobby, likely waiting on his breakfast to be served. I've stepped into a circus sideshow.

I somehow make it into the dining room without incident and flinch a little at the bright fluorescent lights that periodically flicker and vibrate. The floor is waxed linoleum tile, white with a weird blue pattern on each square. Old recycled lunchroom tables fill the area, offering at least a hundred seats throughout the space.

"You must be the new Ralph."

I take in the approaching man with baggy gray slacks and a fluorescent green Hawaiian shirt. He uses a cane when he steps with his right leg, and his hands are marred with at least a hundred scars ranging in depth and width. He offers me his left one. "I'm Pete Kenzie. January, right?"

I lightly shake his hand, which feels as leathery and damaged as it looks. "I actually go by Jan."

"No need to simplify the exceptional. January is a great name. Means 'month of the wolf,' you know."

My sudden curiosity surprises me. "No, I didn't know."

"Yep. And a wolf has powerful instincts, intuition, and high intelligence." He winks at me. "I can already tell your name fits."

Score one for the oddly dressed man who likes blind reptiles. I think this is the first time I've ever felt even a smidgen of pride for my name.

Ralph checks his watch. "We better keep moving. Doors open in an hour."

"We're fine. Got plenty of time." Pete slides his arm through mine and tugs, using me as his stabilizer instead of the cane. "Nora and Mike are a fine couple. They'll show you all the ropes in the kitchen."

We weave around a stainless-steel serving counter that marks the start of a moderate but functional commercial kitchen. There's a narrow island, two wide stainless refrigerator freezers, an eight-burner stove, and multiple sinks and counter spaces, but no Nora or Mike.

"They're in the pantry." Pete points to a small room in the corner. "We keep all the supplies locked up in there. Keeps things from walking off, if you know what I mean." He goes on to inform me about keys and plate setups and then his cousin Benny's schizophrenic toad.

He's halfway through the story when Nora appears, moving at the speed of sound, arms full. Her long blond hair is braided down her back, and she seems to be a pattern girl like myself. Each step is exactly a tile square at a time. No cracks. The fact that she can do it so quickly and without looking is a testament to how long she's been volunteering here.

"Hello and nice to meet you. Pull out the milk and I'll get you going on the eggs." She pauses when she spots Ralph at the doorway. "I thought you were on vacation."

"I am as soon as breakfast is over."

"It is over. For you." Nora waves him away. "Now get."

"But Jan needs—"

"I'm fine," I assure him, though I'm not sure I believe it. "I'll see you when you get back."

He looks genuinely torn. "You have my cell, right? If you need anything, call me. Victoria's co-workers have banded together to cover the schedule, so we're thinking one week, two at the most. Eric will be available, as well."

"I know he is. We've already discussed who's doing what. So stop worrying and take all the time you need."

After Mike joins in the chorus, Ralph finally departs, leaving me alone with the three oddest volunteers on the planet.

Pete must sense my unease because he pats my shoulder. "Don't worry. It's a piece of cake once you get the hang of it."

~

The sentiment *longest week ever* has nothing on the four days I've worked without Ralph. My to-do list is growing longer by the minute, and even Eric felt the need to apologize to me as he promised to include the extra hours I've worked in my next paycheck.

The little above-and-beyond things that Ralph does each day without being asked or recognized are too many to count, and if nothing else comes from his absence, I'm pretty sure the "new minister" they're searching for will get hired sooner rather than later.

The thought of my time at Grace Community ending makes me sadder than I expect it to, which isn't good considering I've been teetering between depressed and lonely all night. Even the text from Cameron asking how my weekend was going wasn't able to pull me out of my funk. Of course, that could have been because despite my very strong hint that I didn't have anything planned beyond lying around and recovering from my busy week, he made no offer to keep me company. Instead, what I got was an *I'm glad you're resting, you deserve it* text, along with a smiley face. Any chance of moving our date up from next weekend to this one is pretty much shot. Oh well. Absence makes the heart grow fonder, right?

I push the torturous thought away and continue my quest for the one item I have no business pulling out. Some people have blankets or lovies that they save from childhood. I have an old AC/DC T-shirt that's two sizes too big. It's the only thing I have from Stepdad #1, and why it brings me comfort after all these years I may never know. Still, I carefully pull the old shirt from its hiding place and inhale the faded cotton smell. The material lost his scent long ago, but on the really hard days, when the pain of rejection feels more powerful than the resolution to hate him, it's nice to believe we have even the slightest of connections.

As it has too many times to count, the old shirt eases the sharp pain in my heart the minute I pull it over my pajamas. I don't even care that I look ridiculous with red flannel arms and legs poking out under ugly stone-washed black cotton.

It's funny how memories only tell part of the story. In my

mind, Stepdad #1 was the coolest guy I'd ever known, even though his choice in clothing screams otherwise. He had a radiant smile and would lift me onto his shoulders every time we'd go on an outing, which was often when he was around. Then he started disappearing. First for a night, then for a week, and then . . . forever.

I squeeze my eyes shut until his face fades from my mind. It happens quicker now than when I was a kid, but it still drains me every time. I slam the closet door with a fist, annoyed by my sentimentality, and escape to the front porch. A cold breeze slaps my face the minute I step outside, and I welcome the numbness, welcome the way it cools the heat in my cheeks and eliminates the moisture in my eyes.

Music is booming from the reception hall, and I know it has to be packed in there, even though the cars have thinned quite a bit since the actual ceremony two hours ago. I embrace the noise and the reminder that I'm here, safe and cared for.

Doreen has been a helicopter mom all week, far more concerned about this wedding than I've been. We argued for ten minutes when I refused to stay at their house, but I wasn't about to set a precedent. Tonight is the start of many more events to come, and I know if we can just make it through this first milestone without incident, she'll relax about my being out here all by myself.

Still, it's no surprise at all when headlights flash across the old rocking chairs and a truck turns the corner toward my tiny parking lot. Uncle Jim has already dropped by twice to check on me. And even though I assured him and Doreen both not twenty minutes ago on the phone that I'm fine and no psycho wedding crashers have taken me hostage, he must be coming for round three.

"Are you going to do this all night?" I call out at the silhouette exiting the truck. "Because I'm pretty sure this is way past your normal bedtime." Uncle Jim is on rancher's hours—asleep by nine and up with the sun. "And I'm guessing you're not going to like me very much when you're sleep-deprived tomorrow."

"Eh. I'll find a way to get over it."

I freeze when I hear the voice that is definitely not my uncle's.

Dillon slams the driver's door and walks toward my cabin, the porch light hitting the side of his face as soon as he reaches the edge of the gravel.

"What are you doing here?" I choke out, too surprised to come up with a nicer greeting.

"Taking pity on your aunt. Dad called and said she's been pacing for an hour." He glances up at me, and I swear he nearly trips when his eyes take in the full picture. "What are you wearing?"

"Don't dis the T-shirt," I snap and then force a smile so I don't give away the significance.

"Sorry." He lifts his hands in surrender. "I just never pictured you as a heavy-metal fan. You have Taylor Swift groupie written all over you."

"I'm not a fan. I just like this shirt." I cross my arms over my chest. There aren't many emotional doors in my life that I open, but the one labeled DADDY is locked with a million dead bolts, and I have no intention of that changing anytime soon. "And don't dis Taylor Swift, either. She's an amazing songwriter."

"Yes, I can see how you would gravitate to her hundreds of breakup ballads." He smiles at me, and I return it with a scowl.

"Okay . . . you came, you saw, you insulted. I believe your obligation has been fulfilled."

"Hardly." He hops up the last step, taking away my high-ground position, and shakes a DVD case. "I've been instructed to stay until the last guest leaves." He checks his watch. "Which I'm guessing at this rate will be close to midnight."

"And how exactly did you get roped into being my baby-sitter?"

"I volunteered."

"Why?"

His smirk grows. "Because the job came with two pans of your aunt's chicken enchiladas."

I open my mouth and shut it again. There's not a whole lot I wouldn't do for a pan of Doreen's enchiladas. "Fine, but if I'm forced to spend the evening watching—" I grab the movie out of his hand and roll my eyes. Could he be more of a Texan?—"Westerns all night, then I better find a nice full Tupperware in my fridge tomorrow."

He actually hesitates, and I smack his arm.

"Fine," he moans and rubs at his flesh. "I'll share, but only because you asked so nicely."

"Go inside before I come to my senses." I push him through the door and then immediately head toward my room.

"Where are you going?"

"Nowhere. I just need to take this shirt off."

Dillon leans against the couch and stares at my face with way too much insight. "You want to talk about it?"

"No."

He continues to stare, and my whole body tenses with the need to beg him not to push. Finally, he straightens. "Well, hurry up then."

It takes me exactly 5.4 seconds to rip off the shirt, shove it back in my closet, and return to the living room.

Dillon's squatting in front of the DVD player, blowing air into the disc tray. "How long since you used this thing? It's full of dust."

"Never. All my movies are digital. Do you want some popcorn?"

Dillon stands, apparently satisfied now with the cleanliness of the movie player. "Only if it's not that no-flavor, air-popped kind."

"Do I look like I've been skipping butter lately?"

"Is there a safe answer to that question?"

"No, probably not."

He tosses the empty case on the coffee table and comes to help me in the kitchen. "Here, let me do it. That microwave is moody."

I jerk the packet away. "I know how to pop popcorn, Dillon."

"Really? Because I'm pretty sure you burned it so bad last week that the stench lingered in here for two days."

Busted.

He reaches for the popcorn a second time, and this time I let him take the bag. "The secret is to put it on fifty percent power for two and a half minutes. Never trust the popcorn button. It lies." He closes the door and mashes the corresponding buttons.

"Dillon?"

"Yeah?"

"Why did you really come here tonight? I know my aunt is an amazing cook, but come on."

He turns, and his mouth tenses to the point I wonder if I've finally asked the one question he won't answer. Seconds pass, but then he rubs at his chin and admits, "Being alone on a Saturday night sucks. And I just didn't feel like doing it tonight." And because it's Dillon, I know he's one hundred percent telling me the truth.

"Even when the company is a Taylor Swift–loving basket case?"

His smile is enough to make all the teasing I endure from him worth it. "Yeah, even then."

And I realize he's right, because somehow the earlier sadness I'd been wrestling with has disappeared, and I'm pretty positive the shift had nothing to do with the AC/DC shirt crumpled in my closet.

"In that case, I guess for the sake of Saturday night, I can also deal with a moody popcorn Nazi who has a dust fetish."

Dillon shakes his head and points to the cabinet. "Just . . . get out a bowl."

"A bossy popcorn Nazi at that." I feign annoyance but do as he asks.

It's a crazy idea, but I think Dillon and I might have just become friends.

NINETEEN

I stand in the center of Ralph's semi-clean office feeling pretty proud of what I've accomplished in just over a week. We certainly have more to go, but hopefully I've done enough to encourage future getaways with his wife.

"Knock, knock." Darcy pokes her head inside Ralph's office and gives me a wide grin. "Cam said you were up here."

"Hey. What are you doing here?" The question comes out more surprised than friendly, even though I'm actually really happy to see her. My female interactions lately have been reduced to women thirty to fifty years my senior.

Darcy steps through the door. "I've come to beg for money. Hence the fancy getup and the appointment with Pastor Thomas." Her hand sweeps down her outfit of black slacks and a white button-up dress shirt. She wears no makeup or jewelry, and her hair is in a ponytail. Add a hand towel over her arm and she'd be ready for table service.

I hold in a laugh and decide right then and there that the two of us need to spend more time together. She desperately needs some fashion help, and I need a large dose of her self-assuredness. "Why are you asking for money?"

Darcy drops into Ralph's old leather chair and slouches, as

miserable as a teenage boy at a baby shower. "I've been accepted to teach English at a Christian school in Guatemala, but you have to have all your funding secured before you can go. And I guess the organization I'm working with has had too many missionaries back out, so they require a full six months of salary to be wired ahead of time. And then written letters of obligation for the last six months of sponsorships. I don't have either yet."

"You speak Spanish?" I'm taken aback by nearly everything she just said, but for some reason this is the question that comes out.

"I'm not fluent, but I can get by. And I know once I'm immersed in the culture, it will come even more." She spins Ralph's chair in a circle. "PT's gonna talk to the missions team and see how much they can sponsor." She crosses both fingers and holds them up. "Anyway, I thought I'd grab you and Cam, and we could go get some grub."

"It's already lunchtime?" I look down at my watch and cringe. "I can't. I have a standing appointment." One I'm forty-five minutes late for. "In fact, I should have been there a while ago. Time totally got away from me." I grab my purse as Darcy stands, her disappointment obvious. "I want to go, I do, but I haven't gone to see Mrs. Cox in days."

Her eyes brighten. "Sandra Cox?"

"You know her?"

"Everyone knows her. She and her husband taught second-grade Sunday school for twenty years. Now that you mention it, I haven't seen her at church in a long time. Then again, we're so big now that I could probably pass right by her." There's a bite to her voice as if she doesn't necessarily love how much Grace Community has grown. It's very different from Cameron, who seems to feed off the influx of people.

"She's at Serenity Hills now." I stop myself before mentioning her blindness, unsure if I'm allowed to disclose medical information.

"Really? Man. That makes me sad."

"You can come with if you'd like. We just read a chapter or two in Luke, and then if we have time, a few chapters from one of her novels. I'm sure she'd love more visitors."

Darcy shakes her head, and it's very different from how Dillon does it. Hers feels doused in admiration, while Dillon's, well, it usually comes with that infuriating chuckle. Then I realize I'm thinking about Dillon and I shake my own head, trying to get the image of his confounded brown eyes to go away.

"Cam's right. You really are something special," she says.

"I wouldn't go that far. I'm just trying to find a little purpose in my life after a year of . . ." I trail off because I don't want to admit to how impulsive and irresponsible I've been. That version of me would never have cared about an old lady. Then again, it's easy to empathize with wounded people once you've been one yourself. I slide my purse over my shoulder. "I'm sorry, but I'm so late."

"Oh, no problem." She follows me out the door and shuts it behind us. I don't think Ralph keeps it locked during the day so I haven't bothered to, either. Besides, the room is clean enough now that it no longer brings total humiliation when someone dares to open the door.

We reach the stairs and descend side by side. "If the church funds the rest of your money, when do you think you'll leave?" I ask.

"This summer is the plan."

"And how long will you stay gone?"

"A year for sure. Maybe two if all goes well. Of course,

right now I have only half of what I need, so it may be just a pipe dream." She rolls her eyes, but I can see the stress in them. She really does want this. Incredible. I can't even imagine spending a day in a foreign country all alone, and here Darcy's willing to do it for a whole year.

"And you think I'm special? You're the bravest person I know."

That makes her smile. "Thank you. I've wanted to do this since I heard a missionary speak at youth camp my freshman year. It's just hard finding a place as a single woman, and now with all the cuts in overseas support, it's even worse."

For some reason, my mind drifts back to the bleeding man in my kitchen and his admission of having so much money that he doesn't need to work. "Well, if the church doesn't come through, you should talk to the Kyles. They seem like the philanthropist type."

Darcy's smile fades away. "No. I'd feel way too weird asking."

"But I thought you've all known each other forever."

She gets to the bottom step before me and waits. "We have, but neither Dillon nor his dad have stepped into church since his mom passed away. Calling them now would feel way too insensitive." She spots Cameron and starts to head that way, but I can't think past her revelation.

"Wait." I grab her arm before she can go farther. "Dillon's mom died? When?"

"Last January. Almost exactly a year ago."

And now I have another reason to hate my namesake.

Cameron's approach halts our conversation. "Hey, we ready to go?"

"Jan has another obligation, so it's just yours truly." She hits him in the arm like an old buddy, yet he doesn't react. He's too focused on me.

"What obligation?"

"I read to Mrs. Cox at lunch. And I'm now an hour late so I really have to go," I say, still totally distracted.

"Okay. I'll try not to be too jealous." Cameron drapes his arm around my shoulder, and unlike every other time before, my body has no reaction whatsoever. All I can think about is Dillon's comment the first day we met, the one that I've resented enough to make me constantly approach him with caution.

"You seem less broken."

He didn't say it to be cruel or judgmental. He said it because he knew exactly how it felt.

TWENTY

I run up the front steps of Serenity Hills feeling terrible, not just because of my tardiness with Mrs. Cox but also in how I've treated Dillon since we first met. Even after Doreen warned me that he was hurting, I've never filtered any of my thoughts and words with him.

Beth, one of the other staff RNs, is talking to an orderly when I pass by the desk heading straight for the green hallway. She's much stricter about protocol and policies than Victoria is so I wave quickly, not wanting any more delays.

"Jan, hold on a sec," she calls, moving around the desk to approach.

I swallow my annoyance and meet her halfway. The nursing home has a pretty firm schedule for the residents, and based on the heavy concentration on her face, I have a bad feeling I'm about to get the boot. "I know I'm super late, but I'd still like to at least visit with her a little while."

"Mrs. Cox isn't here." She lays a hand on my arm, and her normally harsh voice turns soft enough to bring an anxious shiver. "She had another episode this morning and was transferred to Methodist Hospital. I don't know when she'll be back."

My mind races. Her daughter hadn't mentioned any other medical conditions in her prayer request. "Episode? What do you mean?"

"Sandra's had a heart condition for many years now."

I swallow back the tears that have been fighting to come since learning about Dillon's mom. "Can I go see her?"

"Of course. Let me get you her room information." Beth pats my arm and it brings some measure of comfort, though not much. Too many questions swirl in my head. Did her daughter know? Would she get there in time to make things right with her mom?

I grab the scribbled paper Beth hands me and race to my car. Methodist is close, so it only takes seven minutes to get there. Mrs. Cox is on the second floor, down a long hallway that echoes as I walk. I don't think, just move as if it were my own mom in that room and I'm desperate to get to her.

Irritation revs up my adrenaline. This is how the church survives. They suck you in, make you care about people who aren't even related to you, like Dillon and his dad, Ralph and Victoria, and now Mrs. Cox and her daughter. I'm supposed to be working on my own life right now, not worrying about Dillon's grief or crying over an old lady.

But the tears only come harder when I step past her open door. Heart monitor wires stick out of her hospital gown while an IV flows into her bruised hand. She's asleep or unconscious, I'm not sure which.

I sit in the chair near her bed and listen to the beeping of her heart monitor. It's the kind of rhythm that will hypnotize if you listen long enough. I fold my hands in my lap, feeling a restlessness I can't describe. It's in my lungs, my arms, my bouncing leg. I bite my lip, fighting what I feel pressured to do.

"Prayer is a power source," Doreen said.

But I don't believe in it, or in God, or in any supernatural thing that suddenly fixes all problems. I believe in medicine and doctors and science. Mrs. Cox already has all those things.

I stand and pace the room. It doesn't help. In fact, it makes the pressure heavier, my mind filling with the words from our latest chapter in Luke. It flows as if I were reading it now, each verse imprinted, the story flashing like it wants me to respond. The centurion wasn't a Jew, yet he asked Jesus to heal his servant, and Jesus did.

My fingers lace around the back of my head and I sit down. Do the prayers of someone like me even get heard? If Doreen's God does exist, would He bother to listen?

The quiet rising and lowering of Sandra's chest takes the decision out of my hands. I'll do it. I'll pray for her and for her daughter, wherever she is.

I close my eyes and bow my head the way I've seen Doreen do it at the dinner table. The plea flows through my mind. For Mrs. Cox to wake up, for her daughter to be here when she does. I think of Dillon's mom and feel an even greater urgency.

"Please," I whisper. "Don't let her die before they can reconcile."

When I'm finished, I feel completely depleted, as if the prayer took every ounce of my energy. Power source? Yeah, right. More like a battery drain.

I stand, knowing there's nothing else I can do, and touch Mrs. Cox's fragile arm, the one place that has no tubing. "We need to finish our story, so I expect you to be awake when I come back."

A steady beep is all I get in response. At least that's something. Proof that life still exists.

I leave her bed and am halfway to the elevators when a woman rushes past, hair poking out from her bun, mascara smeared under her eyes. She stops and talks to the nurses, her voice frantic. I know immediately she's Sandra's daughter. I'd know even if they didn't look alike, which they do. Her daughter has the same pink oval birthmark on her neck, though it's not wrinkled like her mother's.

I don't linger, not wanting to explain who I am and why I'm here. It would probably only add to her daughter's guilt. The elevator doors open and close, but the sweat on my neck only doubles. All I can picture is Aunt Doreen tapping a foot, wearing a smug smile while she chants, *I told you so*.

Coincidence. It has to be. Because if it isn't, then I just witnessed a legit answer to prayer. The very first prayer I've ever spoken, which makes the situation even more jarring.

I suck in gulps of air when I hit the parking lot. My head feels funny, and I have this sense that something is chasing me but I don't know what. As soon as I reach my car, I lean against the door and close my eyes, trying to rein in the panic. I know what's driving it—guilt. For being here, for praying, for going two months without speaking to my mom. She didn't raise me this way, to be driven by compassion and emotion.

My heart is at odds with itself. Who I was and who I'm becoming are in too great a conflict to do anything but destroy each other. I reach in my purse, grab my phone before doubt makes me change my mind.

She answers on the first ring, and the tears come again.

"Hi, Mom," I say with a choked whisper.

"January," she sighs into the phone. "It's about time."

Talking with my mom always seems to ground me, even if we did spend thirty minutes out of the fifty-minute conversation talking about my stepdad and his vices. Trust me, there are some things a girl just does not need to know about her mother's husband.

Unfortunately, my mom has no need for such discretion. Nor does she have any girlfriends besides me. She blames her beauty, saying most can't handle being the frumpy best friend. I blame the fact that Mom tends to flirt with any male who breathes, even the married ones.

Still, the phone call accomplished what I needed it to. I feel tons better, and Mom and I are speaking. Even if Doreen and anything related to my living here isn't among the things we're speaking about, at least we've established communication again.

I unfold from my Prius and stretch, my muscles tight from sitting during our entire phone call. There was no way I was walking into the church with my mom on the phone. I turn to shut the door and spot Cameron giving Darcy a hug. They're standing by what I assume is her truck, and she wipes under her eyes after they release each other.

That little green villain curls inside me even with her assurance they're only friends. Knowing my luck, his interest in me has made her realize the error of her ways, and lunch was just a chance to get her hooks back into him.

He backs away from her truck but watches it leave the parking lot. That's a sign, isn't it? A man turning to get one last look, or watching the empty road after the car disappears. It takes another thirty seconds for him to notice me, and when he does, I'm not so sure I want him to. Today's been far too much of a roller coaster of emotions to deal with this right now.

"Hey, you just get back?" His face lights with a smile, and my irritation fades. How does he do that to me every time? It's like I have no capacity to be sad or mad or anything but stupidly giddy when he comes around.

"Yeah. How was lunch?"

"Not nearly as fun without you." He lifts a small to-go box. "But I brought you back something."

"Really?" And now I'm blushing. Good grief. I open the styrofoam lid and see a blue-and-pink swirled dessert.

"It's cotton-candy cheesecake." He shrugs when I look up at him, so incredibly touched I nearly start with the tears again. "To tide you over until I can get you out to a Rangers game."

I close the lid and hug the little box to my heart. "Thank you. I don't even know what to say."

"You don't need to say anything." He tucks a piece of hair behind my ear and all my insecurity fades. "Just promise me we're still on for tomorrow night."

"Absolutely."

He slides his arm around my shoulder, a favorite position for him I'm learning. Maybe it's because our bodies are such a great fit. He's tall enough to tuck me against his chest without having to stretch at all. "How was Mrs. Cox?"

"I don't want to talk about it." No way am I diving into that story. I'm still totally freaked out by the whole thing.

"Okaaay . . ." He draws out the word like he's waiting for me to change my mind. I won't. "Let's talk about tomorrow, then. I was thinking a movie, some gourmet pasta, and my famous brownies."

"You cook?"

"I cut open bags and follow directions."

He's so cute, I nearly lean up and kiss him, then remember we haven't crossed that line yet. "Works for me."

His arm falls away when we reach the entrance of the administration building, but only so he can open the door.

"Darcy looked upset when she left," I say as I walk through.

"Yeah, it's been a tough few months, and the stress of fundraising hasn't made it any easier."

"Boyfriend problems?" Okay, I admit I'm fishing, but come on, anyone who's ever watched the CW should know that girl best friends are the kiss of death for a relationship.

"Darcy?" He actually laughs. "No. That girl tosses men aside like stale bread. I've told her a million times that she's far too picky."

I can see that. Darcy oozes the kind of self-confidence that would entice anyone. She probably has no idea what jealousy feels like. Not like me, who's feeling pretty silly right now.

"Cam, that you?" Nate pokes his head out of the band room. "Oh, hey, Jan."

I wave, knowing it's time to say my goodbyes but not wanting to. The last five minutes are the happiest I've been all day, and I don't want to lose the feeling at all.

See you tomorrow, Cameron mouths silently while stepping backward.

My stomach does a jump-spin-kick, and I start my mental countdown once again.

Twenty-nine-and-a-half hours to go . . .

TWENTY-ONE

At exactly 7:05, I knock on Cameron's door and quickly tug my sweater back down. Tonight's date outfit did not come from a box. It's one Doreen helped me pick out, along with the leather ankle boots I'm wearing. Camel-colored with just enough heel to make my legs appear long and slender. The ensemble makes me feel like I could conquer the world. The leggings are lined and super comfy, the sweater's a beautiful cream cashmere that drapes perfectly over my torso, with a multicolored scarf I had to watch YouTube to know how to tie. Basically I'm so fashion-forward I could be a pin on Pinterest.

The door swings open, and my heart stumbles as I take in Cameron on the other side. He looks exactly like he does every day—simple jeans, a casual button-up shirt with the cuffs rolled back, and those dimples that are the perfect mix of shy and sweet.

His eyes drink me in the same way mine do him, and a pleasant warmth fills my cheeks. "Come in," he says, moving to the side.

I step over the threshold and into his world, one not a whole lot bigger than my cabin. "Three of you live here?"

He shuts the door behind me. "Yeah. It's tight, yet somehow we make it work. Bedrooms are the size of a closet, but at least we each have our own."

"You've made it look good." The living room is to my left and is decorated similarly to the praise team room at the church. Band pictures and guitar stands line the walls, except for the one closest to the door. That one has a collage of record covers, probably close to thirty different albums. Some of the bands I recognize—Pink Floyd, Metallica, Journey, U2. "Quite the eclectic grouping here."

Cameron joins me. "Yeah, we call it our inspiration wall. Every one of these albums has a song that's shaped our sound in some way or another."

"Which ones did you add?"

He points to several of them, all artists I've never listened to—Creed, Skillet, Ashes Remain. Christian bands, I'm assuming.

"Darrel's the metalhead, Brian likes the softer stuff, and I'm a product of a family that didn't allow us to listen to secular music growing up." He points to the Metallica cover. "I was seventeen the first time Bryson played me Kirk Hammett's guitar solo in 'One,' and I've never looked at music the same since. I couldn't get the riff out of my head, so I stayed up the entire night listening and practicing until I had it down. Needless to say, my parents were not happy with my iTunes choices after that."

I imagine they'd be even less thrilled with the idea of his joining Bryson's band. There was nothing uplifting about any of the music I heard that night. And from the little Cameron's shared about his family, I get the impression they're all very close.

"You never told me how Bryson took your declining being in the band?"

Cameron's smile fades. "Not well, but he never does."

"He's asked you before?"

"About every six months for the last two years."

That makes me scowl and increases my dislike for the guy. Not that it wasn't high already.

"I still think you made the right call," I say, in case he's having any doubts.

"Yeah, me too." He sounds sure, but I wonder, especially when his hands go deep in his pockets and he stares at the ground.

Not wanting to dampen his mood, I opt to keep any further thoughts on Bryson's band to myself and move into the kitchen. On the counter is a moviegoer's dream: a popcorn popper, several boxes of candy, and a six-pack of Dr. Pepper.

"What's all this?"

"Movie essentials." He walks to the buffet under the TV and pulls several DVDs from a cubby. "I have five options here, but we can also download something new if you don't like any of these. I wasn't sure what your taste included."

"I'm pretty flexible." I take the stack and scan the options, feeling immediately grateful that Cameron's taste in movies is better than Dillon's. Three of the five are Marvel superhero films, two of which I've seen. The other one is a *Star Wars* movie, and the last a chick flick I'm sure he must have borrowed from Darcy. I decide to have mercy on him and pick one that would be fun to watch. "*Spider-Man: Far From Home* is really good." I hand them back. "That's my vote."

"You truly are the perfect girl." He smiles and leans close enough that I wonder if he's going to make a move. I wouldn't mind it if he did. Not one bit.

Unfortunately, he straightens and returns to the living room to put the movies back. "So what do you think? Dinner first, or do you want to wait and ruin our appetite with junk food?"

I look around his surprisingly clean kitchen in search of any signs of cooking. There are none. "There's dinner here somewhere?"

He holds up an index finger and walks to the fridge. Seconds later, he has a meal bag of frozen pasta in one hand and a box of breadsticks in the other. "Sorry, this is my level of fancy."

I'm relieved to see there's actually something he doesn't do well and feel myself relax. "And now you're the perfect guy."

"Yeah?" He shuts the door with his hip and sets our frozen dinner on the counter. "Because if that's the case, I'd like to talk to you about something."

"Okay?" The intention in his voice makes me nearly as uncomfortable as the way he extends his hand toward the small kitchen table. I guess this *something* requires a sit-down chat.

I scoot out the first chair I see and sit, rubbing my arms to ward off the goose bumps. Cameron pulls out another chair and brings it close enough that when he sits, our knees touch.

He takes my hands in his. "I like you, Jan. More than like you."

I let out a relieved sigh and squeeze his fingers. "I like you, too."

"Good." He smiles, and I don't miss the red blush moving up his neck. "Because I'd like to pursue a relationship with you, but first I think we need to define what we are and how that looks moving forward." He says it so matter-of-factly that I don't even think he understands how odd this conversation is.

"You mean like you want to be exclusive?"

"Yes. For starters. But I also feel like there has to be a chance for more or it's a waste of time for both of us."

I'm stunned and slightly weirded out. "I don't think I understand."

He shifts closer, his left knee sliding between mine. "I want to be fully transparent with you. I want a career in music, and that will mean sacrifice on a lot of levels." His voice turns eager. "Is that something you could live with?"

"Of course." Although I don't really know what I'm agreeing to exactly. "I would never keep you from pursuing your dreams."

He drops his head like my words are a huge relief, then lifts it again. His expression changes, his eyes dancing over my face in what could only be described as infatuated admiration. "Then, if it's okay with you, I'd like to move to the next phase."

"Next phase?" I feel certain the thoughts going through my mind are not the same as his. After all, the guy was raised in what appears to be a very strict Christian home. Maybe "next phase" is synonymous for finally getting to first base. If so, I've been on board for that for a while now.

"Yes, the next phase, but only if you're comfortable with the idea. I don't want to take things too quickly. I want to make sure I'm always being respectful of you."

Take things too quickly? If Cameron waits any longer to kiss me, I'm going to grab his lapels and do the deed for him. "I'm definitely comfortable with the next phase." I mean, come on, most of my previous boyfriends hit first base on day one, and they never gave me any kind of heartfelt speech beforehand.

He lets go of my hand, and a second later his fingers are grazing my cheek. "You are so beautiful. I never dreamed I'd be lucky enough to find someone like you."

When he leans in, I close my eyes and feel the press of his lips against mine. They're as soft as his touch, as innocent as his heart, and so gentle that I cast away the guilt that comes with his words and allow the kiss to wrap us both in this place of euphoric denial.

The attraction is so intense I swear I hear music playing in the background and fireworks, or maybe that's dynamite. My fingers slide through his hair, tugging him closer. This kiss feels different: new and forbidden and exciting.

Cameron pulls away abruptly and stares at me like I suddenly grew an extra eyebrow. "That was . . ." He stands, his chair sliding back with the momentum. "I think I'm going to start dinner now."

I'm not really sure if I should feel rejected or complimented by his need to flee. "Did I do something wrong?"

From behind the kitchen counter, his expression turns soft. "No, Jan. Everything about you is very, very right." He smiles at me then, and since the crisis seems to have passed, I stand and join him in the kitchen.

"Can I help you with something?" I ask.

"Sure." He grabs a cookie sheet from under the stove. "Line this with foil and then put two breadsticks for me plus however many you want on there."

I begin my task, taking four sticks from the box, then opting to put one back. Cameron makes my stomach feel too swirly and excited to eat much when he's around.

He pours the bag of pasta into a skillet, the sauce sizzling soon after. "We should probably let Eric know that we're dating."

My hand freezes. "Why? Do you think that it will be an issue?"

"No, not at all. I just don't want it to look like we're hiding anything." He adds a cover over the pan and turns to face me. "Is there someone you'd also like me to talk to, maybe your mom or dad?"

I nearly burst out laughing. "Um, no. I haven't asked my mom's permission to date for close to fifteen years now." As the idea sits, my humor turns to outright dread. My mom would pounce on Cameron. Ridicule his beliefs, his career choice, even his overly sweet demeanor. "In fact, I doubt you'll ever need to meet her."

His brow furrows. "Well, eventually I will. And your dad, too, I hope."

I hand him the pan of breadsticks and try to keep my tone lighthearted. "Tell you what. When I finally meet my dad, I'll be sure to introduce you to him, as well."

There's a shift the minute he processes what I just told him, and I don't like how pity spills into his expression. He takes the pan from my hand and sets it on the counter. Then I'm in his arms, his hug tight, just like it was the night he dropped me off at my house. "I'm sorry," he whispers, as if he can see all of my pain.

I feel a sting in my throat but refuse to let it go anywhere. I haven't cried over my deadbeat dad in years, two decades at least, and I'm not about to start again now. He made his choice a long time ago not to know me, and that is that.

My squirming makes Cameron back away, and his arms fall back to his sides. "Better stir your pasta before it sticks," I say.

He seems confused by my need for space, but it's pretty

simple. Cameron makes me happy. He makes me forget all my problems and issues and believe that the world is a better, brighter place. I don't want to be sad with him or talk about the wounds in my life. There are therapists for those kinds of things.

I spin and grab a box of Junior Mints, needing this heaviness to go away. "Care for a pre-dinner appetizer?" I shake the box and give him a daring smile. *Come on, Cameron, let it go. Please.*

He finally smiles back. "Only a few. I'm slaving over our dinner, remember?"

"I think you're burning our dinner."

Cameron spins around and immediately pulls off the lid. He scrapes the pan with a spatula, but I can already tell he let it sit too long. "Dang it," he grumbles. "I should have turned down the burner. I can't believe I did this."

His frustration makes me giggle. I snuggle up to his back and wrap my arms around him.

"Crusty pasta is great," I tease. "I especially love it when it's super black at the bottom and has that ashy taste." He still seems upset, so I pour several Junior Mints into my hand and attempt to stick them in his mouth.

"What are you doing?" he asks, though it comes out muffled since I'm shoving candy in while he talks. Four pieces fall to the floor, and I'm laughing so hard I have to bend over, my forehead pressed against his back.

I hear the pan move across the stovetop and know before he turns that it's time to run.

He catches me at the couch, mostly because I'm still cackling too hard to breathe, let alone run, and wrestles the box from my hand. His warnings that he'll get me back slide out between our laughter while more chocolate circles are sacrificed in the battle.

We tumble backward, and Cameron is somehow strong enough to control our fall so that we don't hit the cushions with a collective two-hundred-plus-pound thud. Instead, it's a smooth drop with his chest pressing into mine. Our legs are tangled, and just when I see his full hand come toward my mouth, ready for revenge, his lips hit instead.

The kiss isn't gentle or timid this time. It's fast and furious, and I'm pretty sure we've smashed at least ten mints into the leather cushion.

His palm presses against the outside of my thigh, then moves up to my hip until his fingers tickle the exposed skin above my waistline. I let my hands roam, too, sliding up his back, the cotton material stiff beneath my skin.

He pauses, and while I know I should too, that we're feeling more than thinking, I want to stay in this bubble with him, a place where my heart is happy and my beautiful new boyfriend makes all my troubles disappear.

"Is this my . . . ?" He pulls back, and I realize he's found my secret—the guitar pick I've kept on me since we met.

Our bodies untangle, and he sits, allowing me not only to pull the small piece of plastic free but also to sit up.

"Busted," I say, more embarrassed about my little treasure than our romp on the couch. "It's my good luck charm." I suddenly can't look him in the eye but focus on a loose string attached to one of the pillows.

He carefully takes the pick from my fingers and rolls it in and out of his hand like a seasoned magician. "If I recall, this was only good for three lessons. You're going to need another one after tonight. One that doesn't expire."

I look at him now that he's not making me feel foolish and try to take it back. He hides the pick behind his back before I can snatch it.

"What do you mean? I still have two left before this expires." I reach again, but he shifts to block the attempt.

"How do you figure that?"

"We've only had one real date. This one."

He actually looks offended. "What are you talking about? The first was when I took you onstage and sang for you, the second to see the band, and now tonight. Not to mention all the flirting we've been doing at work." When I continue to stare at him like he's from another planet, he scoots closer and takes my hand in his. "Jan, I make it a practice to be very cautious when it comes to dating and being physical. And my losing control just now is a good example of why I'm careful."

"Oh. I thought maybe you hesitated because of your feelings for Darcy."

"Darcy?" His head jerks back. "No. We're tight, yes, but it's never gone farther. Friends only." He comes closer, his eyes studying mine like they might give away all my secrets. "Does our relationship bother you?"

"No, it doesn't bother me," I say, even though it does a little.

"If it ever starts to, promise you'll tell me." He presses our joined hands to his lips. "I want us to be totally open with each other."

His words make me swallow, not just because they feel far too intimate for the scale of our relationship but also because I know even as we sit here, I'm keeping the biggest secret of all. One that would very likely ruin the way he's looking at me right now.

"I'll tell you. I promise."

He leans in for another quick kiss, then stands, tugging me with him. "Time to salvage our dinner."

I follow, my hand tucked into his, and stuff Doreen's warning along with the guilt of my deception as far down as it will go. After all, there's no need to ruin the relationship when it's only just getting started.

TWENTY-TWO

I wake on Saturday morning feeling as if I could star in my very own Disney movie. The sun is shining, the birds are chirping, and my residual smile from the night before can probably be seen from the moon.

Reaching over, I grab my cell phone from the nightstand and check my texts. The first is from Doreen.

We're BBQ-ing today, so come over when you get up. Jim's been smoking a brisket since last night.

I quickly text back.

Yum. Count me in. I'll be over in a few.

There are also two texts from my mom, and I'm in the process of answering back when Cameron's name flashes on my screen. He wants to FaceTime. No way, no how.

I decline but quickly text him back.

Still in bed and it ain't pretty.

He immediately calls me, regular this time.

"You're always pretty," he says immediately after I answer.

"Good morning to you, too." I relish the high that only comes with a new relationship. Maybe that's why I've started so many. It's addicting, the stomach-tumbling anticipation. Like the whole world stops when you hear the other person's voice.

"Is it bad for me to say I miss you already?"

I sit up and rest my back against my headboard. "No. I think it's really sweet."

"Brian sat on a Junior Mint this morning. It was interesting trying to explain that one. Needless to say, we've been banned from eating in the living room." Last night Cameron explained that Brian is the neat freak in the bunch, holding house meetings every time a dish is left in the sink.

I burst out laughing and have to cover my mouth so I don't bust his eardrum. "Are we banned from the kitchen, as well? Because I don't think that pan will ever be the same." After Cameron's dinner attempt, we ended up ordering pizza.

"I may have run to the store after you left last night and replaced it."

"Coward."

"Yes, I admit it. Brian terrifies me." The sound of an engine starting drowns his voice as if he's readjusting the phone. "What are you up to today?"

"Doreen is having a cookout, so I'm about to head to her house." I kick off my blankets and stand, needing to make some coffee. "Wanna come with me?"

"Ugh. I'd love to, but I have to work."

I flip on the kitchen light. "What is this elusive job you always speak of? Very vaguely I might add."

He groans into the phone again. "I don't want to tell you."

"Why not?"

"Because it sounds juvenile, even though it's really a great-paying job with benefits and the hours are flexible. My manager goes to Grace Community and is super supportive of my music."

I add a Keurig cup to the machine and press ten ounces. "You don't have to sell me, Cameron. I'm not going to judge you." Especially since I've tried and failed at practically every profession that doesn't require a degree.

"Okay . . ." His pause is long. "I work checkout at H-E-B."

"I've seen that place everywhere. What is it?"

"It's a grocery store. Like the biggest one we have in Texas."

I put up my hands in defense, not that he can see me. "Oh. We don't have those where I come from." And when I was living with my ex in San Antonio, we either shopped on base or at the Super Target around the corner. Not that I'm ready to give Cameron any of that backstory yet. "How long is your shift?"

"Till seven, and then I promised Darrel and Brian I'd go catch a movie with them." He sounds as disappointed as I feel.

"So I won't see you at all, huh?"

"Unless I cancel, which I'm not above doing."

"No, it's okay. I don't want your friends to hate me already." My coffee finishes brewing, and I carefully take out my cup.

"They wouldn't dare," he promises. "Besides, we have tomorrow."

"What's tomorrow?"

"Sunday." He laughs when he says the word, like it's the most ridiculous thing for that particular day not to be the center of the universe. "Listen, I know you hate crowds and that you've found that small local church you like so much, but maybe you can make an exception now that we're together and come to Grace Community?"

My shoulders lock up so tight, hot liquid spills over my cup and onto my finger. "Ouch. Crap."

"You okay?"

"No, I spilled my coffee." Avoidance 101—change the subject. "Hey, let me let you go so I can clean this up." Avoidance 102—get off the phone.

"All right. I'll text you later. Have fun with your aunt."

"I will. You have fun, too." I hang up and let my head drop back. Keeping my secret just got far more complicated.

~

I roll to a stop in my aunt's circular drive and park behind a truck I could now draw in my sleep. Mr. Kyle is here, probably with his son, and I have no idea how to approach either one of them now that I've learned the truth about Dillon's mom.

I grab my jacket and shut my car door. The weather is incredible today. Sixty degrees, zero wind, and a cloudless sky. It's supposed to drop back down to thirty-eight after midnight, but for twelve whole hours we get perfection. I think of the wedding going on tonight at six and how lucky the bride must be feeling right about now.

"Hello, it's me," I call through the screen door. Aunt Doreen has all the blinds and windows open, and the smell of brisket fills the house. I move through the kitchen, the living room, and then spot the crew on the back porch. Well, not the whole crew, just Doreen and Dillon. Uncle Jim and Mr. Kyle must be out by the smoker.

For some reason, my pulse jumps when Dillon turns and

offers me a half smile. He looks so different I nearly stop mid-step. Gone are the old ratty jeans and stained T-shirts. His hair is styled, his face freshly shaven, and he's wearing a thin gray long-sleeved shirt tucked into dark jeans.

"Good. You're here." Doreen claps her hands together and stands. She pulls me into a hug as soon as I clear the doorway and keeps her arm around me as she turns us toward Dillon. "I'm assuming you two can play nice for a day?"

"Yes, ma'am," he says, and maybe it's the cowboy boots he's wearing, but I swear his accent got thicker overnight. "Our interactions have only drawn blood once."

I can tell he's teasing me, but I don't respond or smile. It's too easy now to see the sadness through his wit and the layer of grief through the brooding set of his jaw.

Doreen studies me closer. "You okay, hun?"

"Yeah. Just tired, I guess."

"Did that rehearsal dinner party keep you up last night?"

I shake my head and keep my eyes from straying back to Dillon. "No, they were either out or in bed when I got home. Lots of activity this morning, though."

"Yes. I'm going to head up there in a little while and make sure they have everything they need." She pats my arm and then releases her grip. I want the pressure back, just like I want to beg her not to leave me alone with Dillon. She obviously hasn't developed telepathy because she makes some comment about the potato salad and scurries into the house.

I stand there, jacket still clutched in my hand, and have no choice but to interact with the only other person on the porch. "Pretty weather today," I say and sit where my aunt just vacated.

Dillon's forehead wrinkles. "What's wrong with you?"

"Nothing."

"You're acting weird."

"No, I'm not." I ball my jacket in my lap and try to stop the frustration creeping up my cheeks.

"Yes, you are." He scoots to the edge of the chair, and his inquiring gaze makes me start to sweat. "Pretty weather? Really? I give you a perfect zingy opening and you throw out that generic response?"

The frustration wins. "Forgive me if I don't keep a script that's been blessed by your superior conversation skills."

He points at me and relaxes back in his chair. "Much better."

My skin is tingling, and my heart is racing with growing fury. "Did you ever consider that maybe I was trying to be nice to you for once?"

"I don't want nice. I want real." The intensity in his tone shuts me down.

I have no road map with him. Thanks to my mom's stellar training, I'm usually good at controlling the tone of a room or conversation, especially with men. But Dillon makes everything so much more difficult than it needs to be. I study my fingernails, noting every split and cuticle.

"You're doing it again," he says.

"Doing what?" I look up and am again pressed with that need to comfort him, or understand him, I don't know, but it's unnerving and I don't like the feeling.

"I don't know how to explain it; you're just different with me today. Why?"

I hug my jacket to my chest like a teddy bear and decide to just go ahead and tell him. It's not like I'm having any luck with subtlety. "I heard about your mom. I'm sorry, Dillon. I didn't know."

He must not have been expecting that response because his head lowers and all that comes out is "Oh."

I don't say anything because I have no idea how to comfort someone who's grieving. Sure, I miss my pawpaw, but it's not even close to the same as losing a parent, especially one so young.

"You know that's what today is all about. Doreen and Jim didn't want us to be alone." His tone eases, as if the pain from the gut punch I delivered is starting to subside. "Like a sunny day and barbecue will suddenly make us forget it's been a whole year."

"I'm sorry."

"Don't say that." His jaw tightens. "I hate it when people say that."

"What do you want me to say?"

"I don't know. Maybe . . . that it sucks. Or that no one should have to bury their mom before they turn thirty and then watch their father completely fall apart days later." He cradles his head and holds it long enough to make my throat constrict. I want to move closer, to comfort him somehow, but the anger he's emoting is too great a shield. Finally, he slides his hands through his hair and looks up at me, his eyes red and apologetic. "Now I should be the one saying I'm sorry."

"It's fine."

"No, it's not. None of this anger is for you." He cracks his neck to the left and right. "It's just this day. This horrible day that cannot pass quick enough."

I remain quiet and he sighs. "I liked it better when you didn't know. It was nice engaging with someone who didn't pity me." His voice goes soft, and I see a glimpse of his pain once again. It's rare; he's learned to hide it nearly as well as I have. "Let me guess, Doreen wanted to prepare you for my crazy today."

"No. Darcy mentioned it in passing. I think she assumed I knew."

"Ah yes, the Grace Community grapevine is alive and well." His bitterness when he mentions the church puts me on the defensive for some reason. I know it's weird because I'm not even a member and have only worked there a little while, but in that time I've seen the heart that beats in those halls.

"It wasn't like that at all. I'm the one who brought up your name."

"Yeah?" That makes his eyebrow go up, and his sadness gives way to the impish grin that makes my cheeks heat. "And why is that?"

"She's fundraising for a mission trip. You were bragging about being independently wealthy, so I mentioned you."

"I wasn't bragging."

"No, of course not. That would be so unlike you." My eye roll makes him smile, which is a nice change from his earlier mood. While I'm not so good at the heavy emotional thing, I am really good at dispelling tension, and I can see that Dillon needs it badly. Unfortunately, my kindness backfires as he turns his focus to me.

"You've settled right in there, I see. Dating Cam, becoming best friends with Darcy."

"We're not best friends."

"But you are dating Cameron." The way he says it, like I've somehow answered a question for him, makes my hands tingle. He relaxes in the chair and even puts his feet up on the ottoman. "Kind of risky, don't you think?" He doesn't have to expand that thought for me to know that he's referring to my agnosticism. Apparently, I have no secrets from this guy.

A chill slides through the screen behind me, and I take a

moment to put my jacket on. Dillon's stare doesn't falter. He wants—no, is demanding—an answer that I'm not prepared to give. I ignore him and turn my head to find something, anything to focus on outside. Two squirrels spiral around Doreen's oak tree, and I hear Uncle Jim's laughter coming from the smokehouse.

"I have to be honest; I don't really see the two of you together."

That gets my attention, as was his intent I'm sure. "Why not?"

He shrugs. "Cam's lived a pretty sheltered life. You haven't."

I don't even bother arguing, because he's right. Our lives up to this point have been distinctly different, but that doesn't mean we're not a fit. "So what? I've dated plenty of guys just like me and they didn't have an ounce of Cameron's character."

"I don't doubt that in the least. Cam's a great catch."

"And I'm not?"

"I didn't say that." He actually looks defensive.

"Then what are you saying?" Because somehow I'm the one who now wants to bury my head and start bawling. Maybe it's guilt—or worse, recognition that I'm holding on to something I don't deserve. Either way, I can't stomach Dillon's perusal.

"I'm saying you need to tell him you don't share his faith. Cam doesn't date casually, so if this thing is progressing, it means he's all in. And there's nothing more painful than thinking you know someone, sharing your life with them, and then finding out it's a lie." The hurt in his voice is so real I can feel it settle under my skin, past my defenses, and into the aching part of my heart.

We're no longer talking about my relationship, but his, and the guilt I felt earlier changes to something deeper and impossible to ignore. Cameron's word choices last night feel heavy on my shoulders. I press my lips together and debate whether or not to expose something so personal to a man who seems to keep zero boundaries. Then again, my only other option is Doreen, and since I gave her my word I'd tell Cameron and didn't follow through, I'm not stepping anywhere near that one. "Can I ask you a question and you be perfectly honest with me?"

"Always."

"No laughing at me, either."

His lips start to turn upward. "Okay."

"What does it mean in Christian circles when a guy wants to pursue a relationship and take it to the 'next phase'?"

Turns out Dillon is a liar as well, because he can barely contain his amusement. "You mean you got the speech?"

"What speech?"

"The one every student was taught to give when we were in youth group."

"I don't understand."

"Yes, that's obvious."

"Dillon." I throw a pillow at him, and it releases the last bit of control he has. Laughter spills into the room, and I can't help but join him, even though I'm fuming.

"I'm sorry." He clears his throat. "I'll translate. Basically, Cam was asking to see if you were ready to pursue the kind of dating relationship where marriage is the end goal."

I nearly swallow my tongue. "You're messing with me."

He puts up his hands. "I wish I was."

I press my fingers to my temples and will the ache in my head to go away. "It's way too fast."

He cocks his head to the side. "Why? Because you're still in love with your ex?"

"No," I say loudly enough to make him flinch, and I drop my hands. "Because it's only been a few weeks and it was supposed to be easy and fun."

"You mean Cam was just supposed to be a rebound guy."

"No," I say again, but I don't have any counter to his accusation.

Dillon slides his feet from the ottoman and stands. "Call it what you want. Either way, you need to tell him why you're here. You owe him at least that much." He heads for the outside door and lets it slam behind him.

I want to chase him down in the yard, tackle him, and beat him up until he cries *uncle*. But I don't. Instead, I just sit here and wonder how the heck things got so screwed up.

TWENTY-THREE

"Still pouting?"

I glance over my shoulder to find Dillon coming toward me and turn back around to watch the pool water glisten in the sun. It's been thirty minutes since our last sparring match and I still haven't quite recovered.

My feet press into the decking, and the swing I'm sitting on moves back and forth. It's one of those freestanding love-seat types that must be new because I've never seen it before.

Dillon sits down next to me, the swing jerking to a stop under his weight.

"You obviously don't know how to take a hint," I say while scooting as far away as possible.

"You'd really ignore me? Today of all days?"

My mouth hangs open as he waits for my rebuttal. I have none. I can't be rude or snub him, not after he played the Mom card. "Okay, we'll call a truce. But no more inquiries about Cameron."

"Nope. Too one-sided."

"How do you figure?"

"I don't get anything out of it." When I huff in disbelief, he twists in the seat to face me. "What? You think your company alone is worth my handing over my ace?"

Oh. My. Word. This man is the most infuriating person on the planet. "Need I remind you that you're the one who approached me?"

His eyes sparkle with challenge. "Just to begin negotiations. Not to fold."

"Fine," I say through gritted teeth. "What is it you'd like?"

"I need a spades partner."

His answer is so unexpected that I'm sure I heard him wrong. "You want me to play cards with you?"

"Yep. Doreen says you're ruthless, and my dad and Jim have been talking smack for the last twenty minutes."

"So get Doreen to be your partner. She's far more ruthless than I am." I lean close and whisper, "One summer, my cousin Isaiah and I were fifty points from winning and she bribed him with no chores for two days. That cheat handed her the game. Jim wouldn't stand a chance."

Dillon laughs, and I admit it feels good to be the one to get a smile out of him, especially considering our earlier chat. "Well, as appealing as it sounds to play cards with three senior adults, I'm afraid Doreen's out of the running. She's headed up to B&L to check on the wedding."

"It's a mile away; she'll be back in twenty minutes."

He laces his arm through mine and pulls me to standing. "Which is just enough time for you and me to school the old guys."

I reluctantly concede. "If we win, you have to serve me dinner and do the dishes."

He shakes his head and chuckles.

I quit walking. "Why do you do that?"

"Do what?"

"I'll say something and you just shake your head and snicker. Why?"

"Maybe I find you funny?"

"No. I thought that at first, but now I know better." My eyes narrow on his face, looking for any clue.

He takes my arm and pulls me along again. "Tell you what. We win and I'll tell you what I'm thinking."

"As you're serving me dinner," I remind him.

"Just come on."

We're both smiling by the time we join his dad and Uncle Jim at the patio table.

"Calling in the big dogs, I see." Jim shuffles the cards and does a fancy bridge, trying to intimidate us both. It won't work. I know his moves too well by now.

"Ruff, ruff." I pop my knuckles and wink at my partner across the table. "Now deal the cards."

Mr. Kyle bellows a laugh, and I see the way it makes Dillon go soft, like the sound is worth enduring this day with his father's best friend. I find myself going soft, too. I'm sure there's a thousand places Dillon would rather be, and yet he's here, side by side with the only family he has left.

We don't win. Not a single game. But I'm not too upset about it, especially since each win seemed to bring Mr. Kyle more and more joy. In fact, I'd go so far as to say that Dillon threw the games on purpose, which ironically makes me respect him far more than I ever did my cousin.

I grab my keys from my purse and walk to the patio to say my final goodbyes. The sun set an hour ago, and Aunt Doreen has the fire pit blazing full blast.

"Well, I'm going to head home," I say, approaching the

group. I lean down and hug Doreen. "Thanks for the food. It was so good, I don't think I'll be able to eat for a week."

"Did you take some leftovers?"

"I did. I'll grab them on my way out." I turn from my aunt to the men and give my best intimidating scowl. "As for you guys, expect a rematch, and this time I'll have a better partner."

"Hey. That wasn't all on me. You're the one who can't cover," Dillon says, feigning hurt. I can tell he's playing it up, and his dad loves every minute of our banter.

"Says the guy who goes nil with a queen and king of spades." I roll my eyes and quickly hug my uncle. "Give the man some training, please."

Jim pats my back. "You're a pretty good, kid, you know that?" His voice is quiet enough that only I hear him, but it still fills me with pride. Jim does not give out idle compliments.

"Thanks. I'll see you in a few days." I step toward the door with a wave, and Dillon springs to his feet.

"I'll walk you to your car," he says.

"You don't ne—"

His hand is already on my back, pushing me past the threshold, so there's really no room for protest. One important lesson I've learned about Dillon Kyle is that there is no changing his mind once it's set.

He doesn't say a word until we reach my car. "I wanted to thank you for today." He leans with his left hand against the roof, his right one holding my container of leftovers. "You were a good sport, and it's been a long time since I've seen my dad this relaxed and happy."

"You're welcome, although I'm not sure your appreciation is warranted. I wasn't faking having a good time. Jim, Doreen, and your dad are fun to hang out with."

He smirks. "Did you leave me out of that list on purpose?"

"Yes," I say, though it's not true at all. Dillon with his guard down is actually a pretty amazing person—lighthearted, sarcastic, even a little funny.

"You know I can tell when you're lying, right?"

I cross my arms. "Maybe you only think you can tell. Maybe you don't know me nearly as well as you claim to. And maybe it's the other way around, and *I'm* the one who's got *your* number." I lift my brows in stubborn challenge, yet I'm having a hard time not smiling.

"Maybe you do," he answers with a little too much seriousness, and the air between us shifts just like it always seems to when we move past the banter and into territory that's best left unexplored.

I swallow. "I really better go."

He nods and opens the door for me, handing me the container once I'm settled in my seat. "Text your aunt and let us know you got back safely. You know how I feel about you being there after dark with all those strangers around."

I'm touched by his concern. "I will. Thank you."

He shuts the door and stands there, unmoving, while I drive away. I'm not sure why, but my hands tremble against the steering wheel and the air feels heavy. I turn on the air conditioning despite it being plenty cold in the car, and the blast of frigid air against my cheeks seems to calm me down.

I take the curvy drive slow and careful, turning on my brights to see the edge of the road. The entrance widens, and I veer right and down the hill to my secluded cabin. The area is well lit, but I still feel the hair lifting on my neck and arms as I turn the last corner. It's then that I'm not so touched by Dillon's concern. His comment about strangers is making me paranoid, and I nearly jump when my headlights fly over a car parked where I normally do. The panic doesn't last long, especially when I see who's sitting on one of the rocking chairs.

I park next to Cameron's vehicle and cut the engine. He stands up when I exit my car and shut the door. "I thought you were hanging out with the guys tonight."

"I was . . ." He sighs and meets me at the bottom of the steps. Dance music from the reception barn fills the silence while I wait for him to explain. "And then I just drove and found myself here." The sadness in his voice makes my heart squeeze. As much as Cameron is different from me, this part of him I understand. The questioning of choices, of life direction, of purpose. "Sorry to pop in uninvited."

"You don't have to apologize. You're welcome here anytime." That gets a tiny smile from him at least. "What happened?"

"Darrel didn't want to go to the movies, so we stayed home and worked on some songs instead." He stares up at the night sky. "I'm still completely blocked. Everything I did sounded like a commercial jingle."

"I'm sure it wasn't that bad." I bite back a smile, feeling pretty sure that Cameron isn't trying to be funny right now.

"Oh, believe me, it was *that bad*. Worse than *that bad*." He steps forward and laces his hand through mine. "So here I am, because somehow, you make everything better."

I squeeze his hand in assurance, the two of us bonded in a way that Dillon and my aunt just don't understand. Cameron isn't falling for *me*, the person. He's clinging to a feeling of hope and escape, just like I am. We're two floating souls, and yet together life feels grounded, at least . . . a little.

We walk up the steps in tandem, and I release his hand only long enough to unlock my door. He follows in behind me as if it were the most natural thing in the world and not the first time he's ever actually stepped foot past the threshold.

"If you're hungry, I have leftovers." I set my purse and the Tupperware on the kitchen counter while Cameron walks around the small cabin, perusing my aunt's artwork choices. He pokes his head in my room but doesn't go in.

"There's not much of you in here," he says, glancing over his shoulder at me. "Not even a family picture."

I shrug. "I guess I haven't thought about it." Not totally true. The fact is, my time here is temporary. Pictures and artwork and even small touches like replacing throw pillows all feel like too much of a commitment.

"Well, I'll have to remedy that." He leans his forearms on the counter opposite me and grins. "You did tell me I was a good photographer, if I remember correctly."

"That I did." I lift the barbecue, but he shakes his head, declining. I'm slightly relieved since I'd planned to eat this brisket for the next several days.

"Do you get cable out here?"

I shut the refrigerator door and watch as he looks for a remote. "It's in the drawer. And no. But I have internet, so you can watch just about anything you want."

"Perfect. Do you like *The Office*?" He flops down on the couch and pats the seat next to him.

I hesitate for a second and then scold myself for doing so. Cameron isn't professing his love or getting on one knee. He simply had a hard day and wanted an escape. Not only is that okay, but I'm glad. I want to be that person for him right now.

Pushing the last of Dillon's warnings out of my head, I toss my coat and shoes aside and curl up next to my new boyfriend. "I love *The Office*."

He leans down and kisses me. It's sweet and simple.

More like a thank-you than anything sensual. I press in, ready to take it further, when my phone blares a song from my purse.

"Oh . . . crud," I say, jumping from the couch. I get to the device just in time to slide my thumb across the screen before he hangs up. "Sorry. I'm home safe and sound. No stragglers from the wedding reception."

"It would have been nice to know that five minutes ago," Dillon says, an edge in his voice. "Next time I'll just follow you there and save myself the headache."

"Ah, but then I'm the one who would get the headache," I tease.

"Doubtful," he says, and I imagine him shaking his head.

"Good night, Dillon."

"Lock your doors."

"I will. Bye." I press the end button and bring the phone with me to the living room. "Sorry. I totally forgot I was supposed to call when I got home."

Cameron rubs the back of his neck, and I can't read his expression. "Dillon was at the barbecue?"

"Yep. He and his dad." My voice turns somber. "It was the anniversary of, well, you know about his mom."

All the tension leaves his shoulders. "Oh, man . . . I knew it was coming up, but I didn't realize it was today. I can't believe it's been a year. How are they doing?"

"Okay on the outside. I'm sure things are much different on the inside."

Cameron's eyes soften as he brushes his thumb across my cheek. "You're pretty incredible, you know that?"

I pull his hand away, feeling a blush coming that brings both pride and guilt. "Hardly. I just really like brisket."

He scoots back into the corner of the couch and tucks me

up against him, his arms tight around me while we watch the show.

I lean my head against his shoulder and close my eyes. I don't care what Dillon says. There's no way that Cameron and I are wrong for each other. Everything about him feels far too right.

TWENTY-FOUR

I'm starting to think that the dividing up of Ralph's duties was determined entirely by what tasks Eric did not want to do. Which has of course left me tending to all the "special projects" that appear to be on life support. Supposedly, Ralph is in the process of assessing which ministries are still viable, and, lucky me, I get to sustain them while he's on vacation—which is now at two weeks, I might add.

It's hard to complain, though, especially when Margie told me that Ralph and Victoria are exploring every bed-and-breakfast from here to Fredericksburg, something she's always wanted to do but never had the luxury to make happen.

So, for their sake, I will grit my teeth and bear today's lovely task—the thrift store on Third Street.

And yeah, I expected some problems, but I had no idea it would be this bad.

Casting the trash bag of clothes aside, I stare at the mounds of donated goods in front of me. Two rooms. No, I'm not exaggerating. Two rooms, easily two hundred square feet filled with clothes, housewares, toys, yard supplies, and knickknacks, all of which are supposed to be sorted, tagged, and moved to the storeroom. Worse, my on-the-job training this morning consisted of a quick thirty-minute walk-through with Eric, who admitted he hadn't stepped foot in this place in over a year.

The thrift store is only open on Saturdays, so Mondays are spent doing inventory sorting and restocking, a task Ralph has taken over since five of the ten volunteers have quit in the past six months. Sheesh. Is there anything that man doesn't do?

I move back into the storefront area and breathe a sigh of relief, even though it smells musty and old in here. Eric explained that the church bought the old downtown building eight years ago, and, based on the cracks in the walls, mold in the bathroom, and buckling floors, I'd say it's one inspection away from being condemned.

Probably the only saving grace is the interior layout. It's fun and organized, reminding me more of a sophisticated vintage store than a donation center. Faceless mannequins wear sample clothes and hold handbags like they're ready for the town. There's a three-way mirror in the back and a couple of fitting rooms.

I bypass the children's section and move to the women's area, fingering a few tops as I walk past and land on a section of boas and wide-brimmed hats. The shelves are sparse, as are the racks, reminding me that I'm supposed to be finding inventory that's sellable in all the piles of castoffs, yet I can't seem to force myself back into that overcrowded dungeon of chaos. My brain hurt just walking through the door.

What were Eric's words again? *"Just do enough to get them by until Ralph gets back."*

Not exactly the most inspirational of speeches.

I wrap two of the feathered accessories around my neck and pick a pair of shades that cover half my face. Arm lifted,

I stick my tongue out like a panting dog and snap a photo. It's silly and stupid, especially when I'm twenty-nine and a half, but I need some of that right now.

A few picture filters later, I text the shot to Cameron.

Bored. I need to be put out of my misery.

Lovely. I especially like seeing your taste buds.

I was going for fashion diva meets poetic tragedy.

Interesting combo.

I grab my phone, dial Cameron's number this time. It rings and rings until I get his voicemail.

A second later, his text pops up.

In staff meeting going over yesterday's service. Can't talk.

I take another picture of me in the boa, this time with the end held up so it looks like a noose, and send it to him.

Torture . . . pure torture.

I can picture Cameron in the room, trying not to laugh while he hides what he's texting.

Stop. You're going to get me in trouble.

Good. Then maybe you'll be exiled like I've been.

Call Darcy. She's been bugging me too.

I scowl at the message. Okay, so yeah, I'm still a little jealous of their friendship. Anyone would be. Still, I dial her number, because at this point I'm willing to do just about anything to keep procrastinating.

"Hey!" Darcy cheerfully answers. "Cam said you might call. Are you working?"

"If you define the life being sucked from my body as working, then yes, I guess I am. I'm stuck at the thrift store all day."

She laughs, and I hear a dog bark in the background. "That sounds like fun, not torture."

"Maybe for you. I, on the other hand, cannot stand disorder." I look toward the back area, where I'm supposed to be working. "And this place is like a dumping ground for every piece of reject clothing in town."

She laughs again. "Sounds like a perfect setting for a preteen moment."

"What do you mean?"

"You'll see. I'm on my way."

"Don't you have pet appointments?"

"Two this afternoon, but I'm free for the next few hours." Darcy is a dog groomer and trainer at a ritzy place called Pampered Pup Salon and Beauty Parlor. They're the kind of high-end establishment that serves dog treats on silver platters and paints doggy nails to match their owners. A trim there costs more than three times what I used to pay my hairdresser. But then again, I didn't get diamond-studded bows put in my hair. "Besides," she continues, "now that you and Cameron are official, we need to get to know each other better."

"Okaaay," I say with some trepidation, because this will be the first time the two of us hang out by ourselves and it's starting to feel a little like a setup. "If you're sure you don't have anything else to do."

"Not at all. See you in a minute."

When I hang up, I can't help but think back on Dillon's warning. *"Dating Cam, best friends with Darcy. Kinda risky, don't you think?"*

"Stop it," I say out loud and shake my head. Dillon Kyle does not know everything, nor does he get to dictate my choices.

I furiously push open the door to the storage rooms and refuse to worry about it for another second.

~

Darcy and I fall into a fit of laughter, and I nearly drop to the stained carpet beneath me. She's wearing a muumuu dress ten sizes too big, a pair of boots that are hot pink with rhinestones climbing up the sides, a child's hat that sits on her head like Charlie Chaplin's, and is making the face of a cheerleader in a selfie contest.

"Hurry, take the picture," she says, then returns to her pucker face. She has the dress hiked up on one side, exposes her bare knee, and puts her thumb out.

I snap away, trying to capture her insanity.

We've been fashion modeling for an hour and dumped out at least ten trash bags of clothing in our quest to finish off her latest ensemble.

"Got it," I say and text her a copy. Knowing Darcy, she'll make it her profile picture somewhere and come out looking like a supermodel.

She tosses the hat aside, pulls the dress over her head, and kicks off the boots. Darcy has no modesty, changing in and out of clothes without restraint or embarrassment. She reaches for the jeans she abandoned. "I would have loved volunteering at a place like this when I was a kid. It doesn't make sense that they might have to shut it down."

"I know, but it sounds pretty inevitable."

"Too bad." Darcy bends over to lace her shoe. "So . . . I need you to keep a secret, okay?" Her voice matches a nosy neighbor's, and again I feel that tug between wanting to trust her and wondering if we're frenemies.

"Okay," I say, suddenly flustered. "What about?"

She hops back up. "Cameron's birthday is coming up, and his mom wants to make it a surprise party. You know, like a huge celebration because it's his last year before the dreaded thirty hits. She's dying to meet you, by the way."

And there it is. The reminder that Cameron and I grew up in very different worlds. His—a perfect family with four well-behaved kids, two cats, one dog, and church every Sunday and Wednesday. Mine—well, let's just say there wasn't any of that.

I can picture it now: *Hi, I'm January Sanders. I've never met my father, and my mom is likely heading toward her fourth divorce, but I'm really a great match for your son. So nice to meet you!* Cue stunned silence and judgmental stares.

"Jan?"

"Sorry." I blink out of my daydream and stand. "Yeah, that sounds, um, fun."

"Are you okay?"

"Yeah. I just didn't realize how late it was getting. I should probably get this cleaned up."

"I can help." She checks her watch. "I have about an hour before I have to head back to work."

"I wouldn't do that to you. At least I'm getting paid to be here."

"Please. My life goal is to move to another country and work for free." She grabs three large empty boxes from the corner and arranges them in a triangle. "Thrift-store items in this one, and the rest in these two. We'll make a game of it. If we can fill the thrift box in forty-five minutes or less, we'll reward ourselves with an ice cream cone from down the street."

And herein lies my conundrum: Darcy calls my boyfriend daily, has admitted to me that Cameron had a crush on her years ago, and is unquestionably a better match for him than I'll ever be, and yet I still genuinely enjoyed hanging out with her today.

"Well, if ice cream is on the line, then it's a deal," I say, pushing aside the unease that keeps wanting to pop up.

She taps her watch and sets it for a countdown. "Okay . . . ready, set, go!"

TWENTY-FIVE

By Thursday I'm beyond ready for Ralph to return to the office. It's not that the tasks I've been given are hard, but they become nearly impossible to finish when Eric sends me new ones every twenty minutes. No wonder Ralph can't get anything done.

At least this is my last breakfast. Ralph's vacation has finally come to an end and he will be returning to work on Monday. Hallelujah! Now if only I could get this stupid lock to open.

Finally a click and the door swings in. I'm in full shiver mode when I close it behind me. The thermostat is down the hall, and I turn it on, even though I know it will be stifling hot as soon as the oven gets going.

I move to the dining room, fumbling through the instructions Nora texted me an hour ago. Nora's dad was taken to the hospital late last night, so it's up to me to get the entire breakfast started before Pete shows up, which hopefully is soon since I'm already running fifteen minutes late.

Thankfully it's a simple meal today. A tub of yogurt, granola, fresh fruit that's already cut up, and muffins that take less than thirty minutes to bake. I set my purse on the cooking counter and head for the pantry, where the pans and dry food are stored.

Palm over the handle, I tug and it doesn't move. I tug and tug, but it's no use. The pantry's locked, the shiny chrome newness making it very clear the lock will not be opened with the only key I've been given.

My heart begins a slow, panicked beat as I check the time. All the supplies are in that room.

This is when a normal person could rationalize, think about obvious places to hide a key, but my mind doesn't work that way. It's why I barely made it through school and quit junior college after just one year. I can't process the mundane, only the random anomalies.

Like I remember that Mike has connected earlobes that are too small for his face. Or that Nora likes to salt in a line, left to right. But I can't for the life of me remember an essential detail like where Pete said they kept the stupid pantry key.

"It will be fine," I tell myself and try to take a calming breath. "Call Nora."

I dial with shaky fingers but get her voicemail. Next I try texting, then stare at the screen when it's obvious she's not going to answer.

Think, January, think . . .

I rush to the bulletin board at the back of the room. Pete once mentioned a list of seasonal volunteers with their phone numbers. Surely his is on there, as well. I find the faded paper behind a church flyer and nearly rip it from the wall. My eyes scan every line searching for Pete's, but a different name pops from the page.

Dillon and Rebecca Kyle. The number is wrong, and the

name next to his feels all wrong too, but it's enough to ease some of the rising hysteria.

I scroll my contact list and dial his cell. *Please pick up. Please.*

He answers immediately, his voice thick with sleep. "You okay?"

"Do you know where the pantry key is?" I say faster than a normal person should speak.

"Slow down." The phone jostles and crackles as if he's moving. "What key? What pantry?"

I don't know why, but something about his voice makes me sink into a nearby chair, tears I didn't even know I was fighting now blurring my vision. "At the breakfast the church serves. I'm supposed to make muffins, and everything is locked inside the pantry."

Dillon's voice comes back smooth and slow. "January, take a deep breath, okay?"

"Okkaay." I do as he says, already feeling ten times more in control.

"Go to the refrigerators and open the door farthest to the right."

I follow his instructions and open the door. A cold blast of air hits my cheek. "It's open."

"Up on the right, inside the butter tray, there should be a key."

I reach up and sure enough my fingers hit metal. The relief is almost enough to make the tears spill over. "I got it. Thank you."

"Are you there by yourself?"

I shut the refrigerator and walk to the pantry. The key slides in easily. "Yes, but Pete should be here soon. At least I hope so. Nora said she texted him the situation." My breath is steady now, and my heart calms further when I see all the supplies I need.

"I'm on my way."

"Dillon, you don't have—"

"I'm on my way. See you in a few minutes." With that, he ends the call, and I'm so glad he's coming I can't even find a reason to be annoyed by his pushiness.

Steady once more, I grab a huge bowl, two massive boxes of muffin mix, and a stirring spoon. My arms are full when I finally leave the pantry and set all the equipment on the counter. Nora taped step-by-step instructions on the muffin boxes, and I go to the stove and set the oven to preheat.

I systematically follow each directive, adding and mixing when needed until smooth batter clings against the bowl. Muffin pans lined with paper sit on the counter, and just when I'm ready to start filling them, a loud bang makes me fling a spoonful across the room.

The bang comes again, harder this time, and I think I hear my name being called. I wipe my hands, rush to the door, and open it to a scowling Dillon.

"Why didn't you answer my call?"

"You called?"

He takes in my flour-soiled clothes, then my hair that's likely in just as bad of shape, and a smile I'm completely not used to seeing covers his face.

"You're a wreck," he says.

"And you're the most tactless knight in shining armor I've ever met."

He chuckles and follows me into the kitchen. It's then I see what he must: the batter streak across the refrigerator, eggshells on the floor since I was too rushed to pick them up, the usual pristine counter filled with empty boxes and sprays of powder.

"Remind me never to let you cook in my kitchen," he says.

"Shut up." I hit him, twice because it feels good, and then sigh at the absurdity of the morning. "I thought you came here to help."

"I did." He eyes the empty serving counter and pulls an apron from a stack of several. Not once did I notice those hanging there. "You get the plates and stuff out, and I'll finish the muffins."

"Are you sure you're qualified?"

He ties the strings around his back. "I'm a single thirty-year-old man. Cooking is kind of par for the course." His reminder that he's unattached brings me back to the volunteer list and his ex-wife's name. Rebecca. Somehow knowing it makes her more real, and I yearn to ask how long they were married and why it ended.

Dillon would answer truthfully if I dared to bring it up. He's a man with no secrets, no apologies, and no nonsense. But I also know he'd take my inquiry as an invitation to do the same to me. Probe into my past, ask me deep, meaningful questions I don't want to think about. So I keep my mouth closed and go back to the pantry and to the task at hand.

We work in companionable silence, and it's amazing how much calmer and warmer the place seems now that Dillon is here. He moves through the kitchen like he's spent his childhood coming here, and before long the serving counter is ready, the kitchen is once again clean and batter-free, and the last batch of muffins is baking away in the oven.

He leans against the counter, waiting for the timer to buzz.

I stack the last of the napkins near the plates and sidle next to him.

"I couldn't have done this without you," I say. "Thank you so much."

"You're welcome."

I catch movement in my peripheral and flinch.

He freezes, and I realize it's his hand, centimeters from my face.

"You have batter." His fingers continue moving forward until they press against the tender skin under my eye. "Right here."

"Oh. Thanks." I duck away and grab a clean towel from the drawer. Once it's doused with water, I use it to scrub my face and get the last of the breakfast off my clothes.

I finish as he's pulling the muffin trays from the oven.

"So what made you think to call me?" he asks, turning the knob to off. "Any of the staff could have helped you . . . including Cam."

Oh. I hadn't even considered that option.

"Six-thirty in the morning is a little early to be randomly calling the people I work with. Besides, your name is on a volunteer list they had on the wall." I don't mention that Rebecca's is, too. "I guess I'm lucky they haven't updated it."

His gaze is unflinching. "I guess you are."

The door in the hall squeaks open, and I hear Pete before I see him. He's singing a Beach Boys tune about Rhonda. I can only imagine it has something to do with whatever crazy creature he's decided to bring today. Even more strange is that I'm looking forward to finding out.

"Come on, this will be good." I tilt my head toward the dining room. "I have a new image when I hear the word *crazy*."

Dillon must be curious as well, because he follows me out of the kitchen just as Pete walks through the double doors.

He holds up what could only be described as a rodent with a heart-stamped ribbon tied in a huge bow around its neck. "Meet Rhonda Pearl. My chinchilla." Pete moves closer and bounces his eyebrows. "Now, come on, squirmy, you can't possibly be scared of this cute little thing."

I cross my arms, and Dillon laughs louder than I've ever heard him laugh before.

Pete redirects his focus to my companion, and his smile grows twice its size. "Well, look at this. The prodigal son is home."

"Not quite, but it is good to see you." Dillon walks over and hugs the older man, careful not to disturb the animal in his hand. Then he actually pets the furry thing. "Hello, Ms. Pearl." His voice changes to sound like every ridiculous pet owner I've ever heard. "You're so sweet. Yes, you are."

A snort of disbelief bursts from my throat. Who knew that big, broody Dillon would turn into mush over a little furry animal?

"Ms. January doesn't like animals too much," Pete says to Dillon as if I'm not in the room.

"I don't dislike them," I say defensively. "I just have never been around any. Nor do I usually encounter them in a place that serves food."

"And she's moody today," Pete says.

"You should've seen what she did to the kitchen."

"Heeeellloooo. Standing right here."

"Well, look at you getting all fiery. It's nice to see there's someone who can push you out of that shell of yours." Pete winks at me, then glances toward Dillon with a look full of implication. "Especially when he obviously enjoys doing it."

My stomach tumbles, but Dillon brushes off the implication like it's no big deal, which makes me feel stupid for reading anything into one of Pete's offhanded comments.

"Come on, old man," Dillon says, slapping him on the back. "I think Jan's had enough teasing for one morning. We have a breakfast to serve, and you've already gotten out of the hard stuff."

TWENTY-SIX

Cameron answers the door still in his work uniform. "Hey, gorgeous. You made it here quick. I just walked in." He pulls me into a hug I eagerly reciprocate.

It's four o'clock on Friday and he just came off a six-hour shift at the grocery store. I know he has to be exhausted.

I spy the empty apartment. "Where is everyone?"

"Gone." He pulls back and winks, tugging me along with him. "Maybe if we're lucky, it will stay that way for more than two minutes."

I follow him to his room and sit on the bed while he shuts the door. It's not bad for a bachelor in his late twenties. His bed is made, and only a handful of clothes litter the floor.

"So, what did you do today?"

I shift and pull my knees up on the bed to face him. "Helped Doreen. She's been a whirlwind getting ready for the spring. I guess the venue gets crazy busy starting next month."

"Yeah, I can see that. The weather being nice and all." He leans over and takes off his tennis shoes. "And Ralph? Any word on if he's actually returning in this decade?"

"Yes." I sigh gratefully. "He's home and will be back in the office on Monday."

"Good." He comes over, cups my face, and leans down to give me a much-desired hello kiss. "Now maybe you can go back to hanging out in the band room with me." He gathers his clothes to take into the bathroom and points. "Don't move. I'll literally be five minutes."

"Take your time. I'm not going anywhere."

After he leaves, I walk around the semi-clean space. On the dresser is a framed photo of the two of us. I pick it up and slide my finger over the glass. It's a selfie he took last week. I'm laughing and he's smiling back at me as if I were an angel sent just for him. Seeing it front and center makes my chest constrict.

I set the frame back down and move on to the other photos. There's one of Darcy and him as toddlers eating ice cream cones, ones from youth camp with his entire gang, most of whom I've met. There's even one with Dillon in it from high school that catches me off guard. He seems so detached now from anything involving the church that I forget he, too, grew up attending Grace Community.

They're the same pictures that were on Cameron's walls the first time I came in here, but every time I look, I see a new detail—a look that feels more meaningful, or in this case, a hand in Dillon's. One that belongs to someone who's been cropped out of the photo. I step closer, wondering if the hand is Rebecca's. Somehow I know that it is and consider what it must feel like to be loved by a man who tackles every task with fierce dedication.

The door opens behind me, and I turn around, feeling guilty for some reason. Cameron's hair is messy and wet. He's barefoot, wearing gym shorts and a Grace Community

T-shirt. He tosses his work clothes into the corner hamper and turns back to me. "Much better."

I study his easygoing smile and marvel that in only a month I went from the darkest pit of depression to being in a relationship with a man who treats me like his treasure.

I walk up to him and put my arms around his waist, grateful to be the one he cherishes.

"What's that for?" He hugs me back, tight and protective.

"Just because you're you," I say, my nose pressed into his chest. He smells like minty soap and deodorant. Like strength and tenderness. Like my fresh start.

He releases me with a kiss to the top of my head. "Okay, you ready for some Michael Scott?" We've been watching episodes of *The Office* together, mostly because it makes us both laugh, and after the chaos of the last couple of weeks, the break has been invaluable.

"Absolutely."

He walks over to his desk and grabs his laptop, and we settle into our places on his bed. Backs against the headboard. The computer propped on a pillow between us. But instead of pulling up the movie website, he shuts the top.

"Everything okay?" I ask.

He takes my hand in his and kisses the inside of my wrist. Tiny bolts of electricity dance down my arm and into the tips of my nails. It makes me want to pounce on him and never come up for air.

I swallow away the impulse and watch as he slides his fingers over the lines in my palm, his eyes transfixed on the motion.

"I'm absolutely dreading my birthday," he says, though it's barely audible above the sigh. "Every morning I wake up and wonder where all the time went. Wonder how it's possible I'm turning twenty-nine and have nothing to look forward to. Not even a prospect of a future in music. I mean, last year at this time, we were making a CD, had a concert scheduled, and now . . . every one of my bandmates seems perfectly content to just settle for Sunday morning. Well, I'm not." His voice cracks with emotion. "I want more. I was *meant* for more." He sets down my hand and attempts to give me a broken smile. "How's that for a confession?"

"I'm sorry." I don't know what else to say or even how to express the way my heart hurts for him. "What can I do to make it better?"

"Nothing. I just hope you don't wake up one day and realize you're dating a failure."

"Cameron . . ."

"I'm kidding." He leans in and kisses me. It's slow and sad, and makes me want to cry because I feel very certain that he isn't kidding. He pulls away and turns his attention to the ceiling, watching it as if it holds some kind of answer. "I keep praying, and I keep getting silence. I mean, God has tested me before, but never like this." He turns his head and looks at me with the same expectation.

Only I don't have any words of encouragement because I really don't understand what being "tested" means. And truthfully, apart from the one freak coincidence with Mrs. Cox in the hospital, the whole concept of prayer still feels a little weird.

"Anyway, enough on that," he says. "Tell me something about you. Something important."

"What do you mean?"

"You never talk about your life, your family. Just the job and your aunt. Tell me something about your childhood."

"I don't know what to say. I went to school, did homework, played outside."

He scowls.

"What? I don't know what you're looking for. My life has been pretty low-key." It's a lie above all lies, but I don't want my past to tarnish our time together. It's done. Gone. Forgotten.

"Cop-out answer," he teases and wiggles his fingers. "Don't make me tickle it out of you." The nice thing about Cameron growing up in a strong home with loving parents is that he never reads too much into my deflections. Truth is, his sheltered existence makes it easier for me to pretend I've had one, too. "So . . . we need to finalize plans for Valentine's Day. I vote for dinner and a really cute dress. Something sparkly and pink."

Ah . . . Valentine's Day. I secretly cannot wait. It's been years since I've had a boyfriend on what is usually a single woman's least favorite day of the year. Which is why I probably will find something sparkly and pink for no other reason than to make his dimples appear. "Only if you wear a suit and tie."

He groans but agrees, his eyes half closed because my fingers are now massaging his scalp. I playfully bring his hair to point, the strands sticking up in all directions. His morning shave has worn off, and I know the T-shirt he's wearing is at least ten years old and his go-to for comfort. It's my favorite look of his: relaxed, happy, and devoid of any pretention. Cameron isn't vain, so to speak, but he does take great care in his appearance, especially if we're somewhere that serves as a good backdrop for social media content.

Quietly enough that he doesn't notice, I ease my phone from my pocket and snap a picture. He's been bugging me about changing the wallpaper on my screen to the two of us, and this one is perfect.

"What did you just do?" He leans up, freeing my other arm.

I quickly save the picture and lock my phone. "Nothing."

"Let me see it."

"Nope. You won't approve and I love it."

"Please, pretty please?" He nuzzles my neck, but it's only to distract me until he snatches my phone off the nightstand.

"Cameron!" But it's too late. He's already off the bed and backing away toward the hallway. "The phone's locked."

"Yeah, but you forget I'm observant." He presses multiple buttons, and I know the exact moment he gets it right because a victorious smile flashes across his face.

"Cameron, come on. You never let me take candid shots of you." My chase is futile. He's too quick, his arms too long.

Until suddenly he quits the game, his hand dropping so he can look at the photo closer. His face falls into a frown while he slides his finger to several more photos.

"What is it?"

His new position allows me to finally see the pictures that have him pausing. They're ones of Dillon and me from earlier today when Doreen had an impromptu painting party. She'd bought three new tables for the reception hall, and they all needed to be sanded, primed, and painted.

I work to keep my voice light. "See, this is what you get when your sixty-year-old aunt decides to steal your phone." There's at least a dozen of the two of us kidding around. In this case, we're flinging paint at each other.

"You guys look like a couple." Cameron locks the phone again and passes it back to me. "When was that?"

"Today. Remember . . . Doreen, the spring wedding whirlwind? It was all hands on deck."

"And Dillon just came running? Doesn't he have other properties to manage?"

"Not really. He's pretty much at B&L all the time."

"That's convenient." Cameron moves around me to sit on the couch, his shoulders as tense as his mouth. "First the whole breakfast hero thing yesterday, and now he's painting reception furniture with you?"

"Don't be like that. We're just friends."

"Dillon doesn't do friendships with girls. In fact, he's the one who used to lecture me all through high school that boy-girl friendships inevitably turn into something more."

I sit next to him, sideways, my right leg bent on the couch so I can get closer. "That was over ten years ago. I'm sure his feelings on the subject have changed." I take Cameron's hand. "I promise you. It's no different from you and Darcy."

He sighs but seems to acquiesce under my touch. "It feels different."

"Only because you are on the other side of it." My voice is teasing, though my tone also conveys an unspoken tension about the subject.

"In that case." His fingers move to my hair. "We'll just have to come up with new ways to reassure each other."

"Do we now?" I don't even finish my last word before we're horizontal on the couch, bodies and legs tangled together.

His kiss is deep and demanding, a dance of insecurity that only physical contact can solve. A dance we get so swept up in that we don't even realize we get company until a gasp and a squeak comes from the other side of the couch.

I abruptly sit up, and Cameron nearly falls to the floor.

"What are you doin—?" He stops when he sees what I do.

Darcy's standing frozen, her hand covering her eyes. "Oh my gosh . . . I'm so, so sorry. The door was unlocked."

I smother a laugh. "You can uncover your eyes, Darcy. We're fully clothed."

Her fingers split until she's sure it's safe to look, and then her arm drops. "You should really have some kind of system to warn unsuspecting visitors."

"We do. It's called a door," Cameron grumbles. "Most people knock."

"I've never once knocked on that door and you know it."

I pat Cameron's shoulder and lean in to whisper, "See what I mean. No different."

He scowls. "It is different." His focus shifts to Darcy. "Have you ever known Dillon Kyle to have friends who are girls?"

"And it stay platonic?" She pauses. "No."

Cameron turns back to me and raises a brow. "I rest my case."

Darcy finds me twenty minutes later in the park outside Cameron's apartment complex. I'm rocking back and forth on one of the swings, my feet digging into the dirt, when she takes the spot next to mine.

"You didn't need to leave," she says.

"I know. I wanted to." Once all the jokes faded away, I noticed Darcy hadn't just shown up on a whim. Her eyes and nose were red, her smile halfhearted. She was there to seek comfort from her best friend, so despite both of their protests, I excused myself and came out here.

Darcy gets her swing moving, slow and steady like mine. "My parents are getting a divorce."

I look at her. "What?"

"That's why I've been so clingy with Cam." She sighs. "I

should have told you earlier, and I'm so sorry if our friendship makes you at all uncomfortable."

"Cameron said something to you, didn't he?" I shake my head. "I wish he wouldn't have."

"No, he needed to. I just thought with us bonding the other day that you might feel differently." She says it with an air of sadness, as if this isn't the first time their friendship has been an issue. "If you want me to stop calling him or coming over when you're not around, I will totally respect that."

I smile at her, touched by her willingness to sacrifice. "I'm fine with you and Cameron, really."

"So there's nothing you want me to do differently? Because I will."

Wow. Cameron must really be uncomfortable with Dillon to push his best friend this hard.

"You're fine. Just maybe one promise?"

"Anything."

"If you ever start to feel differently about Cameron, you'll tell me. That way I never have to wonder."

"I promise."

It's odd, because friendships with girls have never come easy for me, but I absolutely believe her. "So, what happened today?"

"What do you mean?"

"My mom's been through three divorces, and every one of them has been ugly." And even though she'd never been married to my father, Stepdad #1 certainly felt like a parent. They married when I was only three, and I called him Daddy until the court declared them divorced two weeks after my seventh birthday. "I can't imagine what it must be like when it's both of your parents."

"I always thought that my parents getting a divorce when

I was a kid would be the worst possible thing. But I have to say, it's not any easier as an adult. In some ways, I think it's harder." She stares at her feet and kicks the dirt. "They don't even try to be civil around me. I guess because I'm a grown woman, I'm no longer allowed to be sad that I get to spend the rest of my life doing split holidays. And then Mom asks me today what dating apps are best." She throws out her arms. "I mean, come on! The woman is fifty-three years old and wears pantyhose."

"She can try gray-haired-beauties.com. Or hot-silver-foxes."

Darcy spits out a laugh. "Geriatrics-mingle.com."

We both giggle at that one.

"The diets will come next," I say. "And then she'll be borrowing your clothes. And, well, when she does start dating again, come talk to me. I swear my mom was more emotionally spastic than a seventh-grade girl."

Darcy rolls her eyes, but she does seem less burdened. "You really have been through this before, haven't you?"

I shrug. "I'm a pro." Not really the best thing to add to my résumé.

Darcy twists in her swing, causing the chains to cross and uncross. "Did Cameron ever tell you about Lydia?" she asks, looking up at the pattern she's making.

"No." To my relief, Cameron has never asked about previous relationships, and since I have no intention of sharing my history, it feels wrong to ask about his.

"Well . . . she hated me." Darcy's voice is thick with exaggeration. "I mean, like, *really* hated me. She could not accept we were only friends." She looks over at me. "One day she just said *enough* and gave Cam an ultimatum: her or me. They broke up that week."

"Are you giving me a warning?" Because I'm not really sure of the point she's trying to make.

"Just the opposite. I'm asking you to never do the same." The unease in her gaze confirms the statement. "For the first time in twenty-nine years, I don't think he'll choose me."

I shake my head, convinced she's mistaken. "Cameron and I have only known each other a little while. You have a lifetime of history."

"History doesn't trump love."

My hands go cold, but I somehow find my voice. "Well, even if that's true, which I doubt, I'm not the ultimatum type." I know Darcy is trying to reassure me, yet it's done the opposite. My eyes flick to the merry-go-round. "Wanna see how fast we can make it go?"

She abruptly stands. "You better have an iron stomach, because I'm not holding your hair while you throw up."

"Trust me, if anyone is puking, it's you."

"Challenge accepted."

I race her to the piece of equipment and grab a bar just as she does. We run and push, run and push, until we're both tucked down and trying not to fling off the platform. It's a crazy thought, but somehow if I can just keep moving and spinning and going, I can shut out the one word that changes everything: *love*.

TWENTY-SEVEN

Consciously, I don't mean to put distance between me and Cameron, but subconsciously I can feel myself pulling away. It's the little things I find myself skipping, like popping my head in to say a quick hello during the day, or texting him when he's at his second job just so he knows I miss him.

If Cameron's noticed, he hasn't said anything. Likely because his birthday is in two weeks, and with every new day his mood seems to worsen. Even tonight, the first night alone we've had together in a week, he simply turned on the show and has barely said a word.

The tension is so thick that I'm almost grateful when a fist pounds on Cameron's bedroom door. "Hey, Cam! Get out here, you lazy bum."

That is until I recognize the voice. Bryson's.

Cameron flinches next to me. "Ah, crap. I completely forgot I told him to come over tonight."

"Why?"

He sighs. "He needs help with his new song, and . . . well, you know how he gets when he wants something."

I've only been around Bryson twice since we saw his band

play, and my opinion of the guy hasn't changed. He's arrogant, manipulative, and wants Cameron in his band so bad he dangles his success like a golden carrot every chance he gets.

"What kind of help does he need?"

"I don't know exactly." Cameron sits up. "He wants more originality in the opening with a little extra spark in the bridge. Strings would be best, but I think I can come up with a guitar riff that's simple enough for Mason."

"I thought Bryson was firing him."

"Not until he can find a replacement."

Which shouldn't be too hard, considering Mason can hardly play chords without looking at his fingers. "He's still waiting on you to change your mind, isn't he?"

"It's more complicated than that." Cameron shuts his laptop and sets it on the desk as he makes his way over to the dresser mirror. He cringes and goes to work taming his hair.

I still have yet to figure out the dynamics between him and Bryson. I know they've been friends since they were kids, not quite as long as him and Darcy but close. I also know that Bryson crashed at Cameron's house his last six months of high school for reasons Cameron wouldn't elaborate on.

What I can't seem to figure out is why Cameron tries so hard every time the guy comes around. It's like a warped hero-worship mentality that has no validity.

I swing my legs over the bed and stretch to standing. At least I now have an excuse to leave. "I guess I'll head home, then."

"What? No." He turns, abandoning his comb and his unnecessary primping. "I haven't seen you all week." When I hitch an eyebrow, he comes closer and takes my hands in his. "Come on, it'll be fun, you'll see."

"I don't consider watching Bryson fumble over music fun."

"You can't judge the man after seeing only one performance."

"It's been a long week. Go hang out with your friends. I'm good, really."

Cameron kisses me, sweet and gentle, exactly what he knows will make me cave. "One song? Please?"

I roll my eyes because I really am pathetic when it comes to him. "Ten minutes. That's it."

He grins big enough that both dimples appear. "I'll take it."

It takes another five minutes before Cameron agrees he's presentable. The wrinkled T-shirt is covered now by a button-up shirt he pulled from his closet. His hair is gelled into a stylishly messy arrangement versus just being disheveled like before. And even more disturbing is that he straightened the wrinkled comforter as if something nefarious took place while we were watching our show.

Good grief. The most effort Bryson is getting out of me is to not tell him to take a one-way trip to Hades.

"You sure you're ready?" I tease when Cameron finally grabs the doorknob. "I mean, if you want to toss on some cologne or clip your fingernails, I can wait a little longer."

He pushes me through the door. "Very funny."

We walk into the living room and join the three guys already in full music mode. Brian has pulled his keyboard from the wall and is playing with a few chords. Darrel has one leg draped over the recliner chair, his bass guitar cradled in his lap. Bryson is the only one who looks intensely ready to work. He's on the couch with the coffee table pulled close, sheets of music spread out before him.

He makes eye contact with me, and the contempt is mutual. I'm assuming it's because he's figured out it was my influence that kept Cameron from saying yes to joining his band. "Hey, Jan," he says between strums on his guitar. "You don't mind if I steal your man for a little while, do you?"

I force a smile, though I fear it's more of a grimace. "Of course not."

Cameron leaves me to get his guitar from the corner stand while I take a seat on the carpet across the room. Bryson doesn't look my way again, but I use this opportunity to analyze one of my boyfriend's oldest friends. Like always, he's dressed the part of a rocker. Black jeans, a tight black T-shirt, and combat boots. Across the armrest of the couch lies his signature leather jacket. His face is shadowed with a layer of afternoon stubble, and I guess in some circles he would be considered handsome. Just not in mine, especially since I find him to be a walking cliché.

There's a shift, though, when Cameron joins him on the couch. Bryson sits a little straighter. Immediately moves several of the sheets to his left for Cameron's approval. Maybe the hero worship is more than just one-sided.

Cameron plucks a few strings, pauses to draw chords on Bryson's music sheet, then plays around with the notes again. It's fascinating to watch him work, seeing the way he can absorb the sound only to turn it back out better and fuller than when it came in. When he finishes, Bryson nods and practices the addition.

I guess the changes don't affect anyone else because neither Cameron nor Bryson acknowledge the other two guys before counting out the beat.

Cameron is the only one who moves, and the crisp lingering sound of his guitar pulses through me as if I were riding the notes along the page. Listening to him play never gets old. His talent comes naturally, as though he were born to make music and we lesser-talented beings were born to listen to it.

Bryson watches Cameron's fingers, not even noticing that Cameron's eyes are closed, already playing the song he just read by memory. After a few more bars, the piano hums and so does Darrel's bass guitar. Bryson joins in a beat later, and even I have to admit, in this setting, he's better than I expect. He and Cameron seem to feed off each other's talents while Brian and Darrel fade into the background, almost as if they're unnecessary.

The song shifts to the part that Cameron must have added because Bryson stops to listen. The whole room does, because that's what happens any time Cameron uses the full force of his talents. His eyes open slowly, sensually, and land on mine. Flutters hit my stomach, and I'm taken aback by the immediate physical response: flushed cheeks, dry mouth, elevated pulse. A slow, seductive smile appears as if he can sense I'm under his spell, feeding off the music and him . . . mostly him. Because this man in front of me isn't my sweet and faith-filled boyfriend. He's dark and sexy, much like the lyrics that are nothing like the praise music he normally sings. He finally glances down at the sheet in front of him, and I feel my entire body exhale as if it had been a prisoner for those few minutes. No wonder Bryson wants him so bad. On a stage, with a hungry crowd and the right ambiance, I can see how any girl would be helpless under that stare.

The unease I've felt all week multiplies. I stand, and even though I promised him a full song, I can't continue to watch him this way. He keeps on playing, absorbed in whatever world he goes to, while I quietly ease down the hall to grab my purse.

The music comes to a halt, and I hear the guitar being gently laid on the coffee table. At least he's not completely oblivious.

"Jan?" he calls from the hallway. A second later he's at the door. "You're leaving?"

"Yeah. I'm tired."

His brow furrows as he slides his phone from his pocket to check the time. It's only eight and I slept in until ten this morning. "Are you upset with me?"

"No. Of course not." But I am, and I don't even know why.

"What did you think of the song?"

"I think . . . you change when you sing it."

Cameron doesn't take my words as I mean them. Instead, his eyes light up with pride. "I know. It's like it burrows inside of me. You felt it, didn't you? That chemistry Bryson and I have?"

I don't want to admit it, but . . . "I'll concede that Bryson isn't a total dud."

"Not a dud? He's going on tour. A real tour, with multiple cities and an actual bus." Cameron stares at his feet. "Bryson's making it happen for himself, and I'm still standing right here."

"It will happen for you, too."

"I guess. It's just hard not to wonder." Cameron pulls me in for a tight hug, and for some reason I want to cry. It feels as though a goodbye is just around the corner, like the bubble I've been living in is millimeters from a very sharp needle. "Please pray for me tonight. I don't know if I've ever been as tempted as I am right now."

And with that final statement, the needle makes contact.

TWENTY-EIGHT

Mrs. Cox is still in the hospital after having two more episodes and a minor surgery she claims was unnecessary but seems to have fixed whatever was causing the fainting. They're transferring her back to the nursing home in the morning, which thrills me. I know it doesn't make much sense, but the hospital feels ominous, like at any moment she'll be hooked up to a million tubes again and fighting for her life. I haven't run into her daughter since that first day, nor have I inquired as to their relationship. In my mind, I want to believe they've reconciled, so there's no reason to invite any other scenario into the mix.

"Knock, knock, can I come in?" I call. The door to her room is slightly ajar, and I can hear a hum of voices inside. I'm carrying a small bouquet of pink roses and a big Happy Valentine's Day card with a raised heart on the front.

"Oh yes, Jan! They're just bringing me my lunch."

I smile, honored that she knows my voice now. I guess I shouldn't be surprised; she listens to my voice for nearly forty-five minutes every day.

The orderly finishes getting Mrs. Cox settled in front of a

tray of food that looks barely edible. She fumbles for a spoon, feels her way around the plate, and grabs the pudding container. Smart woman.

"Happy Valentine's Day," I say in my cheeriest voice. "I know it's two days early, but I figured you're going to be pretty busy getting settled the next couple of days."

She sets her food back down, and I love how her face blooms with color. It's been pale for weeks, so seeing her this healthy sends a wave of relief through me.

The young man finishes his task and nods before leaving the room. I like him the best. He doesn't try to make small talk like the other nurses do.

"Well, come on and give me a hug," Mrs. Cox demands.

I walk over to her bed and set down the flowers before leaning over to squeeze her bony shoulders.

"I smell roses."

"That's because I just put a vaseful of them on your nightstand."

She shifts and carefully finds the vase, her fingers sliding up the glass until it reaches the first stem. I made sure they removed every thorn, knowing she would feel all the way to the tip of the flower. "They're beautiful," she says after exploring every one of the roses with her fingers. "Thank you."

"You're welcome. I have a card, too." I hand her the gift I didn't bother to seal in an envelope and watch as her thumb caresses the heart. It still amazes me how she uses her other senses to compensate for her loss of sight. Watching her reminds me not to take my eyes for granted.

I take the seat next to her bed. She seems so much stronger today, and there's only one IV still in her arm. "Do you feel ready to leave tomorrow?"

"More than ready. I never thought I'd miss that place, but I guess it's become more like home than I realized."

"I'm sure all your friends miss you, too. From what I understand, you are quite the shark at dominoes."

Mrs. Cox snorts, but I see a smile appear. She isn't able to play many games, but she can feel her way just fine around a game of Chickenfoot.

"Anyway, I should get started, huh?" I pick up the Bible first, knowing her rules by now. I don't know why, but the book feels especially weighty today, burdensome almost, as if it, too, is disappointed in me. I gingerly turn the pages, and my hesitation only doubles. I don't want to read today. Not one word.

"You okay, hun?"

I feel her wrinkled hand on my head. A small pat of affection that makes me swallow back the emotion. "Yeah, I'm fine."

"You don't sound fine. Your voice, it sounds heavy."

I nearly choke at the truth of her statement. That's exactly how I feel, heavy, as if my time of hiding has come to an end and I'm faced with a truth that's a constant crushing weight. I sigh and close the Bible. "A friend once told me that no good would ever come from a lie. But I don't agree. I think sometimes people don't really want the truth. They want to believe the best in people, and smashing that illusion feels just as cruel." I don't know where the words come from; they just spill out of me like a flooded river that can no longer be contained within its banks.

She presses her lips together and contemplates my question. I respect her more for it, for at least attempting to consider my point of view.

"Have you ever been happy in an illusion, Jan?"

I think back to my ex, the greatest misstep in my life. "Yes, for a time."

"And then what happened?"

I wring my hands in my lap and force myself to go back to that miserable place, the place of heartache and depression. The place that left me all but broken. "Reality shattered it."

She nods. "It always does." Her hand moves from the top of my head to my cheek, then to my chin. She lifts my head from its resigned position, and even with her shadowy eyes I feel as if she's peering into my soul. "Just because you choose not to tell doesn't mean the truth won't eventually come out. God is not a God of deception. He may allow it for a time, but ultimately He will reveal His truth."

A shiver of fear runs through me. I don't like to think of God that way—as authoritative and demanding. I like the softer version that Aunt Doreen talks about. The one who listens to prayers and loves even the worst of people.

I clear my throat. "I should probably get started or we won't get to read anything." Once again I open the book and turn the delicate pages in anticipation.

"Jan . . ." She pauses until I look at her again. How she can tell, I don't know, but she seems to know exactly when we make eye contact. "God is also not a God of fear. Whatever you need to do . . . He's right there to help you."

"Thanks." My voice is flat, just like the emotion I suddenly feel. There's different rules for someone like me. I don't get to call on an imaginary higher being for strength. I have to find it in myself. And right now I'm too much of a coward to even try.

Cameron is working tonight, which allows me to continue avoiding the churning ball of anxiety that's settled deep inside. Yet the restlessness won't go away. I can't sit still or eat. My cabin is spotless; I can't even mindlessly clean. Frustrated, I grab my jacket and storm out the front door, slamming it behind me. The weather matches my foreboding. The skies are gray and overcast, the wind sharp and gusting, and the temperature has dropped to the high thirties. It's too cold for a walk tonight, but I don't care. I need the crunch of dormant grass and the smell of winter to remind me I was never supposed to get attached to this place.

I walk faster than I should, my nose and lips turning numb as I press forward. The wind whips my hair to the side and seeps beneath my layers of clothing. I blow on my frozen fingers, my gloves trapping the heat for seconds before it dissipates. The anxiety has turned to anger, and I feel it bloom across my chapped face. I'm angry with my ex for putting me in this position, and with Aunt Doreen for getting me this stupid job to begin with. But mostly I'm angry with myself for allowing my guard to be so incredibly thin that it crumbled the first time I saw Cameron's dimples.

My tree appears at the crest of the hill, yet I pass by it, unwilling to cry for Cameron in the same place I mourned over my ex. He deserves more from me than a repeat of breakups past.

I hurry on without thinking, without watching where I'm going except to check the ground beneath my feet. I walk and walk until sweat forms under my shirt and my limbs no longer feel anything but the fire inside. I'm now on the far end of Doreen's property, past the pretty landscaping and flagstone, past the clearing and into the ragged brush. Shrubbery covers the ground, along with untamed trees whose branches keep catching on the edges of my coat. I break off stick after stick to make a path, determined to get to my destination—Mom's property.

Another mile and I'll be at the barbwire fence placed between the two plots of land, the twisted metal a cruel reminder that two worlds this different can never collide without consequences.

I break through the last set of overgrown branches and halt immediately when hammering splits the air. Only a hundred feet separate me from my escape, but it may as well be fifty miles because Dillon stands at the fence line, twisting and pounding barbwire into a brand-new wooden post. His hits are brutal, each one given with more force than needed to do the task. I can feel his anger with each strike; it reverberates through the trees and encircles him like a dark cloud. It's so intense, I can't seem to move forward or even backward. He picks up another long nail and repeats the motion, his shoulders tight, his free hand gripping the barbwire as if he wants to make it bleed.

And then his hammer slips, and I gasp just as it makes contact with his knuckle. I feel the curse as much as hear it and instinctively back away so that I'm shielded by the nearest tree trunk.

Dillon screams into the setting sun like a man in dire agony, and the hammer goes flying into oblivion. Then he kicks and kicks and kicks at the post until the wood splinters and his freshly repaired fence is back in ruins.

But it's not the only thing that breaks at that moment, and I feel his pain in my heart so fiercely I want to rip it from my chest. My throat burns as his head dips in defeat. Though my sight has gone blurry, I can still see the way his shoulders shake, the way his whole body trembles as if the sobs might crush him right there.

I step back, knowing it's wrong to share this kind of intimacy without his permission.

Every word Dillon's ever spoken floods my mind as I flee from the scene I just witnessed.

"See, that's where we differ. You think telling someone the truth is bad behavior, whereas I think skirting your real thoughts and feelings is the most hateful thing you can do to another person. . . . There is nothing more painful than thinking you know someone, sharing your life with them, and then finding out it's a lie."

With each retreating step, Dillon's pain seeps deeper inside my bones, the gnawing truth no longer deniable. I haven't just been lying to Cameron. I've been lying to myself, wanting to believe I'm not completely selfish for letting this relationship progress under deception. Sandra was right. Illusions are always shattered, and this one is no different. Except for one simple change. This time I will be the one making the choice.

Tomorrow . . . Cameron will know the truth.

TWENTY-NINE

I feel like a dead man walking as I enter the worship center. Cameron doesn't know I'm coming, nor have I answered either of his phone calls today for fear that if I heard his voice, I would chicken out.

The auditorium is empty, minus the people onstage and whoever is hidden inside the sound booth. I'm grateful for the anonymity and slip into a seat in the very back row.

Cameron, Brent, Darrel, Brian, Nate, and a woman I don't recognize are huddled around the piano, Brian tapping out two chord options. They go back and forth, each arguing their position, until finally the group comes to a consensus. Cameron high-fives the woman—apparently they were victorious in the debate—and I have to squash a nudge of jealousy. She's beautiful and has no problem wearing the same type of skinny jeans that nearly chopped me in half. She also has long legs, platform shoes, and wavy blond hair down to her mid-back.

Brent calls to the sound booth that they're going to try again and then kisses her on his way back to the front microphone. Ah, his wife, Kaitlyn. I should have known.

The immediate relief shames me. I've no right to Cameron, not when our entire relationship is built on a lie. And moreover, I need to prepare my mind for the inevitable truth that after tonight, this incredible man will no longer be mine.

Cameron steps closer to the front of the stage, violin in hand, and my heart flutters just like it did the first time I heard him sing. I want to run, but I also want to hear him play one more time before he thinks I'm the devil.

Cameron tilts his head as he lifts the instrument but pauses when his eyes meet mine. I give a hesitant wave, and surprise splashes across his face, followed all too quickly by undiluted excitement. He's glad I'm here. He wants me here. He has no idea what I'm about to do to him.

He grants me a single wink before placing his violin under his chin and his bow to the string. A single note slides through the auditorium, haunting in its depth and perfection. More follow, and chill bumps fill my arms and legs, multiplying when Brian hits his first chord on the piano. Nate's drums come next, a soft roll that vibrates across my entire body.

The three of them continue, working together, the music climaxing, then calming until Brent's voice comes in as the fourth layer, a silky ballad about his King Jesus and revival and seeing His kingdom. Brent pauses, picking softly on his acoustic guitar, giving me only a moment to recover before he sings again, his wife joining him in a harmony so touching the music feels like velvet across the skin. The violin fades, then the piano and the drums. The woman also lowers her mic so all that's left is Brent's voice, his lone guitar, and an empty room so full of emotion that I nearly choke on my tears.

The music isn't just there, it's alive. I feel it under every inch of my skin, inside my bones, down to my fingertips. I feel its pressure, its demand to respond in some way, as if we've become a partnership and I'm failing in my duties. And yet I can't move, too frozen by the ache in Brent's voice, by the simplicity of his guitar, by how much can be felt in such foreign words.

The piano comes back in, then the drums, and finally Cameron's violin. The crescendo has me sliding forward in my seat as if I'm a captive of the music now, willing to follow it wherever it goes. More tears slip down my cheeks, and I don't even care. It feels like such a natural response that I'm not even embarrassed. And then the song ends, and the silence that's left leaves me hollow yet strangely fulfilled at the same time.

How could Cameron consider, even for a moment, trading this type of music for Bryson's?

Brent cheers, and the band claps. They felt it, too, a surge of power so strong that if you bottled it, you could light all of Dallas.

I slide back in my chair, emotionally exhausted, and yet my mind is racing, my thoughts traveling past B&L's reception buildings and patches of trees. It continues until I'm standing back in the brush and watching Dillon break. I want to reach out, bring him here, let him experience the enormity of what I just felt. And then it hits me. He's not like me. He grew up in the church.

I close my eyes and hurt for him all over. Maybe the agony I witnessed was more than the loss of a mom and a wife. It was the loss of an entire way of life.

My resolve strengthens as I watch the six bandmates discuss Sunday morning's set. I have plenty of regrets in my past, but keeping Cameron from this life and his place within it will not be one of them. He deserves the truth. Deserves to be the one to make a decision either way about the two of us.

Brent dismisses the group, and Cameron sets his violin in

its case. He says goodbye to his roommates. A minute later, he emerges from the backstage doorway.

I stand, fidgeting with my purse while my pulse kicks up two notches.

"Hey! What are you doing here?" He doesn't stop when he reaches my row. Instead, he pulls me into a hug and lifts me off the ground. "What did you think?"

"Incredible. Really. I've never heard anything like that before." I ease away, even though I want to hold on longer. "Is that the song you've been talking about?"

"Yes," he says in a relieved sigh. "Brent's scrapped it from the set three times now, and finally . . . it's right." He lifts his hands to my face. "You must be our good luck charm."

I place my hands on his and move out of his grasp before he kisses me. "I can pretty much guarantee that's not the case." I glance back up at the stage, where Brent and his wife are still engaged over a sheet of music. I don't want to do this with an audience, and besides, admitting I don't believe in God while standing in a place of worship feels far too sacrilegious for my comfort level. "Could we go into the hall or somewhere more private? I really need to talk to you."

"Is something wrong?"

"No. I mean, yes, but . . . please, not in here."

His eyes narrow as his mouth moves into a confused frown. "The bridal suite is right outside. I have the keys."

It takes every ounce of self-control not to groan. Wedding venue, honeymoon cabin, now the bridal suite? I'm pretty sure getting married is out of the question, because I have now cursed every location that is supposed to come with a positive memory. "I guess that'll work." I ease from the row and cross my arms so he can't take my hand.

Cameron seems to register every one of my movements,

and his face grows more and more somber with each physical rejection. He points to the exit doors. I lead, though I have no idea where I'm going until we both spill into the hallway. He passes me then, stops at a door ten feet down, and pulls out a ring of keys. His hands tremble, and it takes two attempts before the key slides in and turns. Cameron holds the door open for me. I pass, careful not to touch him, and walk inside the dim room. He hits a switch on the wall, and a huge chandelier floods the space with soft, warm light.

"Wow."

Cameron remains by the door while I stand in the center of a formal seating area with two Queen Anne chairs, a luxurious curved couch, and a chaise lounge. A vanity mirror hangs in an adjacent room, floor to ceiling, framed with intricate gold etching.

"It's a little much for my taste, but the brides seem to like it." His voice is monotone now, and gone is his earlier excitement. He bites at his pinky nail. "So, what's going on?"

I meet his eyes for only a brief second before I have to turn away. I'm not ready. Not yet. Instead, I focus on the lush mauve carpet, searching for a distraction. It comes in the form of a side table. The piece is off-balance, sloped to the right as if unstable. My gaze follows downward, and sure enough, the back two legs show a jagged thin line across the wood. Glued, put back together, and shoved in the corner so no one would notice. "I bet this room holds a lot of secrets," I say absently, imagining what kind of brawl did the damage. Maybe a father and son-in-law. Maybe two bridesmaids fighting over the same guy. Maybe a bride and her mother.

"Jan, why are we in here?"

I look up then, willing my mind to stop the loop it's on. If

I'm not careful, I'll get so obsessed in the origin of the damage that I'll neglect the entire purpose of coming in this room to begin with. "Do you want to sit?"

Cameron's head falls back, and I hear a small thud when it hits the closed door. "Not really."

"I'm sorry. I'm not doing this well at all." I have no idea what to do with my hands, so I set my purse down on the oval coffee table and opt to wring them in front of me. "First, you need to know I think you're amazing."

I can hardly get the words out without choking, which seems to make Cameron mad because his mouth goes tight.

"If you're breaking up with me, there's no need to prolong the agony. Just do what you came here to do."

My body goes rigid. "Breaking up is the last thing I want." Even though I know that's likely what will happen tonight.

The admission seems to lessen the tension in his shoulders, and he finally moves away from the door. "Okay? Then what's with the 'we need to talk' and 'you're such a great guy' speech?"

"Me stalling, I guess."

"Jan . . . there's nothing you can't tell me." He takes my hand and leads us to the love seat. We sit hip to hip, our warmth and closeness another dichotomy to the chasm I'm about to open.

I clear my throat. "You know how I told you that I hate crowds and big churches, which was why I chose to attend a small church by the ranch?"

He nods.

"Well, I lied." I bite my lip and add my other hand to our joined ones. "I made up that church because I didn't want you to know the real reason for my not attending Grace Community." The air turns stale, but I force the truth out. "Cameron, I don't come here, or go to any church for that matter, because . . . I'm not a Christian."

His shock feels like electricity as his hands slip from mine. "What are you talking about?"

"I don't believe in God," I say with more certainty this time, "or in any religious deity." Cameron stares at me, his jaw slack, and now that it's out there, my excuses follow in a rush. "To me, faith isn't a disqualifier in a relationship. It didn't matter that you believed and I didn't. Only that we were happy together."

His eyes widen as he shifts away from me. "Not a disqualifier?" He stands, his face flushed. "But you work at a church. You read the Bible to Mrs. Cox nearly every day. Jan, you told me not to sell out from Christian music."

"And you shouldn't." I can feel his shock, can see the confusion across his face, and try again to help him make sense of what I'm saying. "Cameron, I respect your faith; it's honorable. I just don't think everyone has to share in it."

His mouth hangs open as he places both hands on top of his head. "You're actually serious?" The hands drop a second later and he stumbles back a step. "I've asked you to pray for me. I've shared my deepest fears and insecurities with you. And all this time you, what, pretended to care, pretended to pray? You just sat there and let me think I had a partner through all of this?" Hurt wraps around every word, as if this fact alone is the greatest betrayal.

"You *do* have a partner." I press my hand to my chest in a plea. "I'm still me, Cameron."

But that comment only seems to make him angry. "And who exactly is that? Because this information means that the girl I fell for does not exist!" His voice shakes, and he takes a deep breath before continuing. "You knew I was looking for a serious relationship. How could you think that didn't include my faith? I've dedicated my life to the church."

"I guess I thought we could get past it." I can't bear the disdain on his face and turn away. Even though I knew this reaction was a real possibility, it doesn't make living through it any easier.

"Does Pastor Thomas know? Eric? Ralph?"

I shake my head. "No. No one here does. Well, except you now." I hadn't even thought of that potential outcome—Cameron getting angry enough to get me fired. I probably deserve at least that much. "I understand if you feel the need to tell them."

"You understand." He snorts. "Well, that's generous of you."

We continue to stare at each other in silence until the absence of noise feels deafening to me. I don't know whether to stay or leave or even if pleading will make a difference.

I decide to do the latter and carefully approach him. "I know I should have told you sooner, and I know I'm not what you expected or even someone you would have considered. Honestly, you're not like anyone I ever expected to be with, either. But somehow, we fit. And really, apart from this one small difference, we're great together."

"Small difference?" He stares at me, his breathing heavy. "Don't you understand? Being with you now goes against every conviction I have about relationships. It breaks every promise I ever made to my parents, to God . . . to myself. This isn't a *small difference*, Jan. It's a deal breaker."

His words are a knife through my heart. One I completely deserve because I'm the one who lied. I close my eyes; I can't look at Cameron anymore. He's right. It is a deal breaker. I knew it that first day, and yet I foolishly let myself fall into another impossible scenario.

"You're right. You deserve better." I turn away and grab my purse, determined to keep it together until I get to the car. Yet, despite all my willpower, a tear slips out, rolls down my cheek and onto my shirt. I hate crying. I especially hate crying in front of other people. And now I've done it twice in the span of an hour. "I really am sorry, Cameron. I didn't set out to lie to you. I was going to tell you, but when you hugged me and made me feel so special and respected, I just couldn't. After that, it snowballed and I found myself in this cycle of deception. One I couldn't break without ruining the best part of my life . . . you."

When I turn, his eyes are on me and wet with unshed tears. It's too much. This whole thing is too much. I dip my head and rush by him, desperate to flee this sick feeling in my stomach. I'm halfway through the door when I hear him speak.

"Jan." He doesn't move, and somehow that makes it more wrenching. "I need time to process this."

"Of course," I choke out. "Whatever you need."

We don't say goodbye, although the moment feels very much like one. Instead, I walk away and leave him standing there, his back to me, knowing I did the right thing . . . for once.

THIRTY

There's a wedding tonight . . . of course. After all, Valentine's Day is supposed to be the most romantic day of the year. B&L can probably be seen from space with all the lights on display. They wrap the trees, cover retaining walls, and even hang in strings over the stone wedding altar.

I watch from a safe distance as the couple hold hands and vow to love each other. At least a hundred guests fill the chairs on either side of the aisle, and four attendants each stand by the bride and groom.

Despite my inner pity fest, I do feel happy for them. The weather couldn't be more perfect. Nearly seventy degrees—a miracle this time of year. Good thing, too, because the bridesmaids are barely covered in their matching blue short-sleeved, knee-length dresses. It's the most casual wedding I've seen out here. The girls are all wearing cowboy boots, even the bride. The men are in jeans, boots, crisp white shirts, and leather vests. Only the groom is wearing a tie.

It's kind of nice, though. Definitely more my style than some of the others.

Outside the barn, the band is getting set up for the reception, which promises to be a wild one. The patio has been transformed with two open bars and a temporary dance floor made out of tongue-and-groove wood flooring. The guitarist quietly tunes his instrument, and I move as far as I can from the commotion. I want to hear the officiator's voice, and moreover, being around a musician right now is not exactly on my wish list.

The groom kisses his bride, signifying the end of the ceremony. I'm disappointed because it means I can no longer hide in the shadows. The group will come this way soon, and I'll be exiled back to my cabin, where nothing but loneliness awaits.

Cameron has remained silent all day, and while it's killed me to do so, so have I. He asked for time, a small request considering the situation. At least the tears have stopped. In fact, I'm not sure my body has the ability to cry any more than I already have.

The newly married couple lock arms and begin their retreat down the stone walkway. Two more groomsmen do the same, each escorting a bridesmaid. The third groomsman offers his elbow, and I startle at the resemblance to Dillon. It's uncanny. Same dark hair, same build, same . . . I press my hand to my mouth, unsuccessfully holding in a giggle. It's not a doppelganger at all. Dillon Kyle is a member of the wedding party. On Valentine's Day. Okay, maybe I do appreciate irony when it's not mine.

Curiosity wars with my good sense and wins. I stay in my spot by the trees, watching the entire wedding party finish their march. The officiator invites everyone to the reception, and right on cue the barn doors swing open to reveal multiple tables covered in white linens and carefully chosen centerpieces.

Casual as the attire may be, this wedding is not cheap. Dozens of white roses dot the room, each arrangement stuffed until overflowing. The dinnerware is china with multiple silver utensils, and each table has both champagne and white wine open and ready for consumption.

This isn't the type of party one crashes, especially not in an oversized T-shirt, leggings, and fuzzy boots. And yet I can't seem to retreat. Who are these people, and how is Dillon, Mr. Unsocial himself, one of them?

"I never figured you for the stalking type."

I jump at the voice behind me and spin around so fast I stumble. Heart racing, it takes me at least thirty seconds to register the face of the man in front of me. "Mr. Kyle! You scared the daylights out of me." I press my hand to my heart and work to still my frantic nerves.

"Sorry about that, kiddo. I figured you'd hear me coming."

I might have if I hadn't been completely absorbed with watching his son. I don't say that, of course.

"What are you doing hiding in the shadows?" He raises his eyebrows, and I know he's teasing me. The man spends way too much time with my uncle and has taken on a similar father-figure role with me.

"Watching the ceremony. I do that sometimes." Though rarely do I stay for the whole thing. "What are you doing here?"

"The groom is my cousin's boy." He points to the group taking pictures. "Though I can't say I envy him. It's been quite an interesting couple of weeks."

"Why's that?"

"Well, let's just say the bride is a mite spoiled, and I guess she and Nathan's best friend had words." He rubs his chin. "Anyway, there was a last-minute shake-up in the wedding party, and Dillon got called yesterday to fill in."

The giggles come again. "Oh, I'm sure he loved that."

"Thrilled beyond measure." Mr. Kyle winks, but his smile fades soon after. "It's good, though. He didn't need to spend tonight by himself, especially considering . . . well, he just didn't need to be alone."

It doesn't take a genius to surmise this must be Dillon's first Valentine's without his wife.

We both turn back to the wedding party that's now dispersing. Dillon's already halfway down the hill when I spot him again. His posture is rigid, his steps hurried. There's so much about him that's still a mystery to me. His past, his marriage, his faith that doesn't seem to exist anymore.

"You should come in and hang out for a while," his dad offers. "I guarantee the food is going to be worth staying for."

I pry my eyes away from his son and the questions bombarding my mind. "No, that's okay. I have dinner waiting for me at home." A meal that's likely freezer-burnt, yet it sounds better than a roomful of love-focused strangers. "In fact, I better go before everyone wonders who this crazy girl is behind the trees."

"You sure?" Worry wrinkles his brow, and as touched as I am by his concern, I once again decline.

"Thank you, though." I ease away, but Mr. Kyle continues to watch me. I know without asking that he'll do so until I'm safely back down the hill. He and Dillon are the same that way. Always mindful, always the protector. "Have fun!" I call before making my final turn to leave. "Be sure to tell Dillon he needs to work on his fake smile."

Mr. Kyle grins. "I will. Good night, Jan."

"'Night, Mr. Kyle."

I walk the path home, forcing myself not to look back. I can't worry about Dillon's broken heart—not when I haven't even started to re-mend my own.

~

I'm nestled in my comfy pj's, hair in a messy bun, and watching a movie when a banging starts at my door.

Cameron. Hope fills my chest, and I toss off my blanket. "Who is it?"

"Cupid," says a surly voice. "Who do you think? Open up."

My heart shrinks. Of course it would be Dillon and not Cameron.

"Stupid girl," I grumble under my breath. This is the result of way too many romantic movies. I'm haunted now with images of Cameron on his knees, a bouquet of roses in his hands as he begs me to take him back.

I turn the lock and swing open the door. "Tired of your wedding duties already?"

Dillon dismisses my sarcasm and walks right in. "Get dressed. I need backup at this ridiculous event." Up close, his wedding ensemble borders on absurd. The vest is easily a size too small, straining against his chest like it's hanging on by a prayer. The shirtsleeves are an inch above his wrists and look as uncomfortable as I'm sure they feel. At least the jeans seem to fit, though they're far snugger than his usual work attire.

"Wow, with an invitation like that, how could I refuse?" I shut the door. "Oh, wait, here's how—no."

He grabs a bottle of Mountain Dew from the fridge. A bottle I neither bought nor put in there, but Dillon has pretty much claimed this place as his own during the day. I could pretend I mind, but coming home to a stocked fridge and a clean kitchen is a nice trade-off.

"Besides, I'm not on the guest list."

"Believe me, the least they owe me is a plus-one. I've already been propositioned twice by Erika's obnoxious friends. One even tried to feed me at dinner." He shakes his head like he wants to dislodge the memory. "I didn't even want to go to this thing, let alone be in it." Bottle to his mouth, he chugs a third of the soda and sets the drink back on the counter. The cuff links strain against his skin, red marks already forming where the sleeves end. Sheesh, how does he have any circulation?

Leaving my station by the door, I join him at the counter. He flinches when I reach for his wrist, but I'm faster and tighten my grip. "Hold still. I'm trying to help you." Though it takes two attempts, somehow I manage to turn the cuff link enough to slide through the first button hole. The second one is easy after that.

After I finish both sides, Dillon rolls each wrist. "Thank you."

"You're welcome. That'll be twenty bucks. You can put the money on the counter."

"I fixed your leaky faucet yesterday. Count us even." He folds up one sleeve until it lies securely in the middle of his forearm and then pauses before starting the other one. "Why are you even home?"

"I live here."

"You know what I mean. Why aren't you out on a date tonight?"

"I don't want to talk about it." Especially with Dillon. I return to my indented couch cushion and flop down.

"Okay, then you leave me no choice but to guess." He follows me to the living room, sits on the armrest, and studies me. I want to take the blanket and wrap it around my head so he can't see the remnants of a day full of tears. "Let's see . . . you're not mad, so he didn't stand you up. You're back in your heartbreak flannels and"—he leans forward—"you've been crying. A lot."

How he's figured me out so fast, I'll never know, but once again Dillon has pegged the situation perfectly. "I really do hate you."

He chuckles, yet it's drowned out by the compassion in his eyes. "You finally told him, didn't you?"

"Right again," I mutter. "Now, if this interrogation is finished, I'd like to get back to my wallowing."

"Not on my watch." He's off the couch before his sentence is over, and not only does my TV screen go black, but he manages to confiscate both remotes in the process. "I'm not letting you regress back to the unwashed hair and sob fests by the tree. Get dressed. Between the two of us, we're going to make sure tonight doesn't completely suck."

"I really don't want to," I say, which comes out more like a plea.

"Neither do I, but sometimes you have to force life to go on, even when it feels impossible."

His father's words come back to me, and I realize that Dillon isn't talking about me and my once-again failed relationship. Last year at this time, Dillon had a wife. In the scheme of things, his woes do kinda trump mine. "Fine." I kick off my blanket and force myself to stand. "Give me two minutes."

"Have you looked in the mirror? You're going to need more than two minutes."

I throw a pillow at him, but we're both smiling now, so I guess he wins again.

How does he do it? I wonder all the way to my closet. *How does he make every situation just a little bit better?*

THIRTY-ONE

I emerge fifteen minutes later and know by Dillon's reaction that I cleaned up better than he expected. As luck would have it, I was a regular at the country bar in my hometown and have all the clothes and skills needed for a night of dancing.

"Ready, cowboy?" I ask in my best Texas drawl. It gets me a chuckle and another sweep of his eyes.

"Lose the hat. It's too much."

"Really? I love this old thing." I pull off my favorite accessory and shake out my hair. I still haven't found a hair stylist, so it's an impossible mane of waves right now. "Give me another minute, then. I need to do something with this hair."

"It's fine." His voice cracks and he clears his throat. "You only needed to look acceptable. And now you do."

"Ah, gee." I fan myself. "You're gonna make me blush."

"Just . . . hurry up."

I grab a small purse and stuff my keys, a tube of lip gloss, and my phone inside, but not without checking for any missed texts. Blank. Empty. Just like my love life.

Dillon guides me through the door, locking it from the inside before pulling it shut. He must have gotten rid of the vest while I was changing, and now with the rolled sleeves, open collar, and tight jeans he's definitely a few notches above noticeable.

"I'm not sure you did yourself any favors," I say on our way up the flagstone.

"What do you mean?"

"Without the getup, you look, I don't know, nice. Some women might even say handsome."

A small grin appears. "Some women? You mean someone other than you?"

I don't bother responding. He's too good at baiting me, and I don't have the energy to rise to the occasion. I need to breathe and focus on forgetting about Cameron.

The music grows louder as we climb the hill. Groups gather everywhere, both inside and outside, and the dance floor is full of half-inebriated guests.

"Just play along," he whispers and slides his hand in mine. It's rough and warm and so different from Cameron's that I feel guilty when I wrap my fingers with his.

"Who was it again that said, 'Skirting your real thoughts and feelings is the most hateful thing you can do to another person'?"

He shoots me a deadly stare. "Bridezillas are an exception to that rule."

"So now there are exceptions? That's convenient."

He pulls me along, and it's more than a few prowling women who zero in on our joined hands. Mr. Kyle nearly spits out his drink.

My cheeks burn. "I don't think you thought this through very well. Your family is going to think we're . . . you know, together."

"Who cares? It's no one you'll ever see again."

"I'm talking about your dad, who happens to be best friends with my uncle, who happens to be married to my aunt, who will unquestionably have something to say about this."

"Doreen has something to say about everything."

"Dillon, I'm serious." I halt, and he turns until we're face-to-face. "My aunt and uncle's opinion means a lot to me. So does your dad's."

His gaze softens and so does his voice. "Dad knows what I'm doing. He looks surprised because he said you'd never agree. As for the rest of these people, they think it's their personal mission to find me a replacement wife, and if one more person talks about setting me up, I'm going to lose it."

My frustration fades when buried hurt leaks through his voice. "Okay, fine."

His relief is palpable. "Thank you."

As we mingle our way through the crowd, I quickly understand Dillon's desperation. Whispers seem to follow us, as do the unmasked stares.

"Isn't she lovely? Is Dillon dating again?"

"That wife of his really did a number on him. Glad he's found a new girl."

"They've both had such a brutal year. Didn't expect to see them here."

I grit my teeth but keep silent solely out of respect for Dillon and his dad. How can they not see how uncomfortable he is? Or maybe they think grief makes someone deaf. Idiots.

We find an abandoned table by the dance floor. Dillon collects the empty cups littering the top and the ground below and tosses them in the trash. "How hard is it to clean up after yourself?" he mutters.

"I'm guessing pretty difficult when you can barely stand." I set my purse down on the now-clean surface and subtly point to the trio of women heading our way. Their arms are linked like they need the extra support, and every one of them is swaying.

"Dillon," the tall one calls in a pathetic plea. "I need you. My partner bailed on me."

Either she doesn't see me standing next to him or she doesn't care. Based on the looks I'm getting from her friends, I'm guessing the latter.

Dillon slides his arm around my waist, tight and secure. "Sorry, but I need to spend a little time with my girl."

Not only does that draw a very unflattering pout from the woman, but I get a visual dressing down that practically sends me back to high school. Unfortunately for her, I'm not only fluent in Mean Girl but also hold the reigning title at Northside High.

Snubbing her, I place my palm to Dillon's chest and press up against him. "Dillon?" I coo, fluttering my eyelashes twice. "Dance with me."

He glances down, and the amused lift of his brows almost sends me into a fit of giggles. We somehow don't break character, even when he says, "Whatever you want, my dear."

I do a pirouette on my way to the dance floor and wave sweetly at the three girls, who seem to have sobered up quite a bit. The song is a fast one, and two rows of line dancers are stomping to the beat.

We join on the far side, and while I pick the moves up pretty quickly, Dillon is operating on two left feet.

I sashay to the right and then pull Dillon back in line. "Just watch the person in front of you."

"I am watching," he grumbles. "Every time I get it, they turn."

The song ends shortly after, replaced by a slow ballad that Dillon obviously feels more comfortable with because he sweeps me in a hold that is tight and confident. Soon we're lost in the midst of dancers, circling with the lazy grace of a falling feather. Dillon is a stronger lead than I expect, but it allows me to relax and sneak a peek at the threesome we ditched. They're gone.

Mission accomplished.

"I guess I can now add female repellant to my growing list of Dillon Kyle duties."

"What duties?" He snorts.

"Hmm . . . let's see . . . there's nurse . . . dance instructor . . . spades partner . . . food storage assistant."

"That one's reaching."

"All the same, you keep food in my cabin so it counts."

The corner of his mouth turns upward into a half smile. "Is that all?"

"Nope. One more . . . internet provider."

"Come on, I watched two movies on there, that's it."

"Except those two movies are now in my recently watched file and will dictate my suggested titles forever."

"Good. You need to pull your head out of all those cheesy romance movies anyway." He spins us to avoid a two-stepping couple moving much faster than the music. "None of it is real."

"I know. I just like happy endings."

He grows silent, and as much as I like the bantering, I also can't help but ask the next question. "Dillon?"

"Yeah?"

"Why don't you ever want to go home? I don't mind or anything. My kitchen has never been so organized. But it does seem like you're hiding."

He sighs, and it's so weighty I immediately regret my intrusion. "She's everywhere there. Some weeks it's not so bad. Others, I suffocate on her memory."

We're quiet for a while, both in our heads, aimlessly moving to the music. "Do you think you'll ever fall in love again?" I ask.

"I don't know. Maybe. If I do, I'll be more careful next time. That's for sure."

"I know what you mean. I've wished a million times that my first love had been anyone other than Jason." I flinch at his name on my lips. It's been months since I've allowed myself to utter it.

Dillon spins me out, and somehow our chests end up closer when we reconnect. "Jason?"

"San Antonio guy."

"Ah." He nods, making the connection. "Why is that?"

"Because I think I might be ruined now," I say honestly. "Love scares me. I don't trust it. Even with Cameron. The minute Darcy said the word *love*, I began my retreat." My thoughts drift to the father who never wanted to know me, then to Stepdad #1 who never once called like he promised, and finally to all the many men since who couldn't be bothered to stay. "It's like the minute I get past that reckless, heart-throbbing, throw-caution-to-the-wind euphoria to something deeper, I want to run."

"Do you think that's why you finally told him? To drive him away?" Dillon's voice is soft, even though his words reveal a truth I haven't wanted to admit.

"Maybe. Or to test him. I don't know." Moisture nips at the corners of my eyes, and I fight to keep the tears back. "But if it was, how is that fair to anyone who dares to care about me?"

Warm brown eyes meet mine and I cling to them, cling to

the security I find whenever he's around. Somehow, through all the tumultuous storms and unknowns these past few months, Dillon has become the one unwaveringly honest, steadfast presence in my life.

"You're not ruined," he finally says, his voice roughened by some unidentifiable emotion. "You just need to pick a stronger man. Someone who isn't going to let you hide behind a quip and a smile."

"I'm not sure I'm worth the effort."

"Trust me. You are."

I don't realize we've stopped moving or how close our faces are to each other until a couple bumps into us.

Fire races to my cheeks as the horror sets in that for a few seconds there I'd forgotten the rest of the world existed. I disentangle myself from his arms. *Why would I tell him all that?*

"Dad looks cornered."

"What?" I dare to look back at the man who just completely annihilated my defenses.

Dillon tilts his chin toward the refreshment table, where two women flank Mr. Kyle, who isn't even trying to hide his misery.

The picture is just ridiculous enough to end my embarrassment and douse whatever crazy connection we just had. "Well . . . I am in rescue mode tonight."

Dillon winks at me. "I don't think you'll pass for his date."

"No, probably not. But I'm sure there's some emergency I can come up with."

He stretches his hand out, and I try to ignore the fact that it, too, is trembling. "Alright, Wonder Woman. Lead the way."

THIRTY-TWO

Cameron doesn't text until Sunday night, and when he does, it leaves me no clue as to how he's feeling.

Can we talk or are you busy?

Not busy at all. Would love to talk.

Okay. I'll be there in 20 min.

Nothing more. Not even an emoji, which makes these twenty minutes the longest of my life.

I peer out the window, searching for headlights, but it remains dark except for my porch lights. Grrr. I let the blinds fall from my fingers and go back to the kitchen to reclean the counters.

A hesitant knock comes minutes later, and I feel it all the way to my toes and back up. My hands shake as I toss the paper towel into the trash and wipe the remainder of the moisture on my jeans. "Coming."

I open the door, and my heart reacts as it always does when I see Cameron. It's one of the things I'll miss most when all of this is over—that thrill of anticipation.

"Hey," I whisper.

He's in jeans and a T-shirt, one that's more wrinkled than any I've seen him wear. His hands are shoved deep into his pockets, and he makes eye contact only for a brief second. "Hey," he says back but doesn't move.

The resulting silence is so awful, I throw out, "I'm really glad you came," just to end it.

"Yeah, well, I felt this conversation needed to happen in person." I can't read his expression. It's not angry or sad or even tortured the way he appeared when we last talked. It's just empty, and somehow that feels worse.

"Do you want to come in?" I move out of the way, and he takes his first step across the threshold. It seems to break some kind of barrier because he immediately shoves his hands in his hair and exhales.

"I had this entire speech planned all the way here, and now I can't remember any of it."

Since I don't know if he planned a goodbye speech or an I-forgive-you one, I don't know if his forgetfulness is a good thing or not. Based on his body language up to this point, I have a sinking suspicion I should be grateful for the lack of memory.

"We could sit down?" I offer. Cameron stares at me, his eyes moving from my freshly braided hair to my sock-covered feet. The scrutiny makes me squirm, even though I worked hard to look nice for him. "Or we could take a walk?"

"I don't want to take a walk." He pulls at his neck with his right hand. "I just want to say what I came to say."

Any hope for a positive outcome leaves with those words. "Okay."

He falls back against the kitchen counter as if he needs the extra support. "I resigned from Grace Community this morning."

My stomach drops, as if his words opened up a swirling vortex. "What? Why?"

"Because I'm miserable there and have been for months. I had my resignation letter typed and ready to turn in until you showed up. And then I thought . . ." He presses his wrists to his eyes, and the hardened, curt man who showed up finally disappears. "I don't know. Nothing makes sense anymore."

"Cameron . . ." I rush to him, unwilling to let him suffer alone. "You don't have to do this." I take one of his hands in mine and crush it to my heart. "We can find our way."

He closes his eyes like it physically hurts to touch me. "It's not that simple."

Encouraged by his struggle, I press my head against his chest and wrap him in the tightest hug I can. "So it's complicated?" I swallow. "Aunt Doreen and I have an amazing relationship and we've never agreed on this subject." I look up at him, a fresh wave of tears threatening to ruin my makeup. "Can't we try?"

His thumb slides to my cheek and wipes away the moisture. "I lay awake all last night trying to figure out how I missed such a monumental thing about you. Six weeks." He shakes his head. "I've replayed each conversation a hundred times, and what I realized was that every time we approached anything remotely serious or meaningful, you'd change the subject or make a joke or distract me. And I let you, because deep down I wanted to believe that God gave me this perfect girl instead of the music, when really it was just me filling a void you had no ability to fill."

Ouch. I pull away and stare down at my sock-clad feet.

"I'm going on tour with Bryson. We leave tomorrow." Cameron's decision feels more like defeat than a true choice. "I think us getting some space from each other for a while will be a good thing, at least until my head clears."

Space. I know all about that word. Stepdad #1 used it when he hugged me goodbye. *"I'm just taking a little space from your mom, not you."* I never saw him again.

I back away, practice and instinct taking over. "Go. Do what you have to do."

"I'm not trying to hurt you."

I cross my arms. "Who's hurt? We dated a few weeks. Now it's over. No big deal."

His mouth presses into a thin line, but I don't care. It's not my job to make him feel better about leaving. I walk to the door and hold it open for him. Cameron huffs and takes his final step out of my life. "It didn't have to be this way."

I shut out his voice with a slam.

Christian, non-Christian. It's all the same. Men leave. It's simply what they do.

I call in sick the next day. It's one thing to be a pillar of pride and strength when you're kicking someone out of your house. Another to do it for hours at the very place we met. Not to mention, I feel pretty sure that as soon as I go back, Pastor Thomas will call me into his office and fire me for lying. Cameron and I didn't exactly end amicably, which means he has no reason not to rat me out.

I shouldn't care. The job wasn't permanent anyway, but I do care. I've never fit so well anywhere else. Ralph and I make a great team. He loves people and visiting and going a million miles an hour. I'm good at organizing and administration. Not to mention his time away has turned him into a completely different person. He smiles more readily, speaks optimistically about the day instead of hanging his head, and has even cracked some jokes.

Of course, this could all have nothing to do with me and everything to do with Victoria, but I'm going to believe I had a small part in helping him.

I tug my brush roughly down my hair, half tempted to cut it all off. I need to get out of here. Out of my head and this stuffy cabin that seems determined to break me.

Forgoing my task, I opt for a quick ponytail, a pair of faded jeans, and a thin long-sleeved shirt. Two minutes later I'm driving, and even though I had no conscious thought as to a destination, I end up at the Serenity Hills Nursing Facility.

I want to talk to Sandra about last night, to tell her I told the truth, and maybe even ask her more about the whole conquering-fear thing she mentioned. It's strange. Sandra is blind, and yet sometimes it feels like she sees me more clearly than most others.

Victoria waves when I push through the nursing home doors. It's warm in here, and not just the temperature. Everything about this place makes me feel comforted now. "Jan, hey."

"Hey. How was your trip?" The most I've gotten out of Ralph is a snort and an "It was nice" comment.

She sets down her clipboard and meets me at the counter. "Wonderful. The best vacation we've ever taken. Half the places we stayed had little-to-no cell service. It was like we were in our own little cocoon." Her voice has a singsong quality, and watching her I'm amazed she's the same woman I saw crying in the bathroom. "The Ralph I married has returned." She giggles and presses her palms to her cheeks. "I feel like we're newlyweds again."

She looks like a newlywed. Her skin is brighter, her hair

fixed and styled versus pulled sharply into a ponytail. Maybe it is true that the act of loving another person makes us more beautiful people. If so, I'm sure I look like Medusa today.

"Now tell me about you. Anything new on the boyfriend front?"

I don't want to talk about Cameron or our breakup. "Nope," I lie. "Same old, same old." I keep a smile plastered on my face, even though I want to cry. "I'm really glad you two had a good time."

"We did." She sighs like she still can't believe it's real. "The change is more than I prayed for, but then God seems to be doing that a lot lately."

"What do you mean?"

"Here, I'll show you." She steps around the desk, and I follow her down the green hallway that leads to Mrs. Cox's room. We stop outside her door, where Victoria lifts her finger to her lips, then points to her ear. I strain to listen for what she wants me to hear and then it comes. A voice reading the very passage I ended on in the hospital.

"Who is that?" I ask quietly.

Victoria leans close and whispers, "Rachel. Sandra's daughter. It's the first time she's visited the nursing home in months." Her eyes turn teary, and I find my vision going blurry, as well. I'm reminded of the prayer I said at the hospital, the one I chose to forget because the stakes were too high. To admit prayer works is to admit that God exists, and admitting God exists means that the words in Sandra's Bible are not just a collection of fanatical writings but instructions for living. And, well, there's just too many things in that book that would change everything in my life.

I back away from the door, not wanting to ride this train of thought any further.

Victoria tilts her head. "Don't you want to meet her?"

"No. Let them have their time. I'll try again tomorrow." I feel a sob in my chest and move farther away from both the room and Victoria.

Her expression turns to concern, and I know she can see I'm on the edge of breaking down. "You sure everything is okay?"

"Yeah. I'm just tired. I'll see you tomorrow." With that, I flee. From the hall, the building, the parking lot, until I'm safely locked inside my car. The dam on my tears collapses immediately after. Head against the steering wheel, I let the river of emotion that I've been stifling finally burst forth.

How is it possible to be so happy for another person and so devastated for myself? I'm glad Victoria and Ralph are falling in love again, glad Mrs. Cox's daughter is in there reading to her, but at the same time I feel as if I'm losing everyone I care about.

I pound my head against the leather wheel, admonishing myself for getting too comfortable. I came here to heal, get stronger, and then return to my old life. The one I felt completely satisfied with prior to moving to Texas.

And now I have no idea how I'll ever return to who I used to be.

THIRTY-THREE

The days pass in slow motion, leaving me too much time to think. Too much time to question all the events that have left me sitting on this same bench fighting heartbreak all over again. I once heard the definition of insanity is doing the same thing over and over again while expecting different results. If that's true, my life can be concisely summed up in that one tragic word.

I turn toward the sky, even though I know no one's listening. "Well . . . here I am again. Is this what you wanted?"

There's no answer except the *snap* of cutting shears. It gets louder as I strain my ears to hear, and I don't fight the relief that comes in knowing I'm not out here alone. On my feet once again, I trudge toward the only person who might understand why I'm sitting alone on a Saturday afternoon.

Dillon appears the minute I clear the edge of the reception barn. He's hunched over Doreen's barren rosebushes, the ones that run along the back fence for a good twenty yards. I wait to speak until he lets the tool drop from his hand and takes a swig from his thermos.

"What is your obsession with working on the weekends?"

He sets down his drink and smiles at my approach. "I like

the quiet, and it's rare when we don't have a wedding scheduled." He says *we* like he's part of this place, as if he, too, has part ownership of B&L and the land it sits on. I understand. I've been here nearly three months now, and the venue feels like a part of me, as well. "And," he adds, "it seems to annoy you, which has its own benefits."

I push at his arm, but I can tell by his smirk that he's teasing. "So what's with all the branches?" I ask. There's a small pile at his feet and another one in the nearby wheelbarrow.

"Pruning time."

"Already? Aren't you supposed to wait until it's warm?"

"Nope. Ironically, Valentine's is the ideal week for pruning, but I just didn't feel like doing it then."

"Yeah, I can see how slicing something that day might have been dangerous." A white fluffy cloud covers the sun, and I stamp my feet to keep my legs from going numb. Dillon's wearing a long-sleeved shirt with no jacket, and although he claims he's ultra warm-natured, I know he has to be cold. "Thank you, by the way. I really appreciate you cheering me up that night."

"Anytime." He stretches his arms above his head and lowers them again. "In fact, we should do it again. What do you have planned for June seventh?"

I chuckle. "I don't know. Why?"

His gaze finds mine, and that same confusing heat I felt on the dance floor returns. "There were three days I was dreading this year. You've managed to be at two of them. And despite what this statement is going to do for your ego, I will admit you made them far better than I expected."

Ah. That was actually kind of sweet. "Well, I was going to head back to Georgia around then, but I suppose I could push my plans back a few weeks."

"Good." He goes back to his methodic task, not offering any more details on what event is to take place come the seventh of June.

I could ask, but the last thing either of us need is a tumble back into the past, or worse, to find ourselves emotionally connected like we were on Valentine's Day. So instead, I squat down and watch him work. "Any more run-ins with the stumbling trio after I left?"

"Thankfully, no. But I did snag an invitation I couldn't refuse."

"Really? From who?" I'm going for nonchalant, but it comes out with a bite that makes Dillon's lips curl into a smile.

"Easy, tiger. They know I'm taken." He winks, and I open my mouth to protest but he keeps talking. "My dad's cousin said I could use his hunting lease whenever I want. I'm thinking I might take him up on the offer."

"Oh. Well, good." I don't know why, but I feel a twinge of sadness at the thought of his not being out here. "When do you leave?"

"Not really sure. I figured I'd just let the wind guide me." He shrugs like it's no big deal, but I see the change all over his face. His mouth is relaxed, his eyes soft and absent of the weariness I've come to expect. I wonder if it has something to do with that night by the fence. As if releasing all those emotions allowed him to embrace life again. Or maybe the relief is just from making it through two exceptionally hard days.

"I'm really glad you're going," I say with all sincerity.

He turns his head. "Tired of me already, huh?"

I can tell he's deflecting, yet for some reason I don't want to let him. He's come too far. *We've* come too far. I lay my hand on his forearm. "You deserve to be happy again."

"I'm trying." He clears his throat, and I drop my hand, feeling a little silly now that the moment has passed. Dillon picks up a spare set of work gloves and holds them out. "Wanna help?"

I take the gloves with trepidation. "Won't I mess it up?"

"Nah, it's easy. I'll show you where to cut."

"Okay . . . but Doreen better not come hunt me down when her prize rosebushes don't bloom in the spring."

He shakes his head. "You worry far too much about the little things . . . and far too little about the big things."

"Stop it." I grab the extra pair of shears he offers and point it at him. "We're finally getting along. Don't pick another fight with me."

He lifts his hands in surrender. "Okay. I take it back."

"Good."

He shows me how to grip the branch, how far down to cut, and the correct angle to hold the shears. I do a couple under his supervision, and when I pass the scrutiny, he goes back to the bush he was working on.

Five whole minutes pass, but I can't get his statement out of my head. I pause before cutting. "What did you mean by that? Me not worrying enough about the big things?"

He pauses but doesn't look up. "Don't forget who you're talking to, Jan. You know better than to ask questions you don't want the answers to."

I scrunch my nose, annoyed but not at all surprised by Dillon's warning. "Just tell me."

He sighs as if he can't believe he has to explain it. "You are an incredibly intuitive person. No one can deny that. You see things in people no one takes the time to notice, but you also use it as an excuse to pretend you know people, when in truth you're just guessing. I've told you this before, and I'll say it again—you can't truly know someone from far away, no matter how complex your brain is." His gaze zeroes in on mine, and I feel alarmingly exposed. "Have you ever allowed someone to know you? And I mean *really* know you?"

He watches me, waiting for a response, yet doesn't seem surprised when I don't give him one.

"I want to," I finally say, but then wonder even as the words fall out if it's true. "It isn't easy for me."

"It isn't easy for anyone. Trust is never without risk. You are surrounded by people and yet you choose to exist completely alone. How is that any better?"

I swallow because it's all I can do to keep from crying. He doesn't know what it's like to be disappointed by people over and over again. To love and then be abandoned or forgotten. "My world has been a lot darker place than yours."

"If that's the case, then it should be really easy for you to see the pockets of light."

I immediately think of my aunt, of Sandra Cox and her consistent faith, of Ralph and Victoria and how they fought to stay together, of Cameron, despite the sharp pain it brings, and even Dillon when he's not driving me crazy. "I do see the pockets of light."

"Then why do you insist on staying in the darkness?" He leans closer, conviction coating every word. "I get it. I've been there. Been angry at God, abandoned everything I was raised to believe. But I've found my way back, and I know if you would just let your guard down for one second . . . you would see what I do."

I know his words are meant to bring some religious epiphany or to incite a tear-filled response that will force me on my knees and make me forget all the hardships in the past. And emotion does come, but not sadness or guilt or even surprise that Dillon seems to have found his faith again.

No . . . this time, the only emotion I feel is blinding hot rage.

"You say those words as if my life has been a choice. Like I asked for a dad who couldn't care less if I'm even alive. Or for the only decent stepdad I had to leave the house and never call again. Or maybe I could have decided to simply 'step out of the darkness' when my second stepfather backhanded me after beating my mother." I stand, my voice trembling. "Or when Stepdad #3 came into my bedroom drunk and handsy, pretending I was my mom. You're right, Dillon. Shame on me for not figuring it out."

He gets to his feet, but I back away before he can approach.

"And where do you get off lecturing me? You're divorced. You gave up." I see him flinch. Still, I don't care that my words are cruel. I don't care about anything right now but making the gut-wrenching pain go away. "You talk about finding a strong man, but you're no different. You're exactly like them. All of them. And I am sick and tired of everyone trying to shove me toward a God who has never once bothered to intervene."

My angry words hang between us, my chest rising and falling so fast I can audibly hear each intake of breath. And for once, Dillon doesn't seem to have anything to say. Well, good.

I throw the shears I'm still holding to the ground, followed by the gloves I tear off my fingers. "You're right, Dillon. I shouldn't have asked."

Now it's my turn to leave.

THIRTY-FOUR

I storm through my cabin door, still shaking. My cheeks sting from sprinting against the wind, and my ankles ache from nearly falling twice in my rushing back home. I head straight to the bathroom and viciously grab three tissues for my running nose. No tears have fallen. I'm too angry for them. But as the adrenaline fades, I feel the sobs creeping up like a stealth army approaching the battlefield.

I stare at my red, blotchy reflection the same time I hear my front door slam shut. Why it surprises me that Dillon followed me home, I don't know, but it does. In the months we've known each other, I've said many things that should have hurt him, but only today did I succeed.

He's on the couch with his back to me when I muster the courage to enter the living room. I know he hears my approach because his shoulders tense, yet he doesn't turn or even acknowledge my presence. Not even when I lower myself to the seat cushion next to him.

Elbows on his knees, Dillon stares at the floor, his head lowered. "I didn't give up," he says, unmoving.

Remorse bombards my chest as I study his hunched, defeated position. "Dillon . . . I—"

The shake of his head cuts me off. I guess that's fair. I had my chance to speak. Now it's his.

"Rebecca and I grew up together. Our parents were friends; our circles linked everywhere. Church, school, athletics. And I never once thought of her that way, until one day I did, and this spoiled, crybaby girl became a beautiful, poised woman. We dated my junior and senior years, and it was nothing life-changing but we had fun together. Understood each other. But when we got accepted to different colleges, it was never a question what would happen. We were young and we both wanted to experience life before settling down."

Dillon doesn't move, but I scoot back and find a more comfortable position on the couch. I don't want anything distracting me from the story I've been waiting to hear for months.

"My senior year of college was when they were getting ready to build the new sanctuary at Grace Community. Everyone was so excited. But for me, the building I knew and loved from childhood was getting torn down to make room. The pastor sent out a newsletter inviting us to the groundbreaking, where they'd have some demoed bricks available if we wanted a piece of our history. So I went, and there she was . . . standing with her arms hugging her body and sentimentally crying for the end of an era." He shoves both hands through his hair. "I should have let that be it. One shared moment. But the next day I called her. And then the day after that. And soon we were back together. Older, wiser, and more willing to give up our dreams to be together."

He looks up at me, and the tears pooling in his eyes make

me want to rip my tongue out and slice it apart for being so callous.

"We were married the summer after graduation. June seventh." He looks back down at his feet. "As much as I loved her, and I did, it was a hard match. I had grown up an only child in a male-dominated household. Even my mom wasn't very girly. Rebecca was the youngest of three girls. She was femininity at its core and used to getting her own way. But we made it through that trying first year, and then the second. And after that, I thought, okay, this is going to work. And it did, or at least I thought it did for six years. And then Mom got sick."

His voice trembles when he mentions his mother, and I yearn to reach out and offer some kind of physical comfort. I don't, though, because as much as I want to ease his heartache, I also know that Dillon wouldn't be telling me these things if he didn't want to, and the greatest gift I can give him right now is to let him finish.

"The next five months are a blur to me. I remember them sitting me down and I remember hearing the word *cancer*. But everything else is a movie reel of robotic movement. Survival. First to support Mom and then to keep my father functional when he had no desire to live." Dillon pauses, takes a deep breath, and seems to get his emotion back in check. "And through it all, Rebecca was there. When I'd spend hours at the hospital with my mom, she didn't complain or demand I come home. And then after the funeral, she kept our lives running while I worked seventy-plus-hour weeks to keep the business afloat. I remember thinking how lucky I was." Now his voice turns curt, anger smothering every syllable. "So incredibly lucky to have such a strong, loving wife who could step up like she had during the darkest of times."

I watch as his jaw flexes, watch as his fists release and his anger fades.

"It was three months after we buried my mom that Dad finally came back to us. That day is the first really clear memory I have in that entire season. It was a Saturday, two in the afternoon. He came to work and told me to go home. He said it's time for him to stop being crippled by grief and to find a way to live his life without her. He said Mom would tear his hide apart for letting me shoulder all the burden this long."

I can't help but smile because Dillon sounds so much like his dad that I nearly look around the room for him.

Dillon stretches his neck back and forth like he has to work up to telling me the next part of the story. And since I already know the ending isn't a happy one, I brace myself for what's coming next.

"I picked up flowers on the way home. Tulips, because they are her favorite. Her car was gone, but I knew she had a nail appointment that day, so I figured she'd be home soon enough. The house was immaculate when I walked in, which was very unlike her, and I still to this day wonder why she bothered. Especially when her Dear John letter left me bleeding all over our polished wood floors."

He stands and laces his hands over his head. Even pacing in front of me, Dillon can't hide the fact that this next part still cuts him deep in the chest. Finally, he stops moving and his arms fall.

"All that time I thought she was a saint, she was having an affair with her old college boyfriend. Supposedly they had reconnected on social media and had been talking for over a year at that point. She'd been unhappy for a very long time, she said, and could no longer live a lie. She'd planned to leave me before Mom got sick, but once we got the news, she said it seemed too cruel. But then I guess her lover—" he grinds his teeth, then relaxes his jaw—"finally gave her an ultimatum. Him or me." He shrugs one shoulder like his words aren't the most heinous I've ever heard. "She chose him."

He sits back down, facing me now. "I followed her to her parents' house. Spent the night on their porch trying to get her to talk to me and work it out. I told her I could forgive her, told her we could go to counseling. Begged her not to give up on us." His voice gets deeper, his gaze nearly holding mine hostage. "I fought and fought and fought, every day, until she signed the divorce papers. And then I did what my dad did and tried to find a way to move on without her."

When he finishes, I feel as exhausted as he looks. The room, which seconds ago was filled with anger and adrenaline and pain, now feels empty. As if a great wind came through and wiped all the emotion away.

I scoot closer to take his hand in mine. It's cold and clammy. "I'm sorry. I should never have made assumptions about you and your past." It's the strongest I've ever felt an apology. If I could write it with stars and display it for the world, I would.

He levels a look of half frustration, half disbelief. "Haven't you heard anything I said? You never *ever* have to apologize for being honest. Not to me." He slides his thumb over my skin, and for the first time I truly understand him. And for the first time, I think there might be one man out there who is genuinely trustworthy.

I move to let go of his fingers when his grip tightens slightly.

Those incredible brown eyes penetrate deep inside my chest. "I'm sorry you were raised by scumbags."

Maybe it's the release of so much emotion, or maybe it's

just the matter-of-fact way he sums up my miserable childhood, but his words break some kind of barrier inside. I feel the giggle in my chest first, weak and barely audible, but then it grows, filling my lungs, knotting my stomach. The laughter comes so hard and so fast that I can't get enough air until I realize I'm not laughing anymore, I'm sobbing. And Dillon isn't a cushion away, he's next to me, folding me into his chest, holding me like no man has ever held me before.

And he doesn't let go.

Not when I soak his shirt with snot and slobber, or even when I try to push him away because embarrassment takes over.

It isn't until I've shed every tear that has been stored away for twenty-nine years that Dillon finally releases me.

"And you thought you were just going to cut some rosebushes today," I say, wiping my cheeks as if it would help the mess I've made. My eyes are swollen, and my hair is doing its best to re-create a character from *The Walking Dead*.

"Jan . . ." He pauses until I look up at him, and the concern in his eyes nearly makes the waterworks start again. "There's nowhere else I'd rather be."

Rebecca is a fool, and this will be the last time I ever think or ask about her.

I adjust, putting a more reasonable space between us. "Tell me about your mom. The good stuff," I clarify. "The stuff you like to remember."

Dillon sighs and leans back against the corner cushion. "She had the best laugh. It was like a giggle that went up and down the musical scale." The smile that forms on his lips is sad but welcome at the same time. "Even if it wasn't funny, you'd laugh simply because she'd make you believe it was. And she loved to hug. Me. Dad. Strangers. It didn't matter.

As a teenager, I'd get so irritated by her badgering for affection. And now . . ." He looks down at his hands. "I'd give anything for just one more arm-crushing embrace." He blows out a stream of air and swallows before looking back up. "What I was trying—and obviously failing—to say at the rosebushes is that I understand why you're afraid. Belief takes trust, and trust means vulnerability. This past year I've felt nothing but rage and bitterness for the storm God put me through. It's only now that the clouds have started to thin that I'm able to see some of the beauty the rain left behind."

Heat fills my cheeks when his eyes continue to bore into mine, then embarrassment comes again. I clear my throat and stand before I let myself corrupt this incredible moment of friendship by turning it into something neither of us is ready for. "Are you jumping on the turn-January-into-a-Christian bandwagon, Dillon? Because my aunt has already tried and failed. Not to mention Sandra and Cameron, who has now moved on to bigger and better things. I'd hate to have to run you off, too." Sarcasm seeps through my words, and yet it doesn't seem to deter the stubborn man on my couch.

"I'm not exactly the bandwagon type. You should know that by now. And when you're ready to have a real conversation about faith, we'll have it . . . without the subtleties." He stands and stretches. "In the meantime, I still have a mile of roses to prune, and daylight is wasting. C'mon, let's go."

I cross my arms. "Is there a *please* somewhere in that sentence?"

He lifts his eyebrows. "Do I need to remind you how I got distracted in the first place?"

"Fine." But as much as I huff and puff about being forced to help him, the truth lies just under the surface. Like him, there's nowhere else I want to be.

THIRTY-FIVE

A month goes by without much fanfare or upsets. Cameron didn't tell anyone my secret, so apart from Ralph leaving early whenever he can and floating around like a lovestruck schoolboy half the time, life seems to have fallen back into place as if the ripples of Cameron's leaving never occurred.

Well, except in one area. Thoughts of him still bring a dull ache to my heart, though it gets a little less painful with each passing day.

Dillon never took the trip to the hunting lease. He said it wasn't the right timing, but part of me knows he did it so I wouldn't be alone. I'm grateful, even though he seems more determined than ever to irritate me any time we hang out together, which is a lot these days. Even Mr. Kyle has started inviting us places as though we're a package deal.

I knock on the doorframe and peek my head into Mrs. Cox's room. "Sandra?" She's sitting on her chair, blanket in her lap, listening to some guy talking from her stereo.

Her eyes pop open. "Jan? Is that you?"

"It's me," I say and walk toward her chair. "Sorry I haven't been by in a while."

She presses a button on the remote in her hand, and the voice fades away. "A while? It's been three days." She waves at me with her wrinkled hand. "Come over here. Let me hug you."

Moments later, I'm smothered against her chest, her blouse soft against my cheek. Her hands, as frail as they are, feel like a vise grip around my shoulders.

She slowly lets me go but puts her palms to my cheeks before I can completely stand. "Is everything okay?"

"Everything's fine. We've just been busy at the church getting ready for Easter." I pull a chair over so I can sit closer to her. "How are you feeling? Victoria mentioned you had a cough."

"Oh, please. I'm blessed," she says simply and squeezes my hand. "Rachel came by to see me yesterday." Rachel is Sandra's daughter. I met her two weeks ago, and she was not only very kind but also told me repeatedly how much her mother appreciates my company. It seems absurd now that I ever thought Sandra wouldn't want both of us in her life.

"Good. Did her daughter get the part she wanted in the play?"

"We won't know until next week, but I've been praying."

"I bet you have." I chuckle at her excitement and point to the remote in her hand. "What were you listening to?"

She brightens, picking up the slim metal device to show me her latest toy. "Rachel introduced me to audiobooks. Now I can read whenever I want to."

What a brilliant idea. "That's wonderful, Sandra. What are you listening to now?"

"Oh, it's good," she coos. "A thriller where a man wakes up and his entire family has disappeared."

"Sounds fascinating." I bite my lip to keep from laughing at her ominous tone. "Well, go ahead. I'll listen with you."

Sandra shakes her head and points to the nightstand. "You know the rules by now."

Of course.

I stand and pull her rugged Bible from the nightstand. We've moved on to the book of Romans, and I have an inkling she picked it just for me.

~

Doreen's waiting on my porch when I get home and stands as soon as I put the car in park. I push open my door slowly, slightly concerned I'm in trouble since her arms are crossed and she has the same expression she used to get when Isaiah didn't clean his room properly.

"I've been told there's a person who lives here, but I think she's a phantom."

I walk up the steps and give her a welcome hug. True to her inner fashion diva, Doreen's wearing a pale green off-the-shoulder cashmere sweater and knee-high leather boots over her jeans.

"Sorry," I say. "I know I've been neglectful."

"Neglectful? You haven't been by for dinner in weeks. Not even for my lasagna." She pulls back but keeps her hands on my arms, checking me over as if I'm a long-lost orphan. "Are you avoiding me?"

"No, of course not."

Her brow scrunches. "You sure? It seems like ever since you and your mom started talking again, you've been slowly pulling away."

Now I feel terrible. The last thing in the world I want is to hurt Aunt Doreen. "Coincidence. I promise. Work has been crazy."

"Okay, I'll buy your I've-been-too-busy excuse, but only

because I know what it takes to put on a great Easter service." Doreen follows me inside and scans the small cabin nonchalantly. "One I hope you're planning on coming to?" It's only after that last question that she turns and looks at me with feigned innocence. It wouldn't be Doreen if she didn't try to slip in an invite.

I smile affectionately. "We'll see."

"Well, it's not a no, so I'll take it." She pats my arm. "Now, on to the real reason I came. They're finishing up the gazebo, and I thought you might want to take a walk with me to check it out."

"Absolutely." I toss my purse into my room and grab the extra pair of sunglasses I keep on my dresser. Spring has finally arrived and it's a beautiful seventy-five degrees outside.

When I return to the living room, Doreen's browsing the stack of DVDs Dillon left on my coffee table. "Either your taste in movies has drastically changed"—she holds up a 1950s Western—"or I'm in the twilight zone."

I shake my head. "Those are Dillon's. The man has an unhealthy affection for bad acting and worse story lines."

Doreen presses her lips together like she's struggling whether to say more or not. It's an odd look for her. She usually speaks her mind without much restraint. "You and Dillon seem to be spending a lot of time together lately."

"I guess. Why?" I can't figure out whether she loves or hates that admission, but it's definitely one or the other.

"No reason." And just like that, she's smiling again as if she holds some great secret. I study her with narrowed eyes but don't press further. Doreen and my mom have polar opposite personalities, but when it comes to keeping thoughts and feelings private, the two of them are experts.

We make our way out of the cabin and down the front

steps. "I have an updated venue schedule to give you," she says. "Now that the gazebo is available, I was able to pull two weddings from my waiting list."

"I'm sure the brides were thrilled." Spring in Texas is the ideal time to have an outdoor wedding. The weather is perfect, flowering trees and roses bloom bright, and Aunt Doreen was wise enough to build her ceremony areas behind natural wind barriers.

I study the paper she hands me, scanning the information into memory, and then stuff it safely in my pocket. "There's some big parties on that list."

"I know." She sighs. "I just get so sentimental this time of year."

"I can see that. The Shepherd-Mackey wedding has over four hundred guests scheduled. And you added a new seventy-five-person wedding party just two days prior? Should be interesting."

Doreen pauses to look down at me. "How did you . . . ? Never mind." She shakes her head and keeps walking. "Sometimes I really do envy that brain of yours."

I hold in a snort because I don't feel like getting a lecture from my aunt. Since I was a kid and first showed signs of being . . . different, she's always considered my curse a gift. Rarely do I agree.

Doreen tucks her arm in mine just like she used to do when I was a preteen. "With that many guests, though, I want you to promise me if you ever feel uncomfortable, you'll come straight to the house."

I smile. "I will, but honestly I haven't had any issue with the wedding parties. Everyone's been pretty respectful of my privacy."

"Good." She nods. "I've made it clear to all my brides that

the walkway to your place is off-limits, so it's nice to hear that they've been abiding by those wishes."

As we crest the hill, I can see the edge of the gazebo roof. "Oh, wow. That's huge." The last time I saw the crew working, they had only a few pieces of wood attached.

"I know. Even with the rain last week, they got it done."

"Maybe because you threatened their lives if they didn't have it ready by this weekend."

"Is that what Dillon told you?" She scoffs. "Not true . . . though I did threaten your uncle with no more cooking if he didn't light a fire under them."

"Well, the fire is ablaze." And it's no surprise. Uncle Jim is a mild man by nature, but he can turn very forceful when needed. Just ask my two cousins.

She waves off my teasing. "It's amazing the difference in scale when it's on a drawing versus in real life."

Dillon comes into view, standing on the sidelines, directing the last of the work.

"I still can't believe Dillon designed this thing," I say. The structure itself is artwork. Ornate carvings along the columns, and the roof beams and decking are stunning.

"He's a talented young man, that's for sure."

We stand in silence for a few seconds, both taking in the beauty around us. "This venue is really something special, Doreen."

"Thank you. It's all finally coming together." She sighs. "I just wish my dad could've seen it. And Cassie."

"Pawpaw would've loved it, and Mom . . . well, she's Mom." I squeeze her arm tighter when I sense the shift in her mood. "Me, on the other hand, I'll always consider this place my awakening. I'm not sure if I ever really thanked you for letting me come here, but I'm so very grateful. You've changed my life, really." I shake off an assault of tears that seem to come out of nowhere.

"Not me." She pats my cheek and keeps her palm there for a few seconds. "The power of prayer, my dear."

"Do you think that power will ever work on Mom?" Doreen's been praying for reconciliation for years now, but getting my mom to budge is like trying to turn the *Titanic*. She all but yelled at me on the phone last week when I asked about opening the easement road between the two properties. A small little request so her only daughter didn't have to drive a dangerous curvy road at night. Her response: *"I'm not letting that woman anywhere near my land. Doreen puts on a big act, but when it matters, she'll let you down. Just like she did me."*

"Yes, Jan. One day I believe it will."

I look back at my aunt, her hands linked, her face serene but focused, as if she were in the act of praying right now.

"Doreen, can I ask you something that might be difficult to answer?"

"Sure, hun."

"Mom made a comment the other day, something about you letting her down." None of it makes sense. After their mom died, Doreen practically raised my mother. She was more like a parent than a sister, and up until their falling out, I know my mom loved her, even if she didn't understand or agree with her lifestyle. "Is that what happened at Pawpaw's funeral?"

Doreen's face goes ashen, a common response when I bring up the rift between her and her sister. "No. I let her down years before." She turns and stares out at Mom's land, and I wonder if she's going to change the subject like she usually does. "But that day, I finally told her my darkest secret. A regret I've carried around longer than you've been alive."

My heart speeds its rhythm. "A secret about Mom?"

"No. A confession to your mom. One I don't think she'll ever forgive."

I open my mouth to ask a million more questions, but fate or God or something else must have other plans, because right at this moment, Mr. Kyle decides to make an unwanted appearance.

"Well, you ladies are a nice addition to our crew," he says cheerfully, oblivious to the intense exchange going on. "You ready to be our first guest?"

Doreen turns, and all traces of unease are gone. "Why else would I be here? Lead the way." She smiles brightly at her husband's best friend, and I work to mask my disappointment.

Mr. Kyle turns to me. "You coming too?"

"In a minute." Unlike Doreen, I'm not quite ready to morph into small talk. I face my mother's property the way my aunt was doing before our interruption and sigh in frustration. I've been here for months and that was the most I've ever gotten on the story. My next chance will probably be when I'm fifty.

Dillon appears at my side. "You okay?"

"I'm fine."

"You don't look fine. You look upset."

"Well, your dad has lousy timing." I scowl at him. "And before you ask, no, I don't want to talk about it."

"Careful. If you aren't nice to me, I'll be forced to remind you that you're not wearing green today." He makes a pinching motion with his thumb and forefinger.

I hitch an eyebrow. "*You* celebrate Saint Patrick's Day?"

He twists to show me a large leprechaun on his T-shirt. In one hand is a basketball, in the other a pot of gold. "I've been a Fighting Irish fan since I was six."

"That's pretty bold talk when you live just hours from Texas A&M and Baylor."

"Exactly, which is why today is all mine." He tugs my arm. "C'mon, grumpy. I have a surprise for you."

Darn him. Now I'm more curious than annoyed. "What is it?"

"If I tell you, it won't be a surprise."

I roll my eyes but let him guide me to the gazebo. Doreen is walking around the impressive structure, and I can hear her gushing praises. I can't really blame her—the building is a masterpiece. The structural columns are all made of whitewood that's been beveled to give it a soft, romantic feel. Inside, a white rail follows the perimeter, its edges perfectly straight, and words have been burned into the wood. I move closer and walk as I read the two sentences that continue around the entire circle.

"And now these three remain: faith, hope, and love. But the greatest of these is love."

I turn around, and Dillon's leaning against the entry post, watching me. "Did you write that? It's beautiful."

His lips twitch, and there's a spark in his eyes that tells me he's laughing at me on the inside. "No, I did not write that."

"Forgive me for not knowing poetry," I bark. He's staring at me like I'm the most adorable idiot he knows. It should irritate me, but I know by now that half of what I say amuses him. "Who wrote it, then, all-knowing one?"

"That would be the apostle Paul. He wrote several books in the Bible."

Oh . . . I clamp my mouth shut and scan the words

again. They feel personal. A promise of things I've only seen glimpses of from afar. I glance back to the man who always seems to have more layers than I give him credit for. "Why did you choose this one?"

His earlier smirk dies as he steps closer, his voice turning soft and urgent. "Because I still remember what it felt like to lose my belief in all three of those things." He slides even closer, so much so that his shadow covers me and his breath tickles the top of my head. "And without them, life is very bleak. A shadow of what it can be." Dillon's voice is rough when he adds, "And I'm tired of living in the shadows."

I look up at him, and he meets my gaze, unflinching. I admire a lot of things about Dillon Kyle, but in that moment it's his courage that astounds me. I couldn't do it, reveal the deepest parts of myself all while looking someone straight in the eye. "Well, it's beautiful. Thank you, I needed this."

"Good, I'm glad. But this isn't your surprise. Not even close." He takes my hand and tugs until I'm following him out of the gazebo and down the steps. "Hey, Dad, mind if I take a break for a little while?"

Mr. Kyle and my aunt turn immediately, and my cheeks burn red-hot coals when I see them zero in on our joined hands. I quickly let go and stuff it in my pocket. Doreen already has the wrong impression, and if there's one thing I've come to count on, it's Dillon's brutal honesty. He's never once hinted at anything more than friendship between us, and considering my many romantic failures, I don't blame him. It's actually a relief in a lot of ways. There's nothing to lose, so I don't have to pretend or be anything but myself.

We get a *see ya* wave from his dad that I guess is our green light, because Dillon jerks his head toward the ATV parked several feet from the gazebo. "Let's go. It's been a wet, mushy mess the last few weeks, and today we might just be able to get out there without getting stuck."

"Get out where?"

"You'll see." He pushes me toward the vehicle, behaving more giddy than a nine-year-old on the last day of school.

"Dillon."

"What? Do you not know what *surprise* means?"

I wrinkle my nose but stop resisting and follow him to the ATV. The minute we get to it, Dillon pulls out a couple of aerosol cans from the back. "Hold out your arms and close your eyes."

I comply, only to get bug spray shot in my mouth. "Sheesh." I choke, waving away the cloud of contamination. "Is this really necessary?"

"Yes. The mosquitoes are horrendous this year." He finishes his bug-spray assault and grabs two pairs of boots next, each with a narrow white collar clipped around the ankles. "Here. Put these on. We can throw your tennis shoes in the back of the ATV."

I take the boots and examine the strange contraption. "What is this?"

"A flea collar. It keeps the chiggers away."

"Mosquitoes? Chiggers? What other horrible creatures might I encounter?"

He eyes the label on the boots he handed me, which are clearly marked. *Snake boots.* Great.

I kick off my tennis shoes, having no idea why I'm playing along. "How do you get me to do the most ridiculous things?"

His lips curl into a smile. "Easy. You trust me."

And I guess I do, because a moment later I'm seated behind him, arms tight around his waist as we speed off into the forest.

Just five minutes into the ride, Dillon stops at a gate I instantly recognize, and dread shoots up my spine. "We can't go back there. The owner has *No Trespassing* signs everywhere."

"We both know your mom hasn't stepped foot on this land in years. I could build an apartment complex in the center and she'd never know." He swings his leg over the padded seat and walks to the lock, keys in hand. In two swift turns, it unlatches.

As the gate swings open, I immediately notice that the fencing Mom had installed is useless. Dillon had cut the aluminum along the side and attached it to the gate poles so they moved in tandem, leaving a wide-open gap for anyone to pass through.

And yet I can't seem to move. "But what if she finds out?" I whisper, as if my mother's land has the ability to swallow me whole.

"How would she? There are no cameras, and no one hired to maintain the place. I know, I come out here almost every day." Dillon walks back to the ATV and squats next to me. "What are you afraid of?"

His genuine confusion and concern hits me deep. So often, Dillon seems to know more about my past than I do, but I guess my aunt has been secretive to everyone about what happened between her and my mom.

"Jan?"

"Sorry." I force a smile. "I guess it just freaked me out how overgrown it is."

"Well, no worries." He stands back up. "I've cleared a path so you're safe and sound on the ATV until we get to the lake."

"There's a lake?"

"Yes." Now Dillon is smiling, and not his usual half-sarcasm, half-annoyance smile. It's the kind that goes deeper, maybe emotionally deeper than he's ever taken me before. "And it's breathtaking. This whole area is, once you get past the junk."

He swings his leg over the seat and starts the engine. "You ready?"

No, but I can't tell him that now, not when he's so excited to share the property with me. I guess I shouldn't be surprised; every step I've taken has had Dillon Kyle somewhere in the wings, pushing me farther than I want to go. Why would connecting with my mom's past be any different?

"Yeah," I say, ignoring the anxious swirling in my stomach. "I'm ready."

THIRTY-SIX

The minute we cross the threshold into my mom's territory, I'm ready to take back every word. Dillon's "path" is barely wider than the ATV, and I spend most of the ride tucked into his back, trying to fend off the slapping branches. The only thing I can say about my mom's land so far is that it's very, very bumpy.

I don't look up until we slow to a crawl and the engine cuts off. But when my eyes open, I'm breathless.

"This is . . ." Words fail me because they pale in comparison. Nestled in a valley is a lake that easily covers five of my mother's thirty acres. On the other side, about a hundred yards up a small hill, sits a small horse stable, and up even farther at the very top, where the clearest view likely is, there's a house. Pawpaw's house.

Memories I'd long ago forgotten flood my mind: sitting on his lap while he teetered back and forth on the porch rocking chair, in the small kitchen with Doreen, rolling out dough to make blackberry pie, playing in the attic with Mom's old dolls.

"I used to come here as a kid," I say half to Dillon and half to myself. "There are three blackberry bushes in the back along a stick fence."

"Yeah?" Dillon twists in his seat so he can look at me. "Do you want to go see if they're still there?"

My heart dances with excitement. "Can we?"

"Of course. In fact, my surprise is over there anyway."

"You mean there's more than this?"

Dillon chuckles. "Wow, you really haven't been treated well by the men in your life, have you?"

I smack his arm, even though it's not far from the truth.

The engine roars once more, cutting off the serene quiet, but this time I hardly allow myself to blink as we take the slope down near the water. Dillon seems to know instinctively where to turn to avoid wet spots in the grass and zigzags up the embankment until we crest the hill near the stables.

This close, it's easy to see why none of my memories include horses. The roof has caved in, and both large barn doors are crooked and hanging off rusted hinges. Weeds climb up the side and poke through the broken, dirt-stained windows.

A chill sneaks up my spine, and I find myself holding on a little tighter as we drive by, like there's a darkness surrounding the building that could easily steal my soul away.

The unease fades slowly, then finally disappears once we reach the hilltop. Surrounding Pawpaw's house is a clearing of thick beautiful grass so manicured it looks as if it were dropped from the sky.

Dillon stops a good twenty feet from the house and cuts the engine for a final time. "We're here."

"How is it possible the lawn looks this good?" I ask, willing my shaky legs to stand and keep me upright. "No one has lived here in ten years."

"You're looking at hours of sweat and tears, let me tell you." Dillon pulls a backpack from under our seat and straps it over his arms. "The first time I came, the grass was at my waist. It took me two weeks with a Weed Eater just to get it low enough to mow." He cringes at the memory. "Then I nearly flipped my ATV twice because I'd strapped a push mower to the back."

My confusion must be written all over my face because Dillon's expression turns sheepish.

"If you think I avoid my house now, you should have seen me last summer." He picks at his fingernail. "Having this project kept me sane."

I look toward my pawpaw's house and back to Dillon. "You stayed out here?"

"In the house? No, unfortunately it's structurally unsafe. But I've camped out here a few times." He puts his hands on his hips and sighs, staring across the lake with longing. "I'd love to buy this place someday." He smiles at me, and I don't have the heart to tell him the dream is unlikely to come true. Instead, I listen as he talks about where his new house would go, about the fishing dock he'd put on this side of the lake, and how he'd turn the stables into a greenhouse.

"It all sounds perfect." And it does. Dillon has something most people don't possess: vision. He can see past the hurt and pain into a better time. My mom never had that ability. She was broken when she left Texas, and while she's functioned for thirty-something years since, she's never once thrived. I don't know why I haven't recognized that until today. Or worse, seen that very trait in myself.

"So . . . you ready for your surprise now?"

His eagerness makes me more excited than I let on. "Would you let me say no?"

"No." He winks and takes off running toward the house he just said could collapse at any second. He stops under the sagging porch awning and lifts a tarp to expose a large ice chest and a folded blanket.

"Need some help?" I call out.

"Nope. In fact, look somewhere else or close your eyes."

I pretend to comply but watch his every move through my fingers. He shoves the blanket under his arms, pulls the handle on the chest, and is in the center of the beautiful lawn in ten easy steps.

It takes me only a few seconds to realize Dillon's setting up a picnic for us. He carefully lays out the blanket, then removes a covered dish from the chest, two plates, forks, and a bottle of something.

I press my lips together to keep from smiling and truly close my eyes this time. "Can I look yet?"

"Almost."

I continue to stand there waiting, a cool breeze sending chills to my neck and bringing with it the potent smell of nature. So different from the B&L Ranch. Hardier, wilder. . . . It smells like Mom, even when I know that's impossible.

"Okay, we're ready now." His voice is next to my ear, and I feel the brush of his hands on my arm an instant later. A new wave of chills assaults my arms and legs, which has nothing to do with the wind.

I uncover my eyes as Dillon leads me toward his surprise, and warmth quickly replaces all other feeling. "You did this for me?" In the center of the blanket is a basket of flowers, flanked by two place settings and champagne glasses made of plastic.

"Truthfully, I did it for both of us." He extends his arm, and I sit crisscross, careful not to knock over any of his masterpiece. "My mom loved Saint Paddy's Day. She spent a semester in Ireland while in college, and it became a tradition of ours every year to have a picnic and eat key lime pie." He plops down next to me and unzips the cloth container that must be keeping the pie safe. "We didn't do anything last year. It was too soon, and Dad was still in a bad place, but this year, I don't know, I didn't want to miss it."

I feel an overwhelming sense of humility that he would choose me to share this moment with him. "I'm glad. This is perfect."

"Well, hold that thought until after you see the pie." He makes a face I've never seen before, a mix of embarrassment and humor. "I went a little heavy on the food coloring."

He lifts the top from the pie plate, revealing a circle of neon green edged with whipped cream. I know I should say something kind or at least praise the effort, but instead I burst out laughing. "That looks absolutely disgusting."

Dillon's grin covers half his face. "Yes, it does, and you are going to sit there and eat it anyway."

My laughter comes harder, my words squeaking out between fits. "It's literally glowing . . . like I think you might . . . have used . . . radioactive food coloring."

"It's not glowing, and it's not radioactive. It's delicious. You just have to get past what it looks like." The steadiness in his voice only makes the situation funnier, even though I'm trying with all my strength to pull myself together.

I clamp a hand on my stomach because it hurts and focus on the careful way he's cutting slices, as if every action is a tribute to his mom. It does the trick as significance replaces the humor of it. "Why didn't you do this with your dad?"

Dillon shrugs. "I didn't want to be sad today. And even though Dad tries so hard, grief still comes through whenever we talk about her." He slides a Play-Doh-like slice onto my plate. "Whereas you . . ."

I'd feel guilty except that I know Dillon well enough to recognize he's paying me a compliment. No pretense. The one promise between the two of us.

He fills our glasses with bubbly grape juice, then screws the cap back on. "Can I make a toast?"

I lift my glass. "By all means."

"To things not turning out the way we wanted them to."

"And to little green men, pots of gold, and rainbows at the end of every storm."

Our eyes lock at the same time our glasses touch.

"And to unexpected friendships," he adds in just above a whisper.

My heart doubles its pounding, and my hands suddenly feel intensely warm. I swallow, unsure whether I like or hate the uncomfortable sensation.

Dillon must feel it, too, because he clears his throat and his voice rises. "But more importantly . . . to key lime pie that I pray will not kill us both."

"Hear, hear!" I chime and drink the same time he does. Whatever Irish spell we fell under for that brief second has thankfully vanished.

Dillon lifts his fork and scoops a heaping piece of green sludge. "Here goes nothing."

I know the minute he puts it into his mouth that it tastes better than it looks. His eyes roll back, and his chest caves as if he's experiencing the best moments of childhood in that one tasty bite. My hesitation crumbles as I shove an equally large piece into my mouth.

Flavor tickles every taste bud, the perfect mix of sugar and tartness coming together. Even the slight bitterness of the food coloring isn't enough to lessen the enjoyment. "Okay . . . I concede. This is delicious."

Dillon drops his fork and leans back on his elbows, his feet stretched out in front of him. It's a posture of peace. A posture of acceptance. And oddly enough, a posture of absolute contentment. "How can you look at that water, this land, the sky, and not believe in God?"

I know he doesn't expect an answer, but all the same, that familiar pressure seizes my chest. The same one I felt in Mrs. Cox's hospital room. The same one from the night I heard the praise band sing together. And the same one I've felt every day since telling Dillon about my stepfathers.

"Can I tell you something without you reading too much into it?" I look down at my fingers and fiddle with a chipped nail.

Dillon shifts to his side, his body still horizontal. "Maybe."

I guess that's good enough. "I've been talking to . . . I don't know . . . the sky, I guess. At night and sometimes when I take my walks."

"What do you talk about?"

I lift a shoulder and let it fall. "Things. Feelings. Sometimes I just yell and ask why." I glance at him and then away just as quickly. I feel the heat in my cheeks as embarrassment makes me wish I'd just kept my mouth shut.

"Do you ever get an answer?"

I'm not quite sure how to respond. Audibly, no, never. I would check myself into a psycho ward if that were the case. But inside, it feels different. Less tumultuous. "I guess in a way I do. There's just so many things I don't understand. Mom raised me to believe that faith is ignorant. That Christians were stupid and judgmental and racist. And then I came here, and nothing is what I expected. People are kind and unselfish and willing to move to another country to teach little kids about their faith. The two worlds don't fit, and now I can't figure out where I do, either."

Dillon sits up. "Have you ever asked your mom why she hates this place so much?"

"Many times. She refuses to tell me. I thought Doreen might today, but then your dad walked up and she shut down."

"Ask her again."

I shake my head. "It makes her sad."

"So what?" Dillon's voice comes stronger. "You've built your entire worldview from your mother's past-and-present choices. You have a right to know where they came from."

Now I'm irritated. "I am my own person, Dillon, with my own thoughts and choices. My mommy does not dictate my belief system."

"And yet you just admitted to praying to a deity that you say doesn't exist."

"I said I was talking, not praying."

"Same thing."

I clench my jaw and turn away. "You don't understand."

"Yes, I do. More than you know. I spent the last year questioning my beliefs, demanding answers, feeling angry. And despite how dark it got, I'm glad I did, because now I know my faith is mine and not anyone else's."

I stare down at my fingers again, a tear sneaking out from beneath my eyelid before I can pull it back. "I'll lose her. If I go down this path, I'll lose my mom." It feels freeing to say it out loud, to be honest about the greatest barricade keeping me from taking that leap into the unknown. Yet, at the same time, it feels just as debilitating as it did trapped inside my head.

I hear him come closer.

"You don't know that."

"Yes, I do."

His palm presses against my back, then slides to my shoulder. "Jan . . . I know I'm hard on you sometimes. I know I push when you don't want me to, but this time you have to be the one to push. It's too important not to."

The moisture in my eyes subsides, and I stare at the green pie in front of me. I can't imagine the courage it took for Dillon to stand in his kitchen and make something so heartbreaking. But he faced the giant anyway, because having this small piece of his mom was worth the struggle.

He's right. It's time for me to ask the hard questions. To face my own doubt and stop spending my life tossed back and forth by the wind. It's time I stop pretending and figure out who I really want to be.

THIRTY-SEVEN

I stand in front of Doreen's house for five entire minutes without knocking on the door. Somewhere between packing up our picnic and pulling into her driveway, I lost the raging fire of determination I'd felt on my mom's property.

My phone buzzes in my pocket.

Don't chicken out.

How did Dillon . . . ? I look around Doreen's yard but don't see any sign of him.

How do you know I'm not already talking to her? You could very well be interrupting a really important conversation.

My intuition says otherwise. As does my dad who's currently watching TV with your uncle.

I scowl and put my phone back in my pocket.

Minutes seven and eight tick by, then nine, and finally on ten I reach up and smash my finger into the doorbell.

Doreen's yelling something to my uncle as she opens the

door, then abruptly stops when she sees me. "Jan? Is everything okay?"

I bite my lip and fiddle with the hem of my shirt. "I wanted to see if we could talk more . . . about . . . my mom. If you want to, I mean. I can come back tomorrow."

Her gaze travels from my head to my shoes as if she's scanning every thought and emotion I have. The superpower must have been successful because she nods like a woman with no other options and swings the door wide. "Come in. We'll talk in my office."

The living room is in our path so the required hello hugs are given to Uncle Jim and Mr. Kyle, even though my mind is racing with anticipation.

"We'll be in the back if you need us," my aunt says in a clipped tone, one she seems to get only when life becomes more chaotic than she prefers.

I feel guilty for forcing the conversation but not enough to turn back. The personnel team has narrowed down their search to two pastoral candidates, which means my time at Grace Community is inevitably winding down. And since my bank account is nicely padded again, I really have no reason to stay at B&L, or in Texas, for that matter. If I want to know the truth, and I do, now is the time.

Doreen quietly shuts the door after we enter her spacious office. It used to be Isaiah's room and had dinosaur wallpaper on the back wall when we were kids. Now there's hardwood floors, a massive oak desk, and a small reading nook with two wing-back chairs.

I take the one closest to the door and dry my palms on my jeans. "I'm sorry. I know you don't want to talk about what happened with Mom."

Doreen presses a soft palm against my cheek. "Don't be

sorry. I've felt convicted to talk to you for a month now and haven't. This is God's way of getting me to do what I should have done long ago." Her smile eases the last of my anxiety, and immediately I feel like I always do with my aunt: safe, protected, and cared for.

Once she sits and folds her hands in her lap, I take my opportunity. "Why are you and Mom not speaking? What happened at Pawpaw's funeral to create this rift between the two of you?"

Doreen licks her lips and contemplates my question. "I think we may need to start much earlier for you to understand my answer to that question."

"Okay." I settle back in my chair and watch as memories change the expression on her face from regret to tenderness.

"My mother loved horses. She'd ridden them since she was a little girl. It was part of her identity. So much so that nearly every memory I have of her includes her with riding gear on."

I think back to the stables on Mom's land and know it would break Doreen's heart to see the building in shambles.

"I didn't really take to them, though Mom never gave up trying to get me to ride." Doreen smiles again, though her eyes aren't quite in the present. "But Cassie, she was a natural. From the moment she could walk, that girl was on a horse with Mom. It was a love they shared that was unique and all their own. Daddy and I were on the outside looking in." Tears well up in Doreen's eyes, but she quickly wipes them away. "When Mom died, the shock was so severe, it was as if time ceased to exist."

I know very few details of my grandmother's death, only that it was a car accident at night and that she died instantly. Like many things in our family, sad memories don't get discussed.

"When the world started spinning again, Daddy and I soon noticed that Cassie wasn't the same. She'd disappear into the stables, and we'd have to go looking for her, calling her name. One time I found her curled up on the hay inside an empty stall. She was crying and calling out for our mom." Doreen's voice cracks, and it takes her a minute before she can resume talking. "Dad got strict after that. Told her that if she went into the stables alone one more time, he would sell the horses. Cassie never did again, and only tagged along when Daddy or I would feed them."

"Is that when my mom quit riding?" I ask because I've never once seen my mom around a horse—not even in a picture.

"For about two years, yes. But when she turned seven, Daddy got her an instructor and she started up again. By thirteen, she was a barrel-racing champion, and by sixteen, Cassie was in the stables nearly as much as Mom used to be."

"Then why?" I'm so confused my head begins to pound. Nothing Doreen described is recognizable. It's like this version of my mom died the moment she left Texas.

"Your pawpaw was a wonderful man, but he was also a very flawed man. When times got hard, he'd hide in a bottle or at a poker table. I had just adopted the boys when the bottom fell out for our family. Dad hadn't been paying his taxes for years. Neither the state nor the IRS are very forgiving, and they have an immense amount of power. His wages were garnished, and they were moving to put a lien on our property." Pain washes over her face. "Dad hired an accountant, and they worked a payment schedule out, but it included eight grand up front to avoid the lien. Jim and I had used all our savings for the adoption and had nothing we could give, although I would have sold just about anything to avoid what Dad decided to do."

I know before she tells me. "The horses."

A sad nod. "He couldn't afford the upkeep or the vet bills, and since Cassie had won so many races, the horses were worth a good deal. Even Mom's old mare was given away to a rescue facility to live out her life." Doreen wrings her hands. "Dad knew Cassie would throw herself in front of the trailer if she caught wind of his decision, so he set up the transfer behind her back. And . . . I helped him."

My lungs seize. "You didn't warn her? Explain anything?"

Doreen shakes her head. "Cassie has always been stubborn and hotheaded, and to avoid the explosion we chose the coward's way out." Regret infiltrates every word, but it isn't enough to temper the anger growing inside me at her confession. "I took Cassie shopping that day. Made a big deal about buying her a dress for prom and doing our nails. Your mom may have loved horses, but she's never been a tomboy. She jumped at the chance."

I stand because I feel like puking. So much makes sense now. Why Mom never truly attaches to anyone. Why she always speaks of things and people as being temporary. Why the moment she finds something she loves, she also finds a way to talk herself out of the commitment.

"It wasn't until Cassie went to the stables that I knew we'd made a mistake. I never truly understood devastation until that moment. For Cassie, it was as if Mom died all over again." Doreen drops her head and rubs her temples. "She left a week later. And because she was seventeen, we couldn't do anything to make her come home. For your mother, starting over with nothing was better than facing the man who'd betrayed her."

"She never spoke to him again," I say as if Doreen doesn't already know this fact.

"Cassie thought for years that Dad acted alone. That he lied to both of us, and I never corrected her misbelief because if I did, I knew I'd lose her forever. And you too."

I sit back down, lost in shock and disappointment. "You told her at Pawpaw's funeral?"

"She was so angry at him still. And I felt like if she just took a second to understand why he made that choice and how hard it was for him, then maybe she could find a way to forgive him." Doreen lets out a heavy sigh. "Instead, it just made her hate me, too." She wipes a stray tear from under her eye. "When she learned Daddy had left her the half of the property with the stables, she nearly threw a chair across the room. She lives a torn life, Jan. Loving and hating with such ferocity that she's consumed by it."

I know Doreen is right. I know that's why Mom won't sell the land but also has no interest in ever stepping foot on it again. It's why she has zero tolerance for betrayal and why my being here hurt her so tremendously. I'm her daughter, and yet I've fallen in love with the very thing that caused her deepest pain.

"I don't know where to go from here," I squeak out, too overwhelmed to deal with all the crashing emotion. I'd always put Doreen on a pedestal. She was the wise one, the caring one, the one who had her life in perfect order. All this time I thought Mom was the villain. But it was Doreen and Pawpaw. "This information changes things."

"It doesn't have to." Doreen's voice cracks, which makes tears well up in my eyes, as well. "You have a choice to do something your mom has never had the capacity to do: forgive. No one is perfect. Not you or me or your pawpaw. But that is why I cling to grace so fiercely. Because without it, all we have left is the anger and shame. And that isn't how life is supposed to be lived."

I press my head into my palms, my mind swirling with a concept I've never once seen played out in practice. How do you forgive the unforgiveable? How do you restore thirty years of brokenness? It's an impossible equation.

And yet, even as I sit here, I can't find the rage I know I should feel on behalf of my mother. Doreen has loved me through all my ugliest moments. She's protected me, accepted me just as I am, and has shown me the true meaning of love.

Dillon's words come to me in a rush of clarity: *"And despite how dark it got, I'm glad I did, because now I know my faith is mine and not anyone else's."*

All this time I thought it was a choice between my mom and my aunt, between one belief system and another. But it was never about their stories; it was always about mine. My journey, my choice, my faith.

I sit back up, my heart racing more now than it was before we walked into this room. "Of course I forgive you, Doreen. You are not defined by one mistake." Wasn't that what Luke had been saying in every chapter? What Mrs. Cox kept trying to point out, even though I fought to dismiss each word?

My powerhouse of an aunt breaks down beside me, her face buried in her hands while she cries. I hug her tight, my own soul opening up to the truth that I've turned away from for months. God isn't just an imaginary thing used to make everyone feel judged and kept in line. He is real. As real as the wind and stars and the tears falling from my eyes. I feel His soft touch as surely as if His hand were vivid in front of me.

My aunt and I cling to each other, comfort and warmth surrounding our trembling figures. It feels so right that Doreen and I would walk a path of forgiveness together.

Hers for a mistake made in fear and desperation.

Mine for simply being brave enough to believe.

THIRTY-EIGHT

"Are you *sure* you want to go?" Dillon asks for the second time.

"Yes. Why do you keep asking me that?"

"Well, for starters, you haven't moved in three minutes."

We're standing in front of Grace Community Church on Good Friday, a sea of bodies passing us to get inside. While it's not my first time going to church since that night with my aunt, it's the first time I've come to this one. Dillon and his dad go to a tiny church in Maypearl, or at least they have since the New Year. Lately, Dillon's been dragging me there every Sunday. It's old and smells like stale wood and dirty carpet, but I have to admit, I sort of love it. And even though almost everyone there is over sixty and we sing out of frail hymnals, the small touch I felt in Doreen's office grows stronger each time I walk through those squeaky doors.

"What are you so nervous about? It's not even a real service."

Supposedly the cross service includes Pastor Thomas chopping up a tree and turning it into a fourteen-foot cross. The office has been a colliding mass of chaos all week trying to get ready for the community event.

"I don't know why." I sigh, frustrated, though part of me recognizes the familiar sting of grief. This building does and always will represent Cameron. His voice, his passion, his faith—it's all tied up here.

Dillon eases closer until soon his warm hand is on my back. "You don't have to go," he says softly. "You've already taken significant steps, and this one can wait."

I close my eyes and let out the breath I've been holding. If I had my way, I would turn tail and rush to the car. But Doreen asked me to come, and I know this event is her favorite, beyond anything else Grace Community does.

"No. I need to. Everyone is waiting for us in there." Uncle Jim, Doreen, Mr. Kyle. It was to be a big group outing and then dinner afterward. When I take my first step, Dillon's hand drops from my back. I immediately miss the touch, the strength he always seems to give me.

We ease our way through the double glass doors, past the volunteers handing out church information, and into the auditorium.

The aisles are crowded with bodies. People are everywhere, talking and hugging. It takes three attempts for us to get through a foursome of ladies catching up, after two years I think I hear one say. I stand on my tiptoes, searching for our party, and silently wish I had another four inches on me.

Dillon presses a hand to my side and shifts me away from a toddler stumbling in his attempt to get away from his mom. "Down in the front on the very right side."

I turn and catch sight of Doreen's bright smile and wave. It's a relief, but it also means we have to push back up the aisle and go down the other side.

"I now understand why you like your church to be small. This is a madhouse."

Dillon continues to guide me forward, his hand now on my lower back. "It's not like this on Sundays. Well, maybe this Sunday because it's Easter, but not on a normal Sunday."

We make it all the way back to the main walkway and down the far side of the auditorium when I hear my name being called behind me. And while most people can ignore the summons based on the fact that millions likely share their first name, I cannot. I've still yet to meet another January.

I turn and spot Darcy frantically waving a hand as she tries to get past the same mass of people Dillon and I just pushed through.

"January! Oh my goodness, I can't believe you're here!" She doesn't stop when she reaches me but nearly knocks me over with an enthusiastic hug. It's awkward and sweet, and I realize she was part of what I mourned about my breakup with Cameron. "How have you been?" She releases me from her vise grip. "I've wanted to call so many times, but I didn't know if it would be okay."

"Of course it would be. There's no hard feeling between me and Cameron."

Her chest caves in relief. "I'm so glad to hear that because I want you to come to my party tomorrow night."

"Party?"

"Yes." She rolls her eyes. "The deposit money is due next week, so this is my last attempt to raise the rest of the money." She sighs and then smiles. "And I'm so close. There'll be barbecue and music and games. And it's just twenty dollars per person so it's practically as cheap as going to dinner or the movies." Darcy finally seems to register Dillon next to me and addresses him for the first time. "You should come, too. I mean, if you want to."

"I'll think about it." It's a blow-off answer, but then again Darcy's invite wasn't exactly sincere, either.

"Well, I have to go—I'm helping upstairs with sound. But please come tomorrow. It's at my boss's house. She has fourteen acres and the most beautiful dogs you've ever seen. I'll show you around when you get there." Darcy backs away before I can give my regrets. "I'll text you the address, and be sure to wear sensible shoes." She waves, spins, and disappears back into the crowd.

"Wow. Darcy's more spastic than I remember." Dillon snorts.

"I think she was nervous." I glance back one more time to the spot where Darcy disappeared and then make my final trek to the row of saved seats.

"You made it!" Doreen beams as I take the chair next to her. "I cannot wait for you to see what Pastor does up there." She pats my leg, practically hopping in her seat. "And don't worry, we made sure to get seats far back from the flying wood chips."

"They reach this far?"

"Oh yes. Poor Cameron got showered last year onstage. Never missed a beat with his violin, though. Impressive boy. Looks like they moved him over a few feet this year." She glances toward the stage, and my stomach plummets as I follow her line of sight. Surely it's not him playing this year. Not after resigning . . .

But there he stands. Beautiful, artistic, and completely focused on whatever discussion he's having with the cello player next to him.

No wonder Darcy was nervous. She knew Cameron was here.

Any chance of focusing on the service is long gone. My

eyes refuse to move. They take in his head, his hands, even his shoes. He's the same and yet different in a way most people wouldn't notice but I see immediately. His hair's longer, a shaggy style that reminds me too much of Bryson. And he looks anxious. His finger keeps tapping his leg as if it's searching for a beat it can't find.

"Just because he's here doesn't mean you have to talk to him." Dillon's voice is soft next to my ear. "We can sneak out before the lights turn back on."

I swallow down the heartbreak I'd hoped was gone. It has been nearly two months since Cameron walked out of my cabin, which is two weeks longer apart than we even were together. The pain in my chest should not be so severe.

"No, it's okay," I say, though I really want to take Dillon up on his offer. I know what tonight means for Doreen, to have us all together. I won't take that from her, no matter how painful it might be.

Dillon slumps back in his chair, and I swear his forearms flex like he's barely keeping his hands from curling into fists.

I twist in my seat, grateful for a reason to stop looking at the stage and, more importantly, the man who walked away. "What's wrong with you?"

"Nothing." Dillon rolls his shoulders, but it doesn't seem to relax him.

"Liar. You're practically a statue, your muscles are so tense." I reach out and playfully massage his shoulder. Actually, it's more a tickle, but we both need a distraction.

He flinches and puts up his arm to ward off my assault. "Stop it," he grumbles, but his lips have turned upward. "Seriously." He bats my hand away. "You're not five."

"And it's not *your* ex up there onstage, so I don't get why you're all huffy." I spin back around and fold my arms across my chest. I immediately regret the decision to do so as my gaze travels right back to Cameron. He's sitting now, his face obscured by the music stand in front of him.

Dillon sighs. "I don't like seeing you upset."

I turn my head and smile at the man who's become my best friend. "I'm not upset. Surprised is all."

"I guess this means you're not going to the party?"

"I guess." I look up at the dimming lights but don't feel any less conflicted. Darcy doesn't have a vindictive bone in her body, so why would she invite me somewhere she knew Cameron would be? It doesn't make sense, unless . . . My mind floods with the possibilities: he's left the band, came home, wants me back?

I don't have time to even consider that last thought because the sound of Cameron's violin steals the air out of the massive auditorium. And as it always does when he plays, my world ceases to exist. All I see is the stage, Pastor Thomas, and a cross waiting to be made.

THIRTY-NINE

I didn't run into Cameron at the cross service but know that will not be the case at Darcy's party. At least fifty cars are parked in the field along a cow fence, and two more came in behind me. Hanging lights illuminate the exterior of a massive barn and makeshift stage set up only ten feet away from the structure.

I slam my car door and wonder for the fifteenth time why I chose to come. And even though I still can't conjure a reasonable excuse, a truth I can't deny sits heavy on my shoulders: I want Cameron to know I've changed. I want him to know I now understand why his faith mattered and why he had to walk away. I want to thank him for treating me so honorably when no one had before.

The two couples who drove in after me are now five steps ahead, so I follow them into a space far too big to ever feel crowded. The sweet scent of barbecue attacks my senses, as does the sting of an electric guitar. Black Carousel is onstage, Bryson belting out a cover of "Sweet Home Alabama" to a cheering crowd. I take in the whole picture, Cameron to his right, sweat-drenched hair flopping over his eyes as his hand trails up and down the guitar's neck.

The energy I felt months ago in Cameron's small apartment is closer to an electric current now. It courses through my chest and down my arms. My fingers and legs tingle, and I find myself wanting to scream the lyrics along with the crowd. This is not the same band I saw at the College Street Pub. Not even close. But since standing like a groupie in front of Cameron and Bryson is too humiliating to endure, I ease through the masses until the music becomes a decibel lower and random conversations take up the bulk of the sound.

I find Darcy inside the barn, collecting the cash and handing out paperware for the barbecue buffet.

"One, please," I say when it's my turn at the front of the line.

Darcy glances up from her money box and smiles as bright as the portable lights outside. "Give me two seconds and I'll eat with you." I hand over my twenty-dollar bill, but she shoos it away. "You're my guest. Dinner is my treat tonight." She turns to her partner, a middle-aged lady with weathered skin and her hair in a messy ponytail. Darcy calls her Laurette when she tells her she's taking a short break, and I vaguely remember that being her boss's name. "Okay, I'm ready. Let's hit the desserts before they're all gone."

We travel through the line, and before it ends, my plate is overflowing with brisket, beans, coleslaw, and bread.

"How's the fundraising going?" I ask, mostly because I imagine this much food was a huge investment.

"Beyond expectation. We've already raised fifteen hundred, and the to-go plate requests keep coming." She shakes her head. "When my boss offered to host this thing for me, I had no idea it would be so huge. She got a local barbecue place to donate the food, Grace Community let me use the tables, and the band was free, of course, so all I had to pay for was renting the stage and buying all the paper goods." She sets her plate on one of the few open spaces and plops onto the seat across from me. "Which means I'm done. My goal is finally met. I can't even believe it."

"When do you leave?"

"June second. Forty-five days and I'll be a full-fledged missionary." She bows her head and says a silent prayer so quick I barely register what she's doing. I'm sure her silence is out of respect for me. No doubt Cameron told her my little secret. I should probably say something, or at least give her permission to speak out loud, but it feels too contrived in this atmosphere.

"That's a huge accomplishment, Darcy. You should feel really proud."

"Well, terrified and half out of my mind is more like it, but yeah, I am incredibly relieved." She takes a bite and watches me while she chews. "So how have you been?"

"I've been okay." I could pretend the last two months haven't been a time of complete self-examination, but I don't want to. "Cameron's leaving kind of forced me to deal with some deeper issues." She continues to watch me, not in judgment but in genuine interest. "I've even been going to a small church near B&L Ranch."

"I wondered when I saw you last night if something had changed," she admitted. "Cameron told me . . ."

"I figured."

We're silent for a while and I should let it continue. Unfortunately, self-control has never been my strength. "How is he?" I whisper, knowing I'm probably breaking every ex-girlfriend code by asking.

"Honestly?" She sets down her fork. "I don't really know.

I've been so focused on fundraising lately, we haven't had a lot of time to talk." She stares off toward the now-empty stage. I guess the song I'd witnessed had been their last one. "But considering the way you two broke up, and how testy he's been since, I do think talking would be good . . . for both of you."

While I'm surprised by her honesty, I'm not thrown by her admission. Everything Darcy has done since seeing me at the cross service has reeked of a setup, even down to how she only semi-invited Dillon.

"I'm not sure Cameron wants to talk to me." After all, he's been in town long enough to prepare and perform at two events and has yet to send me even a hello text.

"Well, I guess we're about to find out, aren't we?" She doesn't even finish her sentence before the band walks up and Bryson slaps his hand on the table.

"Where's this amazing food you promised? The term *starving artist* has never been so true." The inflection in his voice makes it clear he's joking, but I still jump. It's enough to bring every pair of eyes my way, including ones that regard me with absolute surprise.

"Jan?"

Since awkward silences have never been my forte, I smile at the guy who helped me see the possibility of a functional relationship. "Hi, Cameron. You guys sounded incredible up there." Lame, lame, lame. If a hole opened up in the middle of the floor, I'd gladly leap into it.

Darcy jumps from her chair and slides her arm around Bryson's elbow. "Let's go get you something to eat, okay?" She drags him and their two other bandmates away, leaving me and Cameron alone to stare at each other.

"Do you want to sit?" I offer.

He shoves his hands in his pockets and shakes his head. "Not really."

"Okay." My heart pounds, embarrassment moving up my neck and into my cheeks.

"We could take a walk, though, if you're up for it."

I blow out a breath and will my hands to stop shaking. "Yeah, that sounds good." And thanks to Darcy I'm actually wearing shoes that won't break my ankles on the uneven ground.

Cameron grabs my half-eaten plate of food and tosses it into the trash can on our way out of the barn. As he always did when we dated, he lets me go first, and that familiar warmth and appreciation returns stronger than I expect. No matter what has happened between us, or even how we leave here tonight, I will forever remember Cameron Lee with affection and respect. He's the first man in my life to ever treat me like a lady.

"You grew out your hair," I say once we've walked past the barn and into the field, where trees wrapped in tiny lights create a soft glow over us. "It looks nice."

"Yeah?" He quickly runs his hand through it, his voice mildly insecure. "Bryson said it would be good if our band had a more cohesive look."

I take in his dark jeans, black T-shirt, and boots. Yep. It certainly looks like Bryson's handiwork. "Well, don't change too much, okay? Some of us like the old you." I don't mean it to be an admonishment by any means, but Cameron must take it that way because he stares down at his feet, his shoulders sagging. "Cameron, I didn't mean that in a bad—"

"I'm sorry," he says over my backtracking.

"For what?"

His head rises, and there's so much regret in his eyes that I feel my chest ache with the need to comfort him. "I shouldn't have walked away from you so abruptly. I should have tried harder to talk to you about all I was feeling. That night I left, I knew I hurt you, but I was still so mad."

Unable to resist any longer, I take his hand in mine and squeeze. "No. You did the absolute right thing. I was lost and you were confused, and trying to fix that together would have just made things bad between us." My words get a small smile out of him. "You were the best boyfriend I've ever had, Cameron. You cared for me, treated me with respect, and I really believe I would not have found my way without our time together." I feel tears sting my eyes and have to swallow them back. "I was wrong. About God, about everything. Last night, when I heard the ax hit the tree and saw the wood chips flying all over the stage, the Cross became very real, as did the recognition of all the ways I've messed up." I swallow again, but a tear still escapes over my eyelash. "I should never have lied to you. Keeping that secret was so incredibly selfish, and I'm so sorry."

He reaches for me then, cradles my head to his chest, and we stay there for several minutes, holding each other one last time.

I hear Bryson's booming voice in the background giving the ten-minute countdown until they have to get back onstage, but Cameron doesn't flinch. He simply keeps holding me as if he's holding on to something far greater than our goodbye.

More time passes, and finally we pull away, slowly, as if neither of us is quite ready to let go.

"We could try again," he says, his voice rough. "We never really got a fair shot before. You couldn't understand my faith, and I was way too sheltered to understand your struggle. Both those things have changed."

"Cameron . . ."

"Just think about it," he says, his voice rising with optimism. "You could join us on tour, be part of the sound crew. We'd experience the whole thing together."

"I have a job here."

"I know, but it's almost over, isn't it? I heard the church is voting on the final candidate next week, so that will be it for you, right?"

I shrug, not wanting to admit it. "Yeah, I guess that's true."

He cups my face, his dimple showing for the first time all night. "Then come with me. It's all still here between us, I can feel it."

For the briefest second, I consider the offer. After all, he's right, the attraction we've always had is still alive and well. And Cameron is a wonderful guy, one I'd be lucky to have. Plus my job is ending, so even that isn't an obstacle. And yet I know without question that my answer is still no.

Carefully, I take his hands and lower them in front of us, squeezing both so he understands this decision doesn't have anything to do with him.

"You're saying no."

I nod sadly. "I'm sorry. If I were to say yes, I would be going solely for you. Following you. Dependent on *you*. And I can't do that again." His eyebrows scrunch like he's confused, and I guess he probably is because I never told him about how I got to Texas in the first place. I've never told him anything real about myself, which is how, in this moment, I know without question that I don't love him. Not like I need to in order to take this kind of step. "It's time for me to make some choices just for me. Can you understand that?"

"Of course I can. I'm living it." A sad shadow crosses over his face. "I just hope it makes you happy." Before I have time to respond to the faint underlying admission that he's not, Cameron swings his arm around my shoulder. "Come on. If you're going to break my heart, you need to at least watch me onstage one time."

I know I'm not breaking his heart. The two of us were never meant to be forever—just stepping-stones on the journey to something more. Maybe it was part of that grand plan Doreen is always talking about, I don't know. But either way, I'm grateful Cameron Lee was one of those stones.

FORTY

I feel emotionally drained when I pull in front of my cabin at B&L, even though the last hour was spent singing and dancing next to Darcy. But that is how goodbyes go. They force you on a cycle from fond remembrance to excited anticipation to terrorizing fear of the unknown. And it wasn't just me. I watched as Darcy went through every emotion several times.

I trek toward my cabin, and maybe it's the darkness outside or just that I'm lost in my own head, but I don't notice the Kyle landscaping truck until I nearly run into Dillon's six-foot ladder by my front steps. I glance around the porch. There's a button-up oxford shirt lying over the rail and a set of keys tossed on the small table between the rocking chairs. "Dillon?"

No answer. I do a quick check inside, but the lights are off. Weird.

"Dillon?" I call louder and take the steps back down.

"Around back."

I follow the sound of his voice until I see him hunched over by the air conditioner, pulling grass out of the ground, the back of a flashlight in his mouth. It takes all my willpower not to laugh. "Um . . . what are you doing?"

He stands, takes the contraption out of his mouth, and brushes off his hands. The shadows from the sensor lights hanging off the roof create a halo around his skin and leave an opposing line of darkness and light across his torso. "The weeds were encroaching, which means you'll get debris in your motor, which means I'll be stuck out here fixing this thing in the scorching heat of summer."

"So at nine o'clock on a Saturday night you suddenly felt the need to rush out here and inspect my air conditioner for debris that won't even become an issue for another month?"

"Not exactly." He pulls on the back of his neck. "I came to check on you because I thought you might be sad tonight. And then after waiting inside for thirty minutes, I got restless and waited outside for a while, but then I noticed the trim above your door was loose, so I fixed that. And then while I was up there, I saw that the molding around your window was chipping, so I went to get a piece so I could match the paint on Monday, and that's when I saw the overgrown weeds around your air conditioner." He shifts again, and the light consumes the darkness on his face. It brightens his cheeks, shows me his eyes. They're hard and glittering, full of something I've seen a thousand times but never made sense of until tonight.

I shake out my hands, trying to get ahold of what I'm seeing in front of me. Dillon's face is the same, his eyes are still that remarkable mix of chocolate and rich gold, and yet he suddenly feels very dangerous.

Then the truth hits me like a sledgehammer, straight on the forehead where denial is impossible: I love this man.

This crazy, wonderful man who's standing in front of me

in a white undershirt that's now smeared with dirt and what I've learned are his "good jeans." This man who listens and pushes and knows the depths of my soul. This man who's seen my tears and shared his own with me. This man who has become so special, the idea of leaving him makes me want to curl into a ball and scream.

And here I thought I'd wised up in the last few months. There's no recovering from loving a man like Dillon Kyle. No tissue box large enough, no walking path long enough. There's only one way these feelings lead . . . to a heartbreak I won't recover from.

"Jan, you okay?"

I look away, trying to get ahold of myself. "Yeah, just fine."

"So, did you end up going to that party after all?"

"Um . . . yeah, it was fun. Darcy got the rest of the money she needed."

"Oh. Well, good."

"Yes, it was." I take a step back, then two and three. When did it happen? When did I fall in love with Dillon Kyle?

"Are you sure you're okay? You suddenly look terrified."

I suck in air, but I still can't take a complete breath. "I'm fine. Just tired. I'm going to bed."

Dillon follows me to the cabin, even though I'm rushing so much I knock over his ladder on my way up the steps.

"Hey . . . stop." He slows only to pick up the fallen ladder and lean it back against the rail. "What's going on with you?"

"Nothing, okay?" I choke on the words as they spill out. "I just want to be alone for a while. I'll talk to you tomorrow." I close the door behind me, but he opens it back up.

"You know I'm not leaving you this way. What happened? Is it Cam? Did he do something?" He catches me just past the couch, his hand firm around my arm. "January . . . please.

Talk to me." There's a vulnerability in his eyes that tears at my soul. It's not his fault that I passed the bounds of friendship, that when I look at him now, I see only what I wish my future could be.

"He wants me to go on tour with him."

Dillon recoils. "What?"

It's not what I want to say, but anything else is too alarming to verbalize. "He says we never got a true shot. That we're both different now so it could work."

"And you agreed to that?" He drops his hands like I've burned them, his voice a mix of bitterness and disbelief.

"Why wouldn't I? It's not like I have a million other options laid out for me. I can't live here and work at Grace Community forever." The terror I suddenly feel is a bell ringing inside of me—an announcement that something is beginning, something's been unleashed. I want to stop it, bottle it up just like I always do when my feelings become too big. But stopping feels impossible tonight, or maybe just impossible with him, I don't know.

"So you're just going to pick up and leave? Follow Cam like you did the last idiot you dated?"

And once again I want to punch Dillon Kyle in the face. "Cameron's nothing like my ex. He's a good guy. He cares about me and he came back. Do you realize he's the only man in my life who's ever done that?" I'm almost shouting, almost in tears. "Why is it so insane that I would consider going?"

"Because he's not right for you! He doesn't see the real you; he never has." He cradles his head like it hurts, then violently drops his hands. "I don't understand why you insist on settling for a partner who doesn't know and love every part of you."

My heart slams into my rib cage. "Because I live in the real world, Dillon! And that person does not exist!"

"Are you serious?" He throws out his arms. "I'm standing right here!"

The room goes silent. I can't think. Breathing is all I can handle, breathing and watching him. "What did you just say?"

Dillon approaches me slowly, his voice calming to a gentle rasp. "Have you never even considered the idea of us?" His fingers gently touch my cheek, his gaze carefully watching for any indication that I want him to stop. "Because I've thought of nothing else since the day I met you. And no matter how many times I fought it and willed the attraction to go away, I only fell harder. And then I didn't want to fight it anymore. I wanted you so bad it kept me up at night."

"You never even hinted . . ."

"You weren't ready." His hand moves boldly, cupping my jaw, framing my ear, fingers slipping into my hair.

"But you said you had no secrets. That you were an open book, and I could ask you anything about your family or your past. But this? *This* is what you choose to keep hidden? Are you kidding me?"

His eyes drill into mine and there's no apology in them. "*This* . . . was too important to rush. I didn't want to be just another guy. I wanted to be *the* guy. The one you trusted. The one who stayed."

I search his face for any doubt, but there is none. Not even the slightest hint that he doesn't mean every word. And even crazier . . . I believe him.

His breath tickles the bridge of my nose as electricity rushes down my spine, barreling through every limb like it can't get to its destination fast enough.

The sensation nearly takes me off my feet, yet Dillon's

holding me steady, his other arm wrapped tight around my waist. "You have no idea how long I've wanted to hold you just like this. How long I've wanted to—"

His mouth covers mine, and suddenly there is no cabin or air or questions.

Like everything else with this man, kissing him is all-consuming. There's no insecurity, no halfway, no maybes or what-ifs. He's as relentless with this moment as he's been with every other before now, and I'm helplessly willing to concede because I don't want empty anymore. I don't want surface or mindless attraction or safe. I want deeper. I want everything with him.

The release is slow, regretful, as if neither of us wants the moment to end, even though we know it must.

His forehead settles on mine; his eyes are closed, his chest rising and falling in perfect rhythm to my own. "I'm not going to give you the speech, but in case you're wondering, I don't do casual."

"There's nothing casual about my feelings for you." My fingers play with the hair at his temple, an unusual display of affection for me, and the intimacy it brings jolts me as much as the kiss.

"Good." And then he's gone, and a rush of cold air hits me where his body was seconds before. I watch him as he rounds the couch, finds my purse, and begins rummaging through it.

"What are you looking for?"

"Your phone."

"Why?"

He finds his target and holds the device up victoriously. "Because you need to call Cam and let him know you're not going anywhere."

I smile because it feels unbelievably good to feel so important to someone else and decide right then to start this relationship out with absolute honesty. "I can't."

His brow scrunches. "Why not?"

"Because it would make me look really stupid. Especially since I already told him at the party that I wasn't going."

Dillon comes toward me, hooks his hand around my waist, and pulls me to him. "You put me through all that panic for nothing?" He kisses my hair, right beside my ear, and I suddenly feel guilty.

"Not on purpose." It comes out breathier than I intend, but his lips have moved to my cheek, a soft brush, barely a kiss but enough to send fire everywhere he touches. "I . . . I . . . just wanted you to see me as desirable. Not as this girl who is a mess most of the time."

"You are a mess." His lips trail up to my forehead, then down the bridge of my nose. "But I love that about you. I love that you never notice the obvious. I love that you trust no one and yet found a way to trust me. I love that you make me laugh when I'm sad and you challenge me to think beyond my failures." Our noses are a millimeter away, his mouth so close to mine now that it feels like a kiss when he says, "I love you, January. Every part. You never have to prove to me you're worthy of it."

He kisses me again, but I can barely respond through the sobs at the back of my throat. How is it possible that this blessing is mine? This broken, cynical girl who denied God her entire life—how could He give me so much?

I don't have an answer to that one. I doubt I ever will.

FORTY-ONE

It's hard to believe I'm the same girl who sat in this office four months ago, rejected and depressed. Now I face Pastor Thomas and Eric boldly, my smile no longer a lie, and my words honest and heartfelt.

"Thank you so much for meeting with me. I know you are both busy." I rub my palms on my skirt, suddenly nervous. I blow out a breath and say a small prayer for strength. "I lied when you hired me."

Eric shifts to the edge of the couch, his eyes intent on mine. "What do you mean?"

"I thought it was insignificant. A little white lie that wasn't hurting anyone." I wring my hands, amazed at how many things I had wrong. "When I came here, I thought God was a myth. A nice story to tell when life was hard. I respected those who believed, but honestly, I felt they were ignorant for doing so." I face Pastor Thomas. "I especially want to apologize to you. You trust my aunt, which meant you trusted me, and I betrayed that trust. I'm so sorry."

Pastor Thomas watches me thoughtfully. "And now?"

"Now?" I shrug because there is no real beginning or end to this journey. "I'm learning what faith looks like. I'm reading, mostly with Mrs. Cox but sometimes by myself. And praying, even though I still feel stupid most of the time." His lips curl upward at that admission, and it makes my face heat up. "Anyway, I heard you just hired a new pastor to help Ralph, and I wanted to make things easy on you. Here's my resignation letter. I know you haven't asked for it, but it feels like the right thing to do . . . considering." With a quivering hand, I give him my typed page of regrets. "Thank you for all you've done for me. I truly enjoyed working here."

Pastor Thomas takes the letter and reads it with such slow deliberation I nearly snatch it back out of his hands. I don't. I stay put, my legs crossed under my skirt, and accept that sometimes doing the right thing is hard.

He rubs his clean-shaven chin, then hands it back with a sigh. "I'm afraid I can't accept this."

My voice comes out shaky. "What do you mean?"

"I can't accept your resignation because I just lobbied the personnel team to get you permanently hired on as Ralph's assistant."

My mouth opens, then closes, much like a fish in the open air. "I don't understand."

"Well, I believe Ralph's words were something like, 'If she goes, I go.'" He smiles then, leaving me more confused than ever. "You've made quite an impact in your short time here, January. I'd hate to see that end."

"But I pretended to be a Christian. I took advantage."

He and Eric exchange a look that's part amusement and part guilt. "Actually . . . you didn't. Doreen told us your position on faith when she approached me about the job." His voice goes soft, soothing. "We knew all along, January. Eric and I both."

I shake my head. "And you still hired me? Why?"

"Because sometimes it's more about loving a person through a hard time than it is about forcing a conversion. God was going to do what He wanted to do. Meanwhile, I was convicted to use every part of this amazing ministry to show you His love."

I'm floored. More than floored, flummoxed. Is that a word? I think it's a word. I look down at my shoes, a guilt I'm becoming very familiar with coursing through me. "But I messed so many things up. Cameron, especially." I look back up at them. "He left because of me."

Pastor Thomas's mouth gets tight. "Cameron left because he wanted to. If anything, you are why he stayed for as long as he did. That young man has his own battle with God to fight through. You can't hold yourself responsible for it."

My eyes fill with unshed tears. I didn't realize how much of a burden I felt over his leaving until now. "Thank you. I don't even know what to say."

"Say you'll take the job."

My heart leaps in my chest. "Yes. Of course I'll take the job. I love it here."

"Okay then." Pastor Thomas stands, so we all do. "I'll let you break the good news to Ralph."

I'm still not quite sure what just happened, but my cheeks hurt from smiling. "Yes, sir. I will."

He chuckles because while he's told me several times to stop calling him *sir*, I can't seem to stop the formality. Call it a Southern thing, but *sir* and *ma'am* are ingrained in my psyche as deeply as sweet tea is.

We all file out of his office, and after discussing details with Margie, I head up to Ralph's office, practically skipping up the stairs.

I push open his door and nearly trip on my way inside.

Ralph and Victoria are wrapped around each other, hands roaming, clothes crumpled, in a kiss that could rival any romance movie.

They part like teenagers caught by their parents, and I'm too stunned to move or gawk or even worry that Victoria is going to see that her random visitor is also Ralph's assistant.

"Jan, sorry." Ralph clears his throat and pats down his orange hair. "I thought you were in a meeting."

"I was," I say, glancing between the two of them. Ralph's face is redder than his hair, while Victoria is trying so hard not to laugh that I swear she's turning blue. Ah, what the heck, let's shatter the ice now. "And I see you took full advantage of my absence."

Victoria can hold it in no longer and spits out a laugh so hearty it makes her double over. Ralph shakes his head and stares at the floor, unable to look at me. Personally, I think it's a beautiful thing, a married couple after twenty-six years still having that kind of passion for each other. We should all be so lucky.

"So you're the famous assistant," Victoria says once she pulls herself together. She steps toward me and gives me a tight hug. "Why am I not surprised?"

I embrace her without hesitation. "Sorry I didn't say anything to you that day at the nursing home. It felt too intrusive."

When we release each other, Ralph is staring at us like we've transformed into headless beasts. "You two know each other?"

That brings another round of giggling.

"A story for another day," Victoria says affectionately.

"Well, I didn't mean to interrupt. I just came to tell you the good news." I glance between the couple, and I know my smile is broad enough to light up the universe. "I'm officially your assistant. I hope that's what you wanted . . ." There's an edge of insecurity in my voice that Ralph must pick up on because his brows scrunch even further.

"Absolutely."

Victoria moves to her husband's side and wraps her arm around his waist. "Thank you, Jan. For all you've done to help him." Her lip trembles slightly, and I know that "him" means "us," which makes me have to blink away unwanted moisture in my eyes.

"It really was my pleasure." I look around the office that's now tidy and organized. We put pictures on the walls two days ago, mostly of his family, and everything in here just seems brighter. "Okay, well, you two get back to whatever it is you were doing."

"Jan," Ralph moans, his face turning red all over again.

"See you Monday!" I save him more embarrassment and walk out the door, offering one last wave before shutting it behind me.

Dillon's waiting for me when I exit the church. He's leaning against my car, his eyes shielded by sunglasses.

"How'd it go?" he asks when I approach.

"Well, they wouldn't accept my resignation." I shake my head. "And then had the audacity to hire me on full-time."

He cups my face and kisses me like it's the most natural thing in the world to do. In a way it's become that, the two of us, an inseparable pair. "Told you so." And he had, several times when I nearly had a panic attack on the way over here.

He opens the passenger side door and I slide in, even though it's my car. One more sign that we've morphed into a true couple.

He drops into the seat and turns on the engine. "Celebratory lunch?"

I reach over and caress the back of his head, still in awe that this handsome, bullheaded man is mine. "Sounds wonderful."

EPILOGUE

"Her veil is fine. Stop messing with it." My mom slaps my aunt's hand away for what feels like the hundredth time tonight. They've bickered incessantly since the start of my wedding weekend, but I can't find it in me to care. What matters is they are both here, celebrating with me as I'm about to walk down a flagstone aisle toward the love of my life.

Aunt Doreen makes one more adjustment and then throws her hands in the air. "There. It's perfect now."

I peer at my reflection in the mirror. My eyes are brighter than normal. My cheeks are flushed. In front of me is a girl who is no longer afraid of what's coming next.

"Can I have a minute with January alone?" my mother asks, and I'm surprised there's no bite in her voice.

Aunt Doreen must be surprised, too, because she nods quietly. "You have about ten minutes before the ceremony starts." She looks at me then, and her face morphs into pride and affection. "You look beautiful, January. The most beautiful bride I've ever seen."

Tears threaten my carefully applied mascara. "Thank you, Doreen."

My aunt gently shuts the door as Mom slides a folding chair in front of me. She's holding a manila envelope, and I can see her hands are trembling.

"I wanted to give you my wedding gift early." As she eases herself into the chair, I swear she seems to age ten years in the process. I've never considered my mom fragile. Stubborn, yes. Selfish, well, most of the time, but she has never been weak. At least not in my presence.

I place my hand on hers and squeeze. "Your being here is all the gift I need. Really. I know what a sacrifice this is." It took three months before I had the courage to talk to my mom about what her father and sister had done when she was younger. It took two more months after that for her to actually tell me her side. It was harsh and angry, but I do think it was also the first step my mom needed to begin to heal.

"All the same, there's something I want you to have. Something that . . ." Her voice fades, and instead of saying what it is, she pulls at the tab on the envelope and slides out some very official-looking documents. "This is the deed to my land. I had it transferred to you."

My breath hitches as I take the paperwork in hand. It's true. Signed, notarized, and sealed. "Mom . . . this is too much."

She sighs and turns to look out the window. "I'll be the first to say I don't agree with your choices right now, especially the religious thing you've got going. But . . . that aside, this land should be loved. It's what my mother would have wanted." She turns back to me, the grief still very strong in her eyes. "And since I have no intention of staying here past this weekend, I think it's time I let it go. Don't you?"

Forget the mascara. Let the waterworks come without barrier. This is the most unselfish thing my mom has ever done for me. Not just the land, but the promise to try to forgive. To mend our family. To one day maybe find the same peace I found when I came to Texas.

I laugh through my tears. "Dillon is going to do cartwheels. He's had a house designed for over a year now."

Her lips press into a white slash. "Don't you dare put his name on this deed. Marriages end every day. This is Sanders land and will remain Sanders land. Got it?"

So, we'll start with baby steps.

"Got it, Mom." I affectionately place my hand on her ageless cheek. "Thank you. It's the most perfect gift in the world."

Her blue eyes meet mine and we're connected in a way only mothers and daughters can understand. "No, Jan, you're the most perfect gift. This guy of yours better know that, too."

"He does," I say through choked sobs.

My mom, never being one for emotional moments, clears her throat and stands. "Well . . . I guess we should get you out there. Your first wedding is always the prettiest, and the most expensive, so enjoy this one."

I don't bother arguing. She doesn't understand. I know because I never understood it, either. Dillon's and my relationship wasn't born out of attraction and intense emotion. From the beginning, it was real, rooted in friendship, strengthened through pain and loss, and now solidified in equal faith. Maybe one day my mom will understand that kind of love and stop the roller coaster she's been on. I know I'll never quit praying for that very thing.

Mom fluffs my dress and pats under my eyes with a brush of powder. When I fully pass her inspection, she opens the door, too choked up to hide that even though she doesn't much believe in marriage, she still understands the gravity of what I'm about to enter. A covenant with a man who I know will never stop loving me.

It's amazing how life can change in a flash. One year. That's all it took to transform my world. I walked into Grace Community lost, broken, and desperately searching for meaning in my life. Now I know exactly who I am.

I take my first step through the door and onto the path I could walk blindfolded until I see Dillon standing by my favorite tree. He's in a dark suit and tie. His hair is trimmed, and his eyes lock on to mine as if we're the only two people in the universe.

Maybe we are. Because in this moment, I'm not running or hiding from something I don't want to face. This time I'm walking forward, intentionally, purposefully.

I guess Doreen was right about God's plan, after all.

And we know that in all things God works for the good of those who love him. . . .

Romans 8:28

ACKNOWLEDGMENTS

Two years ago, I closed my laptop and decided I had written my last manuscript. The next day, I texted my writing partners and told them my decision to quit. Their response? A capitalized "NO YOU ARE NOT!"

Thus began months of prayer where I begged God to release me from this calling. Everything had gotten too hard, my stories too stale, my motivation nonexistent.

And then one day an idea percolated: maybe I can't write the same type of story because I'm no longer the person who wrote that debut novel. My first ten books were all about overcoming shame, forgiving oneself, and finding redemption. Miraculously, through those ten heartrending stories, I found my own healing.

And once I'd embraced the person I'd become and the new message I wanted to share, this story came tumbling out at such speed that I couldn't get the words down fast enough. I had stepped over a threshold and it was time to close the lid on the past I was so ashamed of and embrace the abundant life I now live in Christ.

Perhaps, as you read this story, you found yourself relating to one of the characters. Maybe it was January and her fear of trust, or Dillon and his anger at God, or Cameron and his frustration with waiting. No matter where you are on this path we call Christianity, I know God has a message and purpose just waiting for you.

I'm so grateful that He made me push through to get to the end of this story. I know without question there are many more to come.

So thank you to all those who have helped me on this crazy, unexpected journey:

To Raela Schoenherr and all the Bethany House editors and staff, thank you for allowing me to partner with such an incredible team. You have been my dream publisher for years, and I still pinch myself that we get to navigate my writing life together. I'm so excited for what is still to come.

To my fabulous agent, Jessica Kirkland, for never giving up on me, even when I gave up on myself. Thank you for the many phone calls and motivational speeches. I couldn't have done it without you.

To my amazing writing partners—Connilyn Cossette, Christy Barritt, Nicole Deese, and Amy Matayo—how did I ever write without you? Thank you for all the plotting ideas, the many encouraging notes, and your steadfast belief in me and this story. You four are one of my richest blessings.

To Angel David, Ashley Espinoza, Joanie Schultz, and Kelly Scott, thank you for being fabulous beta readers, even when given an incomplete story. Your input was invaluable and critical to the success of this novel.

To my wonderful readers, you have all been so patient and so kind. I know I still owe you a book in a previous series, but

I hope you now understand why this one had to come first. I pray you have seen my heart on every page.

And finally, to the most important people in the world, my family. You sacrifice so much each and every time I sit down to write. Thank you for forgiving the mounds of unwashed laundry, the many "fend for yourself" dinners, and my habit of staying in story-world long after the workday is over. You make writing possible, and I promise: you all are getting a huge celebratory dinner very soon.

ABOUT THE AUTHOR

Tammy L. Gray lives in the Dallas area with her family, and they love all things Texas. Her many modern and true-to-life contemporary romance novels include the 2017 RITA Award–winning *My Hope Next Door* and show her unending quest to write culturally relevant stories with relatable characters. When not taxiing her three kids to various school and sporting events, Tammy can be spotted crunching numbers as the financial administrator at her hometown church. Learn more at www.tammylgray.com.

Sign Up for Tammy's Newsletter

Keep up to date with Tammy's news on book releases and events by signing up for her email list at tammylgray.com.

You May Also Like . . .

Led to her hometown by a mysterious letter, Genevieve Woodward wakes in an unfamiliar cottage with the confused owner staring down at her. The last thing Sam Turner wants is to help a woman as troubled as she is talkative, but he can't turn her away when she needs him most. Will they be able to let go of the façades and loneliness they've always clung to?

Stay with Me by Becky Wade, A Misty River Romance
beckywade.com

More from Bethany House

After many matchmaking schemes gone wrong, there's only one goal Lauren is committed to now—the one that will make her a mother. But to satisfy the adoption agency's requirements, she must remain single, which proves to be a problem when Joshua appears. With an impossible decision looming, she will have to choose between the two deepest desires of her heart.

Before I Called You Mine by Nicole Deese
nicoledeese.com

After a life-altering car accident, one night changes everything for three women. As their lives intersect, they can no longer dwell in the memory of who they've been. Can they rise from the wreck of the worst moments of their lives to become who they were meant to be?

More Than We Remember by Christina Suzann Nelson
christinasuzannnelson.com

Famous author Josephine Bourdillon is in a coma, her memories surfacing as her body fights to survive. But those around her are facing their own battles: Henry Hughes, who agreed to kill her for hire out of desperation, is uncertain how to finish the job now, and her teenage daughter, Paige, is overwhelmed by fear. Can grace bring them all into the light?

When I Close My Eyes by Elizabeth Musser
elizabethmusser.com

BETHANYHOUSE